BLOOD
of
ZEUS

BLOOD
of
ZEUS

BLOOD OF ZEUS: BOOK ONE

MEREDITH WILD
& ANGEL PAYNE

WATERHOUSE PRESS

ISBN: 978-1-64263-218-7

For Mindy

— Meredith

For Thomas and Jessica.
You're the magic of my life,
the beats of my heart,
the blood in my veins.

— Angel

I saw within Its depth how It conceives
all things in a single volume bound by Love
of which the universe is the scattered leaves.
— Dante Alighieri, *Paradiso: Canto XXXIII*

CHAPTER 1

Kara

THE ONLY THING WORSE than being a demon is being a Valari. Being both means I get to hear every whisper in the room as I make my way into the lecture hall and past clusters of students.

"That's Kara Valari."

"Why does she even bother?"

"They're like the worst people."

I find their faces as I go, not breaking my stride. Sometimes looking people in the eye is the only way to shut them up. They avert their gazes, one by one.

Whispers are easy to hide behind. So are the salacious remarks that no one can hear except me and the guys who've uttered them under their breath. I don't even have to look at them to know I'm not interested. In their case, eye contact might just confuse the issue.

For the sake of everyone's education, I climb the stairs to find a spot in the back of the hall so people will hopefully forget I'm here. As I take my seat, a blonde in front of me pretends to take a selfie. I'm definitely in the background. I can't wait to read the caption.

I've been at Alameda University for three years, but for some, the novelty of sharing a class with anyone above D-list celebrity status never seems to wear off. The beginning of a new term is always the worst. My tolerance after any extended time off campus is dangerously low, and chances are high the Valari name is twisted up with some fresh Hollywood gossip, no less damaging for its brevity in the trash-news cycle.

Of course, I'm not the only one here who was born into a famous family. My grandfather was one of the most renowned screenwriters of his generation. The award statues on his mantel have been long forgotten. Now our family finds the spotlight more often than most, but for far less commendable reasons. Our reputation follows me around everywhere I go, as inescapable as my biology.

I fumble in my expensive leather backpack for a notebook and pen, exhaling a tense breath. I silently reach for a degree of self-control that doesn't come naturally, as raw emotion tries to claw its way past my cool exterior.

I lift my head at the sound of a door slamming, which silences the whispers.

Even from my elevated vantage, I'm fascinated by the towering height of the man who paces into the lecture hall. His expression is hidden with his downward gaze. His mouth is obscured by a golden beard that matches hair tamed in a knot at his nape. Though I expect it's coming, the man needs no introduction.

Within seconds of his arrival, the silence gives way to a hushed hiss, the prolonged echo of his name on students' lips, where mine was moments ago.

Maximus.

Professor Maximus Kane reaches the broad wooden podium at the front of the room in a few long strides. There he carefully deposits a stack of materials from his arms. A familiar shiver of intrigue ribbons through me. I saved this course for my senior year, delaying both the best and worst for last. The best being the highlight of my foray into academia. The worst being the very different life that'll begin the moment I graduate—a life that will be anything but enlightened.

Towering over the podium, he clears his throat loudly, silencing the last of the hushed whispers. Still, his gaze is cast downward toward his notes, affording his audience a moment more to take in his impressive physique. I nip at the inside of my lip because I'm not immune. The only things professorial about Professor Kane are his dark-rimmed glasses and boring sweater-vest, which can't be anything but wildly sexy stretched over his white collared shirt that looks like it might give at the seams if he moved too suddenly.

"Welcome to Advanced Studies in Medieval Literature," he begins, his voice deep and void of humor. "If you're here, you should have completed all the prerequisites for an in-depth reading of Dante's *Divine Comedy*, which is where we'll be spending the majority of our time. If you've managed to get this far in your major by skimming, you should reconsider whether this is the course for you. My expectations of your effort here are commensurate with any other senior seminar. Don't waste my time, and I won't waste yours."

I clip the flesh between my teeth a little harder, creating a distracting throb of pain. I've never shied away from hard-ass professors. In fact, I've sought them out, eager for the challenge. Topping the class and setting the bar high enough to inconvenience my classmates has always been an added bonus.

Except I came here for Dante. Until now, I assumed the professor of English celebrated for his otherworldly looks would be a gentle giant—intellectual and deep but soft-spoken and forgiving, a stark contrast to his notable physical presence. I was fabulously wrong. The masochist in me sends down a dark prayer that he's a hard grader too.

"I will not be your only teacher in this course," he continues. "I'm your professor, but you can think of me more generally as a guide, pointing out themes of note. But if you rely on my interpretation alone, you are robbing yourself of the education inherent in the work, a circle of knowledge drawn by Dante himself. The poem is a journey of the self." He pauses a moment, his mouth drawn into a thoughtful purse. "Journey being the operative word."

He frowns a little and pushes his glasses up the bridge of his nose.

"Moving on. How many of you have already been introduced to the *Comedy* through your other courses?"

Almost every student raises his or her hand. I don't.

My skin heats a little when his scanning of the room

stops on me, but it's a brief pause.

"Since this is a seminar and I will be relying heavily on your contributions to drive our conversation, we'll begin now. I'd like to know, regardless of your familiarity with the text, what draws you to Dante."

Somehow the class grows even more silent, as if people have ceased breathing lest any movement draw unwanted attention to them. I smirk, because just as easily as I can hear words that aren't meant to be heard, I can pick up on the inherent discomfort of humans, from little pricklings of fear to full-on panic.

The professor's gaze lands on the blonde in front of me. "How about you? What brings you here?"

She lets out a breathy laugh and tucks her hair behind her ear, lifting her shoulder coyly as she does. "I don't know. I guess I heard good things about this course."

"Ohh, Professor *Maximus*," a falsetto voice sings out from the crowd, prompting a wave of laughter throughout the hall.

The golden corners of the professor's lips quirk up slightly. No doubt, his presence alone could fill a room with students more fascinated by his looks than his literary insights. He quickly collects himself, lifts his chin, and our gazes meet.

Blood rushes to the surface of my skin.

"You're new to Dante. Why spend the next four months dissecting the *Comedy*?"

The air grows thick with anticipation. The anticipation isn't mine, but I recognize the shift in the mood of the room.

After a moment of prolonged silence, he arches an eyebrow and cocks his head, prompting me to say something. Anything.

"Dante's journey through the underworld is uniquely fascinating to me," I say, which earns some predictable snickers from the audience.

The professor slides his hands casually into the pockets of his dark slacks, drawing my attention to the way they barely contain his thighs. For being an academic, he's remarkably fit.

"Which part of it holds your fascination? The journey through the dark, or the journey to the light?"

I blink and meet his eyes again. I curl my fingers around my notebook as I contemplate his words. His question feels too personal, like somehow he knows something—maybe that *one* thing—about me he shouldn't.

"That's an odd question." I can't hide the defensiveness in my tone.

He winces briefly. "Is it? It's just that I find some people are drawn to dark themes for the sheer ugliness of them. And there are others who are invested in the exaltation of reaching the other side of it."

I'm locked in my own silence, unwilling to tell him what I really think. That he has no idea what he's talking about. That contemplating the allegory is like reading a bedtime story compared to the reality. At least from everything I've been told. He may look like a god, but I'm pretty sure my sources on the subject of hell are better than his.

"Spit it out, Valari," someone shouts out.

My nostrils flare.

The professor frowns in the direction of a boy slouched in the second row. "Excuse me?"

"She's just doing her research, Professor. She's a Valari," the boy says with a cocky laugh. "You know they're all going straight to hell."

The room erupts with laughter. My skin heats fiercely as I contemplate ways I can send him directly there.

"Get out." The professor's sharp command slices into the noise.

The boy laughs awkwardly. "I'm just joking around."

"I don't care. Get out."

He opens his mouth to argue when the professor points to the door.

"I won't ask again. Get the hell out of my classroom."

The fear is back, filling up the few tense minutes the boy takes to gather his things and walk out of the room with wounded confidence. The professor flashes a look my way that feels too intense to be an apology and makes me wonder if the smartass comment unnerved him even more than me.

The moment the door slams with the boy's retreat, the professor doesn't skip a beat. He launches into the life and times of Dante and the historical context of his works. I take notes and try to concentrate on his insights about the outcast from Florence who was, in some ways, like the professor himself. Deeper than he looked and willing to commit to the journey. At least that's the overwhelming aura I get from our instructor. As I keep trying to decipher his intense looks,

I worry I'm no different than every other undergrad here who's fallen under his spell.

An hour later, when he rattles off the reading assignment and dismisses us, I'm almost relieved. I wait for the rows to empty before rising to leave. His back is turned as he erases his notes from the whiteboard. I'm nearly at the door when he says my name.

"Miss Valari."

I turn.

"A moment of your time?"

I walk back to him, clutching the handle of my bag tightly. "Professor Kane."

"Maximus," he corrects. "That's what everyone ends up calling me anyway."

He leans against the desk beside the podium. A plastic Thor key chain dangles from the half-zipped pocket on the front of his soft-sided satchel. The bauble looks nothing like the man in front of me, but I can appreciate that he probably can't escape the association following him everywhere he goes. Why fight it?

I answer with a small smile. "Okay."

"Sitting in on this seminar requires approval. Forgive me, but I don't remember approving you."

My smile tightens. The memory of charming his TA to sign off on my registration request even though I lacked the prerequisites is still quite fresh in my mind.

"Matthew did. You were out of the office. He assured me everything was in order."

He regards me thoughtfully for a moment. This close, I

can appreciate his eyes, a true cerulean so vibrant, one might almost miss their shadows. Shadows are almost always made of secrets, I've learned. Shadows don't scare me, but I rarely seek them out. But something makes me wish I knew what his were made of.

"I teach lower-level lit courses as well," he says, interrupting my wandering thoughts. "How come I haven't seen you before?"

"I'm a classics major."

He nods quietly, looking me over once before averting his gaze quickly. "Sorry for putting you on the spot earlier. I didn't realize who you were."

"Thank you for defending me, I guess. I don't need special treatment, though. My mom isn't going to call the dean or anything."

"That's not why I did it. I don't tolerate bullying in my classes. It's remarkable how often I have to enforce it."

I believe him and respect him even more for it.

"Thank you. Again."

He leans forward and hands me a stapled stack of papers. "Don't forget the syllabus."

When I reach for it, our fingers graze. It's so brief, I wonder if the contact even happened except for the sharp sensation racing up my arm. An odd kind of energy I haven't experienced before—at least not from humans.

I widen my eyes and step back, pressing the syllabus against my chest. Our gazes lock, and for a minute I worry he's felt it too. I swallow hard and try to think of something to say, but his wordless stare renders me speechless.

"See you Wednesday, Miss Valari."

CHAPTER 2

MAXIMUS

"**K**ANE!"

Despite the crashing waves, the screeching seagulls, and the blaring rock music along Venice Beach this afternoon, my best friend's shout is clear across Muscle Beach Gym's weight pen. I look up from the machine I've been working for the last five minutes, crunching a frown as Jesse waves good-naturedly at the regulars taking turns on a punching bag.

"Mr. North," I call back. "You're late."

"And your point is what?" Jesse adds a smirk to his drawl while rolling over in the wheelchair that's practically an extension of him. At least to most around here. Not to me, the guy who remembers him without it.

The guy who put him in it.

For that reason, plus about a million more, our friendship is more like a brotherhood to me—and I know how deeply he returns the commitment.

"Mind-hopping to another planet again, man?" He brakes his wheelchair sharply.

"Yeah, maybe." The answer comes with the vivid memory of one particular brunette. The instant I touched Kara Valari, the rigid control of my mind was overtaken by brilliant color.

One brush of fingers. One exchange of energy. One frisson of time. That's all it took to blast through all my barriers and have me obsessing over that brief interaction with her for hours. Yes, goddammit, over twenty-four of them now.

Not that I'll spill any of that to Jesse. Or even admit it myself. The girl is forbidden fruit. I'm young to be a full-time professor at Alameda, but I'm still that. Her teacher. And her age aside, she's a goddamned Valari. She grew up with silk sheets, marble floors, and personal valet service. My upbringing was defined by a sofa bed, a linoleum kitchen, and boxed mac 'n' cheese, kept warm until Mom got home from twelve-hour shifts at the hospital. LA rent isn't cheap, but she always insisted we stay in the city. Kept telling me it was the safest choice—which I never understood at all. Safest choice from what? Wasn't *I* the monster that needed to be kept clear from everyone else?

"How about that one?" He nods toward the bleachers positioned near the workout zone. Though the seating is a permanent installment due to the numerous lifting competitions held here, most days the stands are just populated with curious tourists and horny locals. Jesse flips his head back, showing off his thick black waves in a blatant bid for the latter. His gaze is fixed on a pair of buxom redheads perched about four rows up. Buxom may be an understatement, but that's how Jesse likes his women, and I'll be the last one to deny the guy his guilty pleasures.

"Not interested."

"You sure about that?" he counters. "Because it's been at least ten years since the last time you did *that*." He points toward the lat pulldown machine I've just vacated. Its horizontal bar, normally curved only at the ends, now resembles a giant horseshoe.

"Shit," I mutter.

"I'm not exactly complaining. The sweet strawberries up there aren't looking at anyone else now." He narrows his eyes, assessing me quietly. "But if our resident Samson needs to get something off his mind—"

I slice him short by cracking my neck. "If you call me that again, I'll tell them you sing Nickelback in the shower."

He directs his attention toward the bleachers again. "With any luck, that nymph on the right will know that soon."

"Somebody's a player today."

"And somebody's avoiding the subject." He fights the late-afternoon sun to pin my gaze with his. "Somebody who hasn't bent a steel rod like it was a pipe cleaner in a long damn time."

And by that, he means years. Several of them. Years in which I've been content. Satisfied. At times, even . . . happy.

But never at peace. I've given up on that part. On the

piece that will lead to *peace*. The explanation of why I'm so . . . different. Because I am. I stick to a world of parchment and pages and predictability, on the inside as well as out, for good reason. Stability means control. And control prevents me from doing what I just did to this weight machine.

If that bar had been a human limb instead . . . like Jesse's . . .

I suppress a shudder. How the hell had I let the control systems slip—so fast, so drastically?

I shove down the memories by looking back to the pulldown bar that looks like a failed arts-and-crafts project. "Overused equipment," I mutter, successfully sidestepping any mention of my distracting student. "Fifty yards off the Pacific . . . good recipe for corrosion. No wonder I wasn't feeling a burn."

"You never burn." Jesse indulges the grumble for a couple of seconds before a smirk overtakes his face again—just as today's version of his dream redhead sashays our way.

"Sounds like we got here at just the right time," she says. The curvy bombshell and her friend look as pleased with themselves as much as they are with us. In breezy dresses and designer sunglasses, they're likely used to being the hunted, not the hunters. But they seem to like this role reversal. A lot.

I openly ignore their flirtations. I can't afford another slip in self-control. When I turn it off, bad things happen, and there are two glaring reminders in front of me. The horseshoe on the lat machine and the wheelchair under my best friend.

Jesse flashes a welcoming grin as the girls lean on the bright-blue rail that surrounds the weight pen.

"I'd say any time is the right time for you."

His line, smooth as whipped cream, has clearly snagged the redhead.

She licks her lips as if some of the stuff got caught there too. "Ohhh, so smooth. That means you're either an agent or a poet."

"Scientist, actually. Unlike Yeats or Hughes, I can tell you all about the Betelgeuse supernova, the Cascadia subduction zone, and anything you want to know about the galactic bulge."

He earns a side-eye. "That's a new one."

He mirrors my look. "It's a real thing, damn it."

The redhead hitches her glitter-trimmed sunglasses to the top of her head. "You had me at Betelgeuse, gorgeous. So . . . where are you boys off to after here?" she asks.

"And do you want some company?" her friend chimes in.

My spine stiffens, but I disguise it by wiping fake sweat off my neck. While Jesse's new friend is nice enough—and I'm sure her pal is too—no way am I up for hours of forced socializing and then awkwardly refusing a trip back to a girl's place for the night.

I don't begrudge Jesse's cavalier approach to sex, but I simply don't share it. Weirdly, it hasn't been a huge sacrifice. The mating merry-go-round just isn't my ride. There's something much more alluring about courting a woman. Learning her secrets. Winning her treasures.

Hell, maybe Jesse's right. Maybe I belong on another planet. Or at least in another time.

"Uhhh," I grit through a smile, hoping it looks contrite instead of constipated. "Sorry. We actually have another thing we've got to be at in a couple of hours. A private event. Downtown."

All of that emerges without a glitch because it's the truth. Tonight is a big night for Sarah and Reg, who are practically family. We're not missing it. I brace for some show of disappointment from Jesse, but his scowl never materializes.

"Oh, yeah." He beams a wider version of his megawatt grin. "The Melora Hall book-to-movie event at Recto Verso."

I instantly want to kill him as *both* women look like they want to jump him.

"You're going to the Melora Hall party?" Jesse's admirer says.

"Seriously?" squeals her little friend.

"And at Recto Verso, too. I love that place!"

"Right? It's so cute!"

As the women trade their exclamations, Jesse and I have an exchange of our own, silent but effective.

Cute? he mouths to me.

What the fuck? I answer, flaring my gaze.

We're on the same page on this at least. Equally proud of everything our bookstore-owning friends have built on Spring and Fifth as well as the praise it's received for the last thirty years—though "cute" doesn't really fit. The reason the studio picked Recto Verso for this event was to lend the project some street cred with the literary and film snobs via the store's trendy-but-intellectual vibe.

"So...we have a request of you ladies." He lets a few beats build up their obvious anticipation. "They likely won't accept Venus and Aphrodite as acceptable names on the event guest list..."

"I'm Misty!" the first one exclaims.

"And I'm Kristy!" says the second.

"Of course," I mutter just for Jesse's ears.

"Perfect," he continues, not missing a beat. By now he's got his phone out of his track pants pocket and extends it Misty's way. "But just to be sure, put yourself in as contacts. Better include your last names and phone numbers too. Just in case I have to text you with an update or something."

"Or something." I'm louder about the repetition, as well as the chuckle I tack on.

"By the way," he says while the girls add themselves to his device, "I'm Jesse, and this is Maximus."

"Oh, I *know* Maximus." Kristy bats her eyes at me. "I graduated from Alameda three years ago. Getting up early for your French Literature class was absolutely worth it."

I clear my throat. Grit my way through another tense smile. "Well...I'm glad you benefited from your time at Alameda."

"As I'm sure we'll all benefit from tonight's fun," Jesse smoothly inserts.

I flash him a grateful glance. I've grown into a semi-hermit because I've had to. He's grown into a halfway decent

16

socialite for the same reason.

"Let's say seven thirty?" he adds. "Festivities start at seven, but who wants to be on time?"

"Seven thirty it is." Misty beams a wide smile. "We need to go home and primp now."

"Ohhh, yes." Kristy nods like a spring-necked dashboard kitten. "Primping is in order." She winks my way. "Down to every last inch."

Three hours later, Kristy is wearing a bigger grin and a lot less clothing. She and Misty nudge their way through the crowd inside Recto Verso. Jesse and I have already staked our claim on one of the store's back corners, the area Sarah and Reg have set up as an LA-infused ode to their home country. There are a couple of mismatched love seats in front of a marble fireplace that's never used and a tall cabinet full of British knick-knacks mixed with sparkly Hollywood curios.

We're happy to grab a spot in front of the mantel's stone pillars and watch the parade of humanity proceeding toward the opposite corner of the store. Other event guests are clustered among the small reading nooks, book-themed sculptures, and tunnels formed of book "bricks" that lead to the area where Melora Hall is posing for photo ops. The leather spines of the novel collectors' section provide a sophisticated backdrop for the author, a lovely woman with big green eyes and mocha skin who greets everyone with the same charm and affection.

"Hi!" Misty greets us in a breathless rush—good thing, since the woman probably shouldn't inhale too hard tonight. Like Kristy, the woman appears to have been poured into her black cocktail dress.

"Well hello there, yourself." Jesse's comment is dotted with surprise, likely due to the full-mouth-press Misty's just leaned over and bestowed. "You look gorgeous."

"Why thank you, sir." Misty giggles, but her expression flattens when some flashbulbs pop, drawing her attention to the celebrity across the room. "Oh my freaking God." She grabs Jesse's hand and twists it in a thousand directions. "Melora Hall is really here!"

Jesse laughs. I join him. Though I'm counting the seconds until it's appropriate to slip away and hide out in Sarah's office for the rest of the night, the excitement in the air is a little contagious.

As if my thoughts have conjured her, a welcome sight of a woman seems to materialize from the middle of the throng. "Just wait until you see the rest of the crowd," she says in a distinct London clip.

The sound of that accent alone is enough to ease my nervousness. Tonight, Sarah—the woman who's been running my favorite bookstore for as long as I can remember—is dressed in a pastel pink sweater paired with gray tights and prismatic Doc Martens. There's a single streak of darker pink at the front of her otherwise silver hair. She's the only woman on the planet who exudes English schoolmarm and ex–punk rocker at the same time.

"Misty and Kristy, it's my pleasure to introduce you to

Ms. Sarah Reitz-Nikian," Jesse says. "She's one half of the kick-ass couple who own this place."

Kristy smiles. "Pleased to meet you, ma'am."

"And you as well, m'dear," Sarah answers.

But a similar greeting doesn't spill out of Misty. We're all curious onlookers as the woman's jaw nearly plummets to the floor. "S-S-Sorry," she finally spurts. "I'm—I'm so sorry. But holy crap, you weren't kidding about the crowd!"

"What?" Kristy leans over, using the motion as an excuse to slide her hand across my stomach. "What is it, honey?"

"Not a *what*," Misty counters. "A *who*. Oh, holy shit. I think it's really her."

"Who?" Kristy pushes at my ribs, seeming to need me for balance as she tiptoes on her stiletto shoes. "Where?"

"Right there!"

"Where? Oh, wait. Now I see. Oh my word!"

Out of pure curiosity, I follow their gawks to the classics section with which I'm so familiar.

I recognize her instantly because the vision of her hasn't stopped tormenting my imagination for the last twenty-four hours. Not her sweet face. Not her petite body that I have no business sizing up the way I did once we were alone in my classroom.

"I can't believe it." Kristy gasps. "It's Kara Valari. I can't remember the last time she's made a public appearance."

I pull in a hard breath through my nose, struggling for a way to distract the two women who should be focused on the event's headliner starlet, not the reclusive beauty belonging to one of Hollywood's most notorious dynasties. Because if I'm wagering any guesses from her unremarkable outfit, Miss Valari isn't here for a photo op.

"What do you think she's doing here?" Misty utters with starstruck awe.

Sarah crosses her arms and peers over her shoulder. "Her sister, Kell, is quite good friends with many of the guests tonight, especially Ms. Hall. She's around here somewhere too."

I think Kristy might stroke out with this news. She unpeels herself from me and reattaches herself to Misty. They crane their necks in unison, intent on spotting the other Valari in the room.

Well . . . hell.

This new twist has handed me the best opportunity to escape—but no way is that part of my plan anymore. Not now, with Kara Valari in my sights.

After giving Sarah a friendly hug and heartfelt congratulations about the turnout, I signal Jesse that I'll be back. Which, at this point, may or may not be the truth.

Using my size to my advantage, I cut a path through the crowd until only a few people stand between Kara and me. Her lip is clipped between her teeth, her brows pulled together in concentration as she stares up at the highest shelf before her.

Seemingly oblivious to the people mingling around her, she lifts herself up on her tiptoes, her fingertips barely making contact with the spine of whatever book she's after.

I maneuver until I'm there, inches away. And I don't realize the gravity of what I'm doing until it's too late.

CHAPTER 3

Kara

I RIP MY HAND back when he grazes my skin. The hot bolt of awareness inspires a flash of concern first, then melts into something even more unsettling when I realize it's Professor Kane—well, Maximus—beside me.

His polite gesture isn't paired with a friendly smile. If I didn't know better, I'd say he felt the singe of energy between us too. But that's impossible. Normal people don't feel things like I do...except he looks like I feel—stunned and fascinated.

He stares down at the book like it offended him before offering it to me. I take it, careful not to touch him.

"Thanks."

He doesn't speak for a moment, his blue-eyed gaze boring into me like I'm a problem he can't solve. It doesn't help that this place is jammed, forcing us into a proximity that feels too personal. Especially as I find myself taking in details about him I couldn't appreciate before. The ring of deeper blue around the irises of his eyes. His muscled forearms, visible now with his sleeves rolled up tightly. Most noticeably, his hair falls in messy coppery waves past his shoulders, giving him a wild and untethered look, far from the buttoned-up professor I met yesterday.

The din of the crowd is pierced with the squeal of an excited Piper Blue fan on the other side of the store. Maximus looks over briefly before turning his attention back to me and the book in my hand.

"Required reading?"

I blink a couple of times before I latch on to his meaning. "Oh." I tuck the heavy hardcover under my arm. "Not really. Just looked interesting, I guess."

The corner of his mouth quirks up. "Greek rituals are interesting?"

"I'm a classics—"

"Yes, I know. Classics major. You told me that already." He rests his elbow on the edge of the shelf dedicated to the Roman Empire. "It's just that everyone's here to gush over celebrities, and you're over here in your own little world."

"And that's interesting to you?"

Those rings of cobalt seem to intensify. "It is."

I fidget with the textured edge of the book, a little floored that he'd notice. "Is that why *you're* here? To gush over celebrities?"

His smirk broadens. "No. I'm friends with the owners. I grew up down the street. They're basically family."

"So is Piper. She and my sister have been inseparable for years."

"That's nice of you to come and support her."

I fail to mask an eye roll.

He laughs. "What?"

"Piper has enough fangirls. She doesn't need moral support. My sister's determined to put me in the spotlight every chance she can. I was promised a lift home after class, and here we are."

"Little bit of a detour."

I wrinkle my nose. "Little bit."

"You could just leave, you know."

I shrug. "I like books."

"I can tell. How's Dante treating you?"

I feel my cheeks color, though I can't reason why. His question is simple enough. "I'm enjoying it," I finally manage.

His next words are lower. Almost...intimate. "You don't have to tell me that just because I'm your professor."

"I wouldn't lie about it."

His gaze drops from my eyes to the book and seems to wander over more of me. I take in an uneven breath because this feels dangerously like flirting. With my professor. Not that I'm parked on any moral high ground about it, but I'm not in a position to get entangled with anyone. Especially Maximus, with his sweet eyes and electric touch and soft-looking mouth...

Umph.

Suddenly I'm shoved from behind, launched against his massive frame. Lightning fast, he wraps his arm around me to keep me from tumbling sideways into the people near us.

"Oh my God, I'm so sorry!" someone says.

They could be a mile away, because all I can hear is Maximus's heavy exhale as he cinches us infinitesimally closer. His hand, huge and warm, is on my waist. His scent, like a summer rain rushing over my senses. Then his voice, breathy and low, is in my ear.

"Fuck."

It's barely a whisper. A word I can feel more than hear as I struggle to process the sensory explosion of this much contact. My heart beats excitedly, like it's responding to a fun new drug designed to keep me amped all night. I brace my palm against the expanse of his chest and force myself into a state of composure. *Calm down. Focus.*

Except this is more than butterflies. This is a phoenix in flight. The hard hook of attraction that's impossible to pass off as anything else now. A live wire I don't want to let go of but desperately need to before he gets the wrong idea.

I steady on my feet and step back slowly. His touch falls away, and I'm almost mournful as I drag my gaze up to his. I'm ready to thank him for his quick reflexes, but the words die in my throat. Suddenly my skin burns as fiercely as the heat in his eyes. Then I realize his earlier slip wasn't meant to curse the offending klutz who ran into me. In fact, I don't think he meant to say it at all.

"You all right?" he says, his voice taking on a raspy quality that I can feel on the surface of my skin. And other places.

"I'm good."

Too good. Buzzing with euphoria good. About to rip his clothes off good.

I should thank him for saving me from the fall. Then I should walk away and take great pains to never get this close to him again.

"Kara. There you are. *Seriously.*"

My sister's dramatic drone breaks the spell. Maximus runs a shaky hand through his hair as she sidles up beside us in head-to-toe Gucci.

"It's a miracle the paparazzi get any pictures of you at all. You find the weirdest places to hide out. You're nowhere near the action," she rattles on.

Before I can make introductions, Maximus mumbles something I can't make out and turns into the crowd, creating distance between us that I'm already conflicted about. A little voice reminds me I'll see him in class tomorrow, which shouldn't be such a thrilling prospect. Not after I nearly seized with pleasure from a few seconds of body contact.

I try in vain not to follow him as he finds a place to stand on the other side of the store. The farthest possible spot from me. Wise. I need to remind myself of that at least a thousand more times.

I silently promise to stick with my seat in the back row of the lecture hall going forward. This can't happen again. He's too dangerous to the walls of my self-control.

"Come on. Let's go get a pic—" Kell's deep brown eyes widen slightly. "Whoa. Do you smell that?"

I swing my gaze back to her. "What?"

Her nostrils flare with a couple short sniffs. "Lust and ..." She frowns. "Anxiety?"

I lick my lips nervously. "That's me. I'm anxious."

"I know what you smell like, K-demon. That wasn't you."

"Don't call me that."

She gracefully flips her slick wall of black hair over her shoulder. "Kara, you're the only one of us who needs to be reminded of it."

"Okay, well, we're in public." I can barely gesture for effect without hitting someone with my hand.

"The public hasn't called us worse?"

I roll my eyes and breathe out a sigh. "Whatever."

"So ..." Her gaze wanders over the crowd. "Who was Mr. Lusty? That's not like you to get someone all wound up."

"It's no one. He's my professor. It's not like that."

Her pretty red lips form a shocked oval as she spots Maximus. "You're kidding me. *He's* your professor?"

"Yes," I hiss quietly and turn my back to him, hoping to hell he doesn't notice the most tolerable of my siblings blatantly pointing and staring at him like an unselfconscious toddler.

"Wait a motherfucking minute," she says almost breathlessly. "That's that superhot literature professor, isn't it? Shit. I tried to get into one of his classes too. I got stuck with some old hag with a hard-on for Whitman."

"Kell, Professor Ferguson is the poet laureate."

She waves her hand dismissively. "I don't even care. On to more important matters..." She studies me closely, as if I have evidence on me. "Are you putting the moves on him? I honestly never thought you'd flirt for grades. That's just not like you."

The growl that rumbles deep in my chest is drowned out by the crowd, unlike her unhinged remarks that can be clearly heard by nearly anyone with any interest. And tonight, with the media mingling like bees in a hive, the shop is swarming with people who want fresh dirt on the Valaris.

"Considering I've had one class with him so far, no. Not to mention...you know." I wave my hand in tiny circles and stare at the bookshelf beside me, briefly wishing I could find a way to hide between the tomes. Maybe find a secret door in this enchanting little bookstore that can take me away from LA to another plane of reality where my life isn't already charted for me.

"What the hell are you talking about?" Kell's flawless face is wrinkled with confusion.

"I'm *promised*. And so are you, by the way. Did you forget that tiny detail?"

When she crosses her arms and averts her gaze, I know she hasn't forgotten. If anyone can appreciate the vow we were bound to at birth, she can.

"You can do other things in the meantime," she mutters without much conviction.

"What's the point?" I wear my emotions too close to the surface, along with every base impulse. And when it comes to sex, having it with just anyone isn't an option. I may hate being a Valari, but that doesn't mean I can pretend I'm not one.

When humans break their vows, feelings get hurt. Hearts get broken. When demons break vows, someone gets punished.

Kell taps her red lacquered nail on her tooth. "Yeah." Her eyes brighten after a moment. "Well, once you meet, you know, whoever it's going to be and seal the deal, you can hook up with whoever you want. You just need to finish this stupid degree and get on with it."

"Why don't you get on with it?" I challenge.

She scoffs. "I *will*. Eventually. I'm just trying to wait a respectable amount of time before I settle down. I'm not an old maid like you."

"You're barely a year younger than me."

She shrugs, a small show of admission. "I hate people telling me what to do. Maybe in a few years I won't care so much."

Unlikely.

In fairness, her worry mirrors my own. We have no idea who we'll be matched with when the time comes. But every full-blooded demon I've ever met has fit a particular profile. Cocky and charismatic and not to be trifled with. They're talented liars with vicious tempers, sent to strengthen a bloodline weakened by my human ancestors.

I've spent a good part of my adult life trying not to think about it.

"Come on." Kell nudges me gently, the same inevitability painted across her features. "Let's get out of here."

CHAPTER 4

Maximus

"**D**AMN IT."

It's not the first time I've spat it tonight. Not even the first time since climbing out Sarah's office window, onto the fire escape, and then up here to the roof. I'm certain it won't be the last.

What the hell was I thinking?

Pretty sure it won't be the last time for that line either. And I can't answer it, because thought had little to do with the force that drew me across the store and into her personal space in that crush of a crowd—even after I'd spent the better part of the day attempting to erase every thought of the girl from my mind.

Except one.

Student. Hands off.

Which doesn't help me right now. None of the pieces inside that feel all wrong.

But when she was in my arms tonight, everything felt right.

More right than things have felt in a long damn time.

I growl out more profanity before sinking my ass onto the concrete lip that surrounds the building's massive air-conditioning unit. With another guttural sound, I claw the hair away from my face.

"Get your shit together, Kane."

The night swiftly swallows the sound. Even on a Tuesday night, Downtown LA is just waking up. People are laughing. Restaurants are bustling. Cars are honking. A local cover band warms up for their first set of the night in the bar three doors over. Their sound-check song is "Don't Stand So Close To Me."

Of course it is.

And just when I think the situation can't get worse, the door from the building's interior stairwell opens. A swath of fluorescent light spills out over the roof, and from that light a silhouette emerges. A petite frame topped by a head with long cornrows.

"There you are."

Reg strolls over and plants herself beside me. "Thought I might find you here." She plucks at the black flowy pants that Sarah probably forced her into. Her grimace betrays how she likens the things to spider webs. The knit top and cropped jacket don't fare much better, victims of her shrugging and squirming. For a few seconds, I watch her do it. I'm not used to this look, such a departure from the cargo pants and book-centric tees that have been her daily norm since the day I walked into the store nearly nineteen years ago.

I was a reclusive, terrified kid then. She was restocking the bestsellers section, and when she said I could keep any book I wanted if I helped her out, a friendship was born.

I let her silently fidget through another minute or so before I break the silence.

"What're you doing up here? Aren't you supposed to be hosting a party?"

She answers with nothing but a frustrated sound.

"Guess I wasn't the only one who'd had enough of the mob," I mutter.

"You said it." A dry laugh escapes her. "Funny thing is, Melora Hall seems the most sane of the bunch."

I'm surprised, but I know all about preconceptions. "Maybe the biggest voices in the jungle have the least to prove."

She shifts her gaze from the sparkling skyline toward me. "Or the most."

I stiffen.

She focuses harder on me. She gets it. I know she does. She knows I still have to think about this shit nearly every day. Being the giant in the room, in many senses, doesn't give me the freedom to do whatever I want. It means I'm forever proving to the world that I'm better than my instincts. It means stressing about smashing all the china.

Or the walls.

Or the people.

"Do you really want to know why I'm up here?"

There it is again. That quiet funnel of her concentration, making me want to fidget worse than her. "If I say no, you'll tell me anyway."

She smirks and then bumps my shoulder. "I'm here because you are."

I shrug, hoping to appear more detached than I am. "Just needed some air. I'm fine. Honestly."

Not remotely, but I hope she buys it. Inside I'm a mess. A turned-on, conflicted mess that I can't begin to explain to this sweet woman with her unconditional loyalty to me.

"You're not," she answers flatly. "I have eyes, you know. I saw you with that Valari girl."

She says it as if she already knows thoughts of Kara have been slamming my frontal lobe for the last hour.

That quickly, my libido succumbs to another tsunami of memories. The crush of the crowd. The nearness of soft skin in a flimsy sundress. The smell of that skin, a succulent mix of roses and cinnamon and smoke. The same heat that was thick in her huge brown eyes, taking me in like we were the only trees still standing in a burning forest.

But playing with fire means someone usually gets burned.

I turn quickly from Reg. "It wasn't what it looked like."

"Famous last words?"

"The room was crowded and noisy." I jam my hands into my pockets, awkward as it is from my seated position. "You didn't see what you thought, Regina."

Her inhalation is so sharp, it sounds like a whistle. "Did you just go there? With the full name? Because even mighty

Maximus can't escape a shot of hand soap instead of creamer in his next cup of coffee."

I try hard not to laugh. The woman usually pulls the first day's shift at the store's coffee bar, so I know she can—and would—make that happen with the latte I always pick up on my way to campus.

"With all due respect, Ms. Nikian, you still didn't see anything."

She lifts a dark brow. "Just like I never did when you nicked cookies out of the display?"

I submit to a chuckle. "Something like that."

Her expression softens. "I've never seen you look at someone like that."

I close my eyes, trying like hell not to show her any of my truth before meeting her penetrating stare. "For the last time, whatever you observed—"

"Before you give me your best lie, remember I've known you nearly your whole life. Now tell me, why are you flirting with a Valari?"

The way she slants the name prompts a defensive clench of my jaw.

"Is there something about her family name that especially bothers you?"

She winces slightly. "Call me curious. That's all." She reaches up and tenderly palms my cheek. "Of course, I can't help but think she's not worthy of you."

She purses her lips into a half smile, and the thunder between my ribs has turned into a wad of warm mush. Damn it.

"You really are bound for better than her, you know." And just like that, her smirk vanishes beneath a small surge of new emotion. Something that hits my perception like vehemence. Even violence. "So much better."

Those last words have me tense again. "Not exactly what I'm worried about, Reg."

"Then what is it?"

My thoughts are tripping again, all over the pretty girl downstairs who I had no business putting my hands on, accidentally or otherwise. I stopped trusting myself with people a long time ago. Despite the gnawing hunger for contact and ... *more.*

"She's a nice girl. From what I can tell, probably better than most people give her credit for." I wince, stopping myself short of saying more. "I just can't get involved with anyone right now," I finish with a note of defeat.

"This is about Jesse, isn't it?" Reg's voice, while laced again with vexation, holds something new. A hint of challenge.

My only answer is my silence. I stare out across the building tops toward the vast darkness on the horizon that's the ocean. Normally, that liquid space brings a strange certainty—a calmness—to my spirit. Right now, it signifies everything I don't know about the world. About myself.

"After all these years, you still haven't forgiven yourself," she utters softly.

I brave a look in her direction, ready to explain that I never will. But the quiet ferocity and devotion in her eyes stop me from saying all I want to.

I paralyzed my best friend. I nearly killed him. I'm unforgivable.

I take in a measured breath. Another. Still, I fight to quiet the internal tirade that wants to spill free and replace it with something Reg will accept. She deserves that much, but I've never been able to give her the actual words. She and Sarah have never let me down, not since that first day I wandered into the store, wondering if anyone would see me as normal again. Not after what I did to Jesse.

It didn't matter that I hadn't meant to do it. That we'd only been playing with the rough zeal of typical eight-year-olds. The damage had been done, and I'd never be the same person again.

"Forgive and forget," I finally say. "But what happens when you can't forget?" I rub a couple of fingers across my forehead, pushing in until it hurts. "I'm never going to be able to forget what happened. Even if I didn't see him all the time, I wouldn't be able to wipe that day from my memory."

That day.

The one that still haunts so many of my nightmares.

Every single one of its details.

The bees humming over the playground field. The warm wind, bringing the first scents of summer. The heady taste of freedom. School was out, and Jesse and I had big plans.

Plans I'd ended. For good. In one moment. On that day.

After that came more awful days. The confusion. The guilt. The fear. No one would talk to me about what Jesse's fate would be. I didn't know until much later that all hopes for repairing the damage to his spinal cord were lost. That he'd be in that wheelchair for the rest of his life. That they'd roll him out of the hospital and he'd start spouting a string of stupid one-liners so I wouldn't notice every hard gulp in his throat or the doomed sorrow in his eyes . . .

"It was an accident, Max. You were eight years old!"

"Doesn't matter," I grit out.

"Of course it ma—"

"It. Doesn't. Matter." I turn from her and hunch over, gaining momentum to drive my fist into the ledge. Instantly I regret the wide crack I've opened up in the concrete. For a guy who's vowed to hang on to control in any way possible, the stuff is tumbling like sand from my fist. "It didn't change the outcome."

She huffs out a frustrated sigh. "Everyone makes mistakes, Maximus. Life is full of them. We've all done things we wish we could take back."

"It's more than that."

So much more than a simple misstep or an embarrassing moment to keep me up at night. There will never be enough well-meaning words or affectionate stares to douse my self-loathing when it comes to what I did to Jesse.

"Is it? Or are you so determined to martyr yourself that you refuse to make peace with something that Jesse already made peace with a long time ago?"

"How do you know he's made peace with it?"

She gives me a pointed look, silently calling me on my shit. We both know better. Jesse loves life. He made a conscious choice to do so, refusing to be a victim or a charity case—and calling me on that shit more than anyone else over the years. He's made peace with his circumstances and expects me to do the same.

But even as I think about it, a stubborn part of me refuses to fully fly that banner. Somehow the prospect of letting it go makes room for it to happen again. And I could never live with that.

As silence falls between us, Reg tilts her head back and closes her eyes. The beads in her braids reflect the streetlights, winking like stars of purple and blue across her head.

I distract myself from the growing pressure in my chest by giving her a good-natured shoulder bump. "You know if Sarah finds out we both ditched her and came up here, she's going to be pissed."

She smiles. "You're right. And I'm pretty sure if you don't get back down there, she may have to pry Jesse's little admirer off him with a crowbar."

I stand, stretching out the stiffness in my muscles. "I'm sure that won't be necessary. But I'll give him a wellness check just in case."

I extend my hand and help her upright. But she doesn't let go right away. Instead, she beams another stare that conveys much more than her love and concern. It holds a hint of determination that's making me itchy to end our chat.

"And the girl?"

"She's a student, Reg. I was just saying hi. Drop it, all right?" *Please, please fucking drop it.*

"Do you like her?"

I groan in frustration and strongly consider bolting for the door, but ultimately there's no outrunning Reg or a conversation she's determined to have.

"Sure. As a student." I sigh heavily. "Hell, I don't know." I thread a nervous hand through my hair, reminding myself to shut the hell up before I give Reg more ammo.

"Is that why you're up here?"

"No, I'm—"

I'm ready to feed her a line about wanting to escape the crowd, same as her, but I have a feeling she's too suspicious to believe it. I give her hand a little squeeze and let it drop between us.

"I'm...different, Reg," I finally mutter. "You and I both know it."

"There's nothing wrong with being different."

"If you're me, there is."

"You're dead wrong." She rocks back on one foot, tossing me a harsher regard while folding her arms neatly across her chest. "And one day, someone's going to prove you wrong in the very best way, whether you're ready for it or not. Probably not this girl, but someone will someday. So my advice to you, Maximus Kane, would be to get ready for it."

I force a tight smile to mask the twist of fear snaking its way through my insides. Fear that she could be right. That despite all my efforts, someone might get too close. Fear that I might let them.

Because, damn it, those fears have a face now. A beautiful, unforgettable one.

And it belongs to Kara Valari.

CHAPTER 5

Kara

A HEAVY MORNING FOG lingers in the valley between the house and the big block letters posted into the mountain on the other side. I don't have to see the sign to know it's there—a constant reminder that Hollywood is home. Our family's chosen headquarters away from the kingdom we're doomed to serve for eternity.

I pull a thick throw blanket around my shoulders, chasing away the chill of damp air on the deck overlooking the reservoir. Even in September, Southern California mornings are too cold for my liking.

The door slides open behind me, a sure marker that my quiet morning is about to come to an end. The patio furniture beneath me shifts loudly when my housemate plops herself down, a tall coffee mug in her hand.

"You're up early," I say, a little impressed that Kell hasn't skipped a beat from last night's event. Her hair is already flat-ironed, her makeup is meticulously contoured, and her outfit is crisp, brand-new, and skintight. It's almost as if she and the paparazzi have an arrangement that she'll give them what they want if they give her what she wants—tantalizing photo ops without the unflattering angles.

She flicks her thumb over her phone screen and starts scrolling through her social media feed. "I have an eight o'clock class."

"You signed up for that on purpose?"

She starts typing a comment. "Introductory Astronomy. At least I'll get there early enough to beat traffic."

True enough. The journey from our house in the Hollywood Hills to campus isn't always predictable. I drag my hefty copy of *The Divine Comedy* onto my lap. "All right. I'll get ready now and ride in with you. We can stop by to see Gramps after my last class. Today's his birthday."

She whips her stare up, concern suddenly sharpening her features. "Kara. Don't call him that."

I bristle inside but try not to show it. Holding on to affection for our grandfather has always been a delicate matter. And I'm only delicate for his sake. Being the only unfortunate human in a family of black souls, he has enough working against him without me raising suspicions that he means more to me than he should.

"We'll go see Gio," I correct, putting added emphasis on the name we've been forced to call him. I'm chafing on the inside. Why does it have to be this way? It's as if he's just a stranger taking up space in the guesthouse of our family's estate. I wouldn't be surprised to find out Mom is charging him rent.

Kell glances back down at her phone, an unpleasant scowl ruining her picture-perfect look. "Mom won't like it. You should go in a few days."

"I'm not going to walk in with a sheet cake and balloons. I just want to stop by and wish him a happy birthday. You know no one else will. And you can distract Mom. I'm sure she's too focused on other things to even remember the day has any significance. It's just another day all about her."

She rolls her eyes with a soft sigh. "Fine. Just leave me out of it, okay?"

Her focus is glued to her phone for a couple more minutes. Kell and I might share a house and a fate, but we're nothing alike. Just like human siblings, we've turned out differently. The problem is, I'm *too* different. Money and clothes and excess are supposed to satisfy me. No one understands why I regard it all as little more than convenience. I'd be happy with less, but a lifestyle supported by the ever-growing Valari fortune is the check I'm expected to cash in exchange for my obedience. Refusing it isn't optional. There's no other way.

I clutch the book to my chest and stand, forcing myself not to break the morning calm by sharing these frustrations with my darkly enlightened little sister. Her illumination on the path straight to hell is the crazy, if sad, irony of the day.

"Give me ten minutes," I finally say. "Make it fifteen."

No sense in denying that I'll be paying a little extra attention to prepping for class today. I'm a demon, not a zombie.

Maximus hasn't looked at me for the better part of an hour. Still, the professor holds every second of my attention. Especially now, as he reads the final stanzas of Canto III aloud, his voice as rich and intense as I've ever heard it. In fact, everything about him seems more intense this morning.

One might suspect he didn't get enough sleep, or coffee, or that he's simply having a shitty day. But the way he tore his gaze from mine as I walked into the lecture hall makes me wonder what's really happening behind his invisible walls.

My conversation with Kell this morning—not to mention our impending visit to Gramps tonight—linger in my mind, but I can't seem to focus on anything except the way Maximus furrows his brows as he reads, gesturing as he goes, like the words are a symphony his fingers need to conduct. Even from this distance, I can feel the passion vibrating from him, an almost imperceptible energy, a subtle but dangerous shift like the tectonic plates that rumble the ground beneath our feet at least a dozen times a day.

"And all pass eagerly, for here, Divine Justice transforms and spurs them so their dread turns wish: they yearn for what they fear."

He continues, finishing the last lines with perfect cadence. Their meaning shoots a stinging arrow through the heart I know I have, even if its longings and purpose never seem to align the way they should.

An air of finality and expectation fills the silence once Maximus claps his copy of the book shut. Students fidget, no doubt anticipating questions they may not be equipped to answer. He paces wordlessly along the front row, whether deep in thought or committed to building the anticipation, I'm not sure. Finally he pauses and clears his throat and begins to speak.

"So Virgil and Dante are at the gates of hell. Charon is ready to ferry the souls of the damned across the river. Yet Virgil claims they all pass eagerly. Why is that?"

I twist my fingers together until I've wrung the blood from them. The urge to speak and have his eyes on me goes to war with attracting everyone else's attention. That and I've already decided that interacting with the professor, even from the back row, is more dangerous than his passion for the text. I'm far too intrigued by him.

As if he can hear my unspoken thoughts, he finally meets my eyes in the crowd. I think he purposefully cast his stare out for mine, lingering long enough to make my blood rush. My nerve endings tingle. My senses careen.

"Kara?"

My name from his mouth shouldn't affect me the way it does in the wake of his reading. Still, my heart slams against my ribs. Once, twice, before I find my voice in my suddenly arid throat.

"Well . . . Virgil is explaining that hell isn't a punishment. It's what the souls of the damned truly long for. It's a deliberate choice." I swallow hard before continuing. "Which is why the damned don't deserve Dante's sympathy."

I've lingered on the passage since I read it days ago. Hearing it pass through Maximus's lips—lips I've spent too much time thinking about lately—almost turns it into an accusation. Except there's no way for him to know how the topic affects me. Snide remarks from my classmates aside, he could never understand my own turmoil about the choices I'm going to make. Choices I'm expected to make.

He nods briefly. "Very well put."

I exhale a breath, enjoying a surge of satisfaction as he goes on to wrap up the lecture, noting the next set of reading assignments.

"If anyone has any questions, or if you'd like to begin exploring themes for the first term paper that's due in a few weeks, I will have office hours immediately after this class on Mondays and Wednesdays, as well as Tuesday afternoons. I'm on the fourth floor of the Archer Building."

He dismisses the class, and as much as I want to disappear as swiftly as I can, the traffic jam makes it impossible. I wait impatiently as every hot-blooded human takes their time filing out of the hall. As I finally rise to leave, Maximus's voice carries through the hall.

"Kara. Wait a minute. Please."

I turn, practically compelled to the action by the rough vibration of his last word. The door closes behind the last student leaving, but I hardly notice. I try not to blatantly gawk at Maximus, propped against the edge of his desk. His long legs are bent, straining the khaki fabric containing them. A few strands of hair fall loose around his face from the messy knot at his nape. So casual and imposing all at once, except his hands, which he uses to clutch the desk tightly like he might fall.

I carry myself down the steps, slowly, enjoying the view.

"What is it?" I ask almost breathlessly.

"Why do you always sit in the back?" His voice is restrained, like there are a hundred questions resting beneath that one.

I think a moment about which version of the truth I should give him. Or which lie.

"People like to take pictures of me. You've already seen firsthand that having me in class can be a distraction. I stay in the back so it's less disruptive. I can't help who I am, but I'd rather it not get in the way of my education."

He taps the toe of his leather shoe twice. "You are a distraction."

I wince. "What exactly are you trying to say?"

He shakes his head slightly. "I mean... I can see how it could be worse. It's just a shame. I think you're one of the only students really engaged in the class, and it's hard to have intelligent discourse with you when people are more interested in..."

"Selfies? Shouting insults?"

"Yes. And I've seen the way people look at you."

We share a long stare. The moment drags until every air molecule in the room feels like a nuclear-charged atom. His eyes and their potent blue fires only fuel my impression. Instantly I realize he's not just talking about the hecklers. The attention I attract isn't always made of spite.

"Like the way you look at me?"

I don't know why I say it, except maybe I need to know how to interpret these interactions between us. Do I affect him the way I secretly hope I do?

"I'm sorry. That's not what I meant," he says quickly, the sound rough in his throat.

"For a scholar, you're having a hard time saying what you mean."

He folds his arms across his chest, like he's protecting himself from my presence, even though he's the one keeping me here.

I widen my eyes when I notice the subtle indents in the metal where his hands once were. I take a step closer, too curious not to investigate the marred desk. Except he quickly settles his hands back into the grooves that perfectly fit his tense grip.

I glance into his eyes, tortured and shadowed, full of answers he's not giving me. The inexplicable anguish there draws me another step closer. I'm not sure what keeps pulling me forward until we're nearly touching. Defiance? Pure recklessness? I reach out, holding my breath as my fingertips brush across the rough fabric of his vest.

His breathing changes, but he doesn't push me away. His knuckles whiten as the metal in his grip bends audibly. It's enough to distract me from our thought-shattering physical connection. It's enough to make me wonder if maybe he feels it too. If maybe he's as different as I am.

CHAPTER 6

Maximus

"Kara."

I'm not sure if the word is even audible. It feels more like a pulse of my instinct. A ripple through my bloodstream. As if primal parts of myself have been waiting for her arrival...

Here. So close.

Then even closer, as she turns the press of her fingertips into the push of her whole hand. The heat radiating from her is nearly tangible, like flames spreading across my chest and directly into the organ that throbs there. It seems to stretch for more of her beautiful fire. Her fierce, forbidden heat...

"*Kara.*"

She's heard me now. That's clear in her pause, but she doesn't withdraw. Suddenly I'm relating more to Dante than I ever imagined. Do I cross the river—willingly—into the flames, or stay on my shore? Do I steer safe from the sins

I'll confront on the other side?

"Maximus."

Her response is also nothing more than a whisper. It's wrapped in her unique scent, the cinnamon and spice making me lick the inside of my lips. Then the outside.

Holy shit. I'm in trouble.

"Please . . . don't . . ." she utters softly.

A growl spills from me while I contort the top of my desk into modern art and tear divots into the floor with urgent plants of my feet.

"You're kidding, right? Because if I try any harder not to touch you—"

"I meant . . . don't push me away."

Air rushes from my nostrils.

A gulp tremors down the column of her throat.

"Maximus . . ." she rasps, ending it with a lilt that almost seems a question. One born in desperation.

"What?" I murmur. "What is it?"

"Tell me I'm not the only one who's feeling this. Please . . . tell me."

I emulate her swallow as she splays her hand along the side of my throat.

"I knew it," she whispers.

I'm stunned into another long silence. I validate the feeling by examining her face again. She's really not afraid of me. Of the force I've exerted on the metal in my hands and the concrete beneath my feet. If anything, my loss of control has tripped some new switch for her senses. Her breaths are a frantic tattoo. Her stare rakes my face, her pupils nearly eclipsing their dark chocolate irises.

She inhales with purpose, as if we're on a plummeting plane and I've handed her the last working oxygen mask. "But why do you keep trying to hide it from me?"

I'm falling. Losing altitude, swiftly and violently. Which way is up? And do I even care?

No. I have to care.

I manage to raise a hand. I form my fingers over hers and squeeze tight. "Because we can't..."

"What? At least acknowledge it?" She pushes at my jaw with shocking strength.

At least I don't have to hide that from her. At once, she answers my bafflement with a full, sweet smile. Like it's perfectly normal for her to be handling my face like she's a pixie-sized bulldozer.

I slam my eyes closed.

"Am I wrong?" she persists. "Open your eyes, look straight at me, and tell me I'm wrong about that, and I'll walk away right now. I'll never mention this again. I'll just keep to myself at the back of the class for the whole semester. We can have a blast talking about hell for a couple of hours each week, and—"

She gasps as I tunnel a hand into her hair and pull at her scalp. Hard. And that's it for all the color in her eyes. The awareness in her stare has blocked everything from my view except her ink-dark need.

"You think hell is just for the pages of a book when you're near me?" I ask.

Her touch gentles. Her fingertips are in my beard,

seeking contact with the skin beneath. "Hell is something I thought I knew—until you touched me the first time."

Now she's done it. Obliterated any hope I had of issuing the denial she dictated. But I'm also just as certain of another truth—and the importance of saying it aloud. Speaking it will make it easier to abide by.

I hope.

"All right." I untangle my hand from her silky ebony strands. "You're not wrong. This is definitely something..."

"Something?"

"Different."

"Okay," she states with quiet resignation. "Different..." But there's a question in that repetition too. A demand she's not about to let me ignore.

"Yes." I use a beat to ram my thoughts back together before finally gritting out, "And dangerous."

I disconnect from her touch completely and stride around the podium I rarely use, but I'm damn happy for its bulk in this moment. I start gathering up paperwork, realigning it all fifteen times just for something to keep in my hands. Something besides her succulent curves and soft skin.

"Because you're my professor?" She lets out a little huff. "I'm not exactly a freshman out of high school. Even when I was, life had taught me some tough lessons already. And I'm pretty sure we're not the first teacher and student, even here at Alameda, who have—"

"It has nothing to do with that."

She folds her arms. The sight isn't one I need right now,

since the action pulls down her cotton blouse and exposes her cleavage in all the best—goddammit, *worst*—ways. Once again, thank fuck for the podium—and how the wood hides my obvious arousal.

"Meaning exactly what?"

"I don't know." And that's the bald truth. "I can only say that I've already thought about it more than I care to admit. About . . . whatever the hell is going on here and what it would be like to tell our invisible Charon to take us to the other side." I almost laugh at myself. I'm the guy who likes studying poetry, not composing it.

Kara adjusts her weight from one foot to the other. She seems unsure and certain at once. Bold one moment and ready to bolt the next. What I want and what I need are two different matters as well, and I worry it's the same for her.

"What did that feel like?" She captures her bottom lip beneath her teeth. "Imagining that jump with me?"

I push air out harshly through my nose. "It felt a thousand kinds of wrong."

But a million kinds of right.

But I clamp that part inside despite the wince across Kara's face. A pain that's pure torment to witness. But I can't elaborate on what I've said to her. I can't explain how I know this to be a truth I can't cross—only that I *do* know it, with primal certainty. I'm as certain of it as the fiber of my muscles and the marrow of my bones. She's gotten to me even in those places. Awakened parts of me that deep . . .

Besides, Kara's already got a full plate of psychological crap thanks to her own birthright. The more I look at her family tree, the more I wonder how the woman has remained halfway sane. But my brooding has now given her cause to reattach her mask of surreal—even slightly scary—resignation. Maybe that's for the best. The more time I spend with Kara Valari, the more I don't want it to end.

But the more I know that it has to.

"Will that be all, then, Professor? I'm meeting my sister, Kell, at the library to study." She pops out a hip and cocks her head in challenge.

I lift a skeptical brow. "You know that's an oxymoron, right? 'Kell Valari' and 'study' in the same sentence?" The comment, simply meant as my awful way of lightening the mood, accomplishes the opposite. I deserve her glare, to which I respond, "All right, that wasn't fair. I don't know Kell—"

"Damn right you don't," she levels.

"It's just staff cafeteria gossip," I fill in. "They should know better. *Hell...*" I scrub a hand over my jaw. "*I* should know better."

She contemplates my piss-poor apology with an all-too-quick stare. "I'm leaving now," she announces flatly before pivoting on her stilettoed boots and making her way back to the desk risers.

The air is thick and silent while she gathers her things and then pushes through the doors at the top of the stairs.

It takes me all of two seconds to admit I already crave her again.

I take the risers two at a time, hoping even her scent has lingered...

What I encounter is less expected. A gem-encrusted earring glitters like illuminated blood on the industrial gray carpet, right in front of my boot toe.

Her earring.

I'm sure of it because my hand was just twisted in the glorious hair that tumbled around the gold, ruby, and diamond piece—which is more than a collection of stones set into an intricate design. It looks like an old family crest. A fierce medieval wolf looks to be running across a sky of the diamonds and holding one in each of his pointy paws. His slitted eyes and curling tongue are fashioned from the dark crimson rubies.

It's one of the most unique pieces of jewelry I've ever seen. Something about it clutches at the darker parts of me, strong enough that I'm squinting harder at it, fighting to make out the tiny Latin words bordering the oval...

Until I realize that every second I'm stalling is another second she's rushing farther away.

I clear the distance to the door with a hell-bent-for-leather leap. Nearly in the same movement, I bust through the portal.

"Kara!"

But in the space of chasing her and marveling at the delicate thing she left behind, she's vanished. The hall is empty, not offering me a single clue to follow. Which shouldn't piss me off as much as it does.

I'll see her here again in a matter of days. That should be too soon after what's just happened between us. But I have to face the truth. I have to acknowledge the line I just crossed with the girl, despite every alarm and warning and threat my common sense screamed at me. Wisdom I knowingly shoved aside.

A truth I can no longer deny.

I'll keep crossing that line. I'll trespass that boundary again and again and again until I can figure out why Kara Valari is unlike any other person I've ever met.

And why she isn't terrified that I'm not either.

CHAPTER 7

Kara

"WHAT'S GOING ON? YOU'RE too quiet, even for you," Kell says, scrolling through dozens of songs on her playlist until she settles on the one that seems to satisfy her enough to look up at the road.

We're at a dead stop. I stare out the window of her cherry-red Bentley to the sea of unmoving traffic, unsure what to tell her. I'm too caught up in my own thoughts. In Maximus. He probably thinks I rebuffed him, and I should be fine with that. If he only knew it was pure desperation that got me out of there before I did something even more reckless. Like press my lips against his just to see if I could unleash more of his strength.

His strength.

I close my eyes and relive the moment I still can't fully believe. I've seen things... Things that wouldn't necessarily be considered normal, or earthly even. But I've never seen a human turn laminate into dust under his heels. I've never

had a man put his hands on me with that kind of power—
the power to keep me there.

I shouldn't want more of that. But hell, I do. I'd give
just about anything to be back there right now, standing
between his thighs, his fingers tangled in my hair, watching
the battle in his eyes as he tries so hard not to touch me but
fails.

Suddenly there's more than our inexplicable attraction
pulling my thoughts toward him. It's the kind of fascination
I reserve for academics and ancient texts, except I'm driven
to figure Maximus out at least a hundred times more.

Who *is* he?

I shake my head slightly, wondering if he might have
told me if I hadn't run out of there.

"Kara," Kell snaps just as the cars ahead of us start to
move again. Miracle of miracles at this time of day on Sunset
Boulevard.

"What?"

"You've had your head in the clouds since we left the
library. You were weird this morning too. What's going on
with you?"

"Nothing. I'm fine."

"Same thing you said when I asked you how Medieval
Lit was."

"Because that was fine too."

Kell stares back at the road and taps her shiny red nails
against the steering wheel. "Are you messing around with
that professor?"

I gasp, partly in shock that she'd suspect it. Even after the run-in at the bookstore, despite the fact that Kell and I live together and share a campus, I'm convinced she's too self-involved to ever put the pieces of my personal life together. For once, I truly hope that never changes.

"He's my professor."

"He's also head-to-toe sex, so I wouldn't blame you one bit."

"*Kell.*"

"What? Sister, your gasps are saying no-no-no, but your scent is screaming—"

"Nothing," I cut in. "I'm just tired and hungry, okay? Keep your nose to yourself."

"Hmm." She's shockingly diplomatic about that. "Just be careful."

"Why would I need to be careful?" I'm still defensive, which feels like the smart choice. "There's nothing going on."

She slants a skeptical look my way. "You're the most sentimental of all of us. Just don't get too attached to him. He's not like us."

"You're jumping to a lot of conclusions."

"I'm just saying…"

"Do you want me to start sniffing into your personal life?"

Her stare turns dark, part warning and, judging by the new energy in the air between us, part worry, but she says nothing more.

I exhale a relieved breath when traffic starts to move, bringing us closer to Beverly Hills. The journey toward the family home doesn't usually elicit the same reaction, but tonight I'm more eager than ever to see my grandfather. I just have to figure out how to bypass my mother.

Finally we pull up to the broad dark wooden gate, which opens almost intuitively, as if the house knows we're welcome guests. Kell speeds along the stone drive and parks in front of the house like she owns the place.

The butler emerges from the early evening shadows like a ghost materializing out of thin air.

"Miss Valari." He tips his head toward me first, then greets Kell with a tight smile. "Miss Valari."

"Hey, Dalton." She tosses her hair over her shoulder and breezes past him without making eye contact.

I touch his arm briefly on my way inside, bringing some warmth to the dark gray eyes that seem to match his suit perfectly. His rigid posture softens slightly.

"Is Gramps home?" I keep my voice to a whisper.

He nods once before following Kell's journey through the wide arched doorway with his gaze. "He hasn't left the guesthouse all day. But your mother is expecting you."

I clamp my teeth together. "Great."

He responds with a subtle shrug, to which I can only sigh and carry on behind my sister, who must have tipped off my mother at some point today. I didn't inherit my family's thirst for vengeance, but I feel the strong urge to make my little sister pay for setting up the intentional minefield.

For now, I follow her inside the mansion that, for all the warm colors of its Tuscany-inspired decor, sends an instant chill down the length of my spine. The slow clicks of my heels clash with the determined stomp of Kell's as we cross the marble foyer, heading for the cream-and-gold luxury of the huge living room on the other side.

"Mom!" she yells before we're even halfway across.

I wince at the loud sound, waiting for the next impending assault. I brace myself at the unintelligible murmurs that are paired with the distinct yips of my mother's furry companions. Then her voice, as sharp and unforgiving as I've ever heard it.

"Jaden will get that part if I have to drive down to the fucking studio myself."

She storms out from our left after throwing open the double doors of her office. Two assistants flank her, dressed in crisp, stylish suits, looking every inch as panicked as Veronica Valari expects them to be.

As if they're in fervent agreement, the estate's resident gang of teacup Chihuahuas begin barking animatedly.

"Should I email someone?" the lanky blond one asks as one of the dogs gets underfoot, nearly tripping her.

Instantly I feel sorry for the girl. She's fairly new. But if she's lasted a month already, she should know what she's gotten herself into.

"No. You are to call him right now before he gives that other no-talent the part," my mother hisses, her dark eyes growing a shade darker. "The head of the studio owes me a favor. Reach out to his people and let him know Veronica Valari wants to speak with him today. Don't take no for an answer."

The blonde nods rapidly and moves back into the office,

which seems to close the door on that subject enough for my mother to recognize her daughters have arrived.

Her eyes brighten and her glossy lips spread into a wide smile. "Girls!" She draws out the word and walks toward us, spreading her arms wide. While the action tests the panels of her black satin suit, the garment's buttons hold firm across her chest. Thank God.

Kell, with a look reflecting our mutual relief, meets her halfway. She bestows a seemingly sincere kiss on her cheek.

"How are you, Mother?"

She answers first with a dramatic groan. "Your poor brother has been running around to these auditions forever, and I'm done watching him get passed over. By our *friends* no less."

My mother's sole mission in life has been to rebrand our family. As her children, we're more than flesh and blood. We're commodities. Arms of the empire she's intent on building around our talents and looks and the mostly forgotten notoriety of my grandfather's career. The decades-old scandal that nearly killed him is hardly pop culture news. But in Hollywood, his name can still open doors. If my mother finds one closed, she has a tendency to bulldoze through it. Like now.

She absently motions me toward her. I go begrudgingly and accept the brief and emotionless embrace. As I expected, she's fully immersed in her day of micromanaging the people who will let her, Jaden included. The youngest of us, he seems to lack a shred of ambition in any direction. That he committed himself to anything for six months should shock us all. But my mother is dedicated to bringing us all into the spotlight, one way or the other.

"What if he doesn't get the part?" Kell asks, tilting her head attentively, when deep down I know she's just placating the woman. We all are.

Veronica answers with a dark smirk and taps Kell's cheek lightly. "I'll take care of it. Don't doubt it. So anyway, tell me about the book signing at Recto Verso. I saw the photos with you and Piper. They were fantastic."

Mother hooks an arm into Kell's and starts leading her toward the office. The remaining assistant and the three little beasts follow along attentively. I keep my feet planted in place until they're all out of sight and I can barely hear my mother's exaggerated tones. If I didn't want to get away from our visit so badly, I might almost feel hurt over the brush-off. But like so many other times, if I stay quiet and very still, Veronica usually forgets I exist. Just like she does my grandfather.

A recognition that lends me strength for my next decision.

I pivot quietly and head through the back of the house, thrilled when I don't see anyone getting between me and my destination. I leave out the servants' kitchen and cross the turf that wraps around the ridiculously large pool until I reach the guesthouse several yards away.

I open the door with care. Just as cautiously, I step inside and then shut the door behind me.

"Gramps?"

I follow the low hum of a television coming from the

sitting room. I find him there, dozing on the couch. His head is angled away from me, but the buttons on his shirt shimmer with flecks of fading light with his even breathing.

I grin and glance up at the old black-and-white movie playing on the flat-screen above the fireplace. The guesthouse is well-appointed, of course, if unnecessarily isolating.

I take the remote carefully from his lap and turn the volume down.

He grumbles and rubs his nose vigorously. "What?" He blinks a few times before his frown is replaced with a look of surprise. "Kara!"

"Happy birthday, Gramps."

"Oh…" He lets out a heavy sigh, and I try not to notice the way his eyes shine when he replies. "Thank you, sweetheart. You know you didn't have to come all the way out here for that."

Didn't have to. Shouldn't have. But here I am.

I take a seat on the couch beside him. "How was your day?"

"Eh." He tilts his head back and forth a few times and gestures up toward the television. "Just me and Liberty Valance celebrating today. But that's okay by me. It's one of my favorites."

"I remember." I look up as a young Jimmy Stewart graces the screen just before it goes black.

Gramps drops the remote on the wooden side table. "What's on your mind, ladybug?"

I warm at the endearment, even though I shouldn't. I shouldn't even be here talking to him. And I definitely shouldn't be bursting at the seams with questions I have no business asking.

He touches my chin, lifting my gaze to his. His eyes are a faded blue, the kind that remind me of gloomy seas and rainy days. They seem to reflect his goodness and all his heartache at once. I reach for his hand and hold it between both of mine, focusing on the softness and the way his veins protrude through the thin skin.

"Hey," he gently prods.

"Hey." My reply is a wimpy rasp. At the moment, I can't do any better.

"Kara. Come on. It's me. What's up?"

I pull in a sigh. The better question is, what's *not* up? But I evade the question with something easier to say. Words I've whispered to him a million times before.

"I hate that you have to stay here all the time."

He gives my hands a squeeze. The motion says nothing but everything. He's probably evading bitter thoughts of his own.

"You know I've escaped from worse places. I can leave anytime I want." He winks, but my heart breaks a little at the same time.

"I wish Mom was nicer to you. It shouldn't have to be like this."

He nods thoughtfully. "When I found out your grandmother was a..." He grimaces briefly before locking his gaze to mine. "Listen. I had a choice, Kara. We *always* have a choice. And when she finally told me about her designs for our children and grandchildren, I had the chance to leave. But I refused to think of the family we'd made as a punishment. Even if Veronica and the others aren't exactly warm, I'd still rather be here than anywhere else. You're my family. You're all my family, no matter what anyone says."

I drop my head to hide the sheen of tears building. I stare down at our hands and swallow hard. Neither action helps me now or stops the emotion creeping its way to the surface.

I hate this. So much of this. I know Gramps does too, in his own way, but he's so much more adept at pushing it down. At concealing the gravity of it all.

My grandmother's deceit is the only reason I'm alive. It's why I'm a Valari with demon blood flowing through my veins. And even though she's long returned to the place that sent her to begin with, if all goes to plan, I'll have children of my own one day who will despise their humanity as I was taught to. Every generation a triumph and a punishment. A lesson for anyone who thinks they can get out of hell for free.

"Gramps ..." I try to piece the words together somehow, though I know there's no right way to say it. "I ... I met someone."

The grooves between his brows deepen. "Who? A friend?"

I hesitate. "I'm not sure how I feel about him right now. I guess that's the scary part."

He pinches his lips together and slips his hand from my grasp, using it to rub the back of his neck. The knot of anxiety I've been holding on to about Maximus tightens painfully.

"I haven't known him very long. We just met a couple days ago."

He closes his eyes a moment. "Oh, Kara..."

"I know," I whisper.

"Please, *please* be careful. Your mother..."

"I *know*. Trust me. I haven't told anyone but you. No one understands what's at stake more than I do."

He shoots me a serious look. "Except for me. *I* know. And I care for you more than—"

He stops himself, but we both know the truth. What we have is one of the few treasures he has left. The relationship we're not allowed to acknowledge. Not inside the gaudy mansion nearby, and definitely not in the world beyond that.

But the same instincts that bring me to the guesthouse to have moments with Gramps are the ones that draw me to Maximus too. Some might call it being rebellious, but I call it free will. Of course, the powers that be won't see it that way.

Privately, I can scold myself into following the rules all I want, but when I'm in the same room as the man who looks like a god, I don't seem to have much willpower at all.

Maximus. My senses long to keep repeating the syllables. My body craves the ineffable shivers they bring.

"There's something about him," I say, unable to hide the subtle pleading in my voice. "There's this energy between us that I can't describe. It's almost like he could be one of us, but I know he's not. I could *feel* that. This...well, this is different."

He stares at me intently. "Are you saying you don't think he's human?"

"I honestly don't know. I'm not sure he even knows."

"Have you asked him about it?"

I shake my head. I've been too busy trying not to claw my way up his massive body. Too busy pretending I have a shred of control around him. But after tonight, I'm not sure I can pretend any longer, regardless of his protests.

"Not yet. But I don't think I can stay away until I figure it out."

CHAPTER 8

MAXIMUS

JESSE'S OFF-KEY HUMMING ECHOES off the walls. I wince across my dining room table, the main piece of furniture in the dining nook of my downtown LA apartment.

When I only have to take a step to grab my next slice of pizza off the kitchen counter, the setup is primo. However, when I have to debate grabbing headphones to drown out Jesse's musical contributions during our weekend paper-grading marathon, it has me wishing I'd signed a lease on a place in the building with more square footage.

But being on the top floor means I get vaulted ceilings and a balcony with no roof, for which every inch of my looming frame thanks me daily. But right now, as the guy continues to prove nothing music-related will ever be on his résumé, this place feels entirely too small.

"Dude," I interject, finally unable to take any more. "If this is payback for our session in the pen at Venice this afternoon..."

"Of course not," Jesse says while tapping on his laptop. "I don't waste my time on payback. You know that. The second that word gets tossed around, you start to suspect shit."

"Should've known better than to ask." Some things in this world, like death, taxes, the Santa Ana winds, and my best friend's snark, will never change. While I can do without pondering the first three, especially as the winds whip a strong gust across my balcony, life wouldn't be complete without the latter.

He waggles his brows. "But you *are* going to ask how things went last night with Stacey, right?"

"Stacey?" I rock my head back. "Who's that?"

"Come on, geezer. Keep up. Stacey? From Sacramento? Comes down here once a month for business and her favorite hottie on wheels? You've met her before."

His description jars some memory fragments from a few months ago, but I stick to my original thought. "What happened to your strawberry girl from less than a week ago? Misty, right?"

"Well, I didn't kill her, if that's what you're asking. Though at her place after the Recto Verso party, I did wonder a few times. Damn. When that girl gets off, it's like the Metro's barreling through. Her nipples turn hard as—"

"Okay, okay. Got it." And holy shit, do I—because as soon as the guy evokes the imagery, all my brain can do is overlay it all onto an image of Kara Valari.

Kara . . .

The enchantress with the firestorm gaze that I can't

banish from my mind. The searing touches I can't wash off my skin. The energy, connective and captivating, that I can't erase from my senses. Even after I think back to the glaring *Absent* next to her name in my ledger from yesterday's class. Which, of course, makes my current state of mind even more pathetic.

Jesse takes another chomp of pizza—another staple of weekend paper-grading marathons. "So what about you and Kristy?" His gray eyes twinkle with dastardly glee.

"Ah, *here* comes the payback."

He chuckles. "I could be a legit douche right now and decide how deep to really twist the knife..."

"Or not," I counter.

"Or maybe I could just change the subject." His cheeky head tilt doesn't have me relaxing. At all. "But maybe that's two birds with the same custom stone...if the new subject is a certain member of the Valari dynasty?"

I give in to a new grimace, baring my teeth this time. An overreaction, to be sure, but I'm incapable of controlling myself. "The hell are you getting at, North?"

"Whoa there, cowboy. If you don't want to talk about Kara Valari and how you and she were eye-fucking the crap out of each other at the Recto Verso party, fine by me. I just hope you're being honest with yourself about the nuclear reactor you became around that girl."

"Goddammit." Even with my gaze averted and my posture slumped, it feels like the bastard has hurled a comet through the middle of my chest. I fist the front of my T-shirt, not wanting to acknowledge the truth—truth that peppers every syllable of my best friend's next statement.

"Well, damn. Maximus Kane, I do declare! Are you actually keen on the lovely Miss Valari?"

I glance up and wince. "I don't know what the hell I am, man."

"Meaning?"

"Meaning that 'keen' isn't the first word that comes to mind in this situation."

"So I should go back to the nuclear reactor metaphor?"

"Maybe. Probably." I jerk my hand higher, dragging it through my hair. "She's a student, for God's sake. And she's part of that strange family..."

"Strange." For reasons I can't fathom, his retort is bitter. "And you think that... why?"

"We're still talking about the Valaris, right?" I counter.

"They're taking advantage of some lucrative business opportunities. What's so strange about that? Building the brand while they can. Young and trendy has a shelf life. If they're smart and savvy enough to be conscious of that and are riding the comet before it sheds all its crystals, more power to them."

As he gets his astronomy geek on, I reach into the side pocket of my carrier bag and pull out Kara's earring. As soon as the thing catches the light and sparkles against my palm, Jesse abandons his Valari Clan public service announcement.

"What... is..."

"You were saying?" I drawl. "About young and trendy?"

"What the hell is that?"

"It's Kara's. But before you get the wrong idea, she lost

it in my classroom. I tried chasing her down to return it, but she'd already disappeared."

"Why didn't you just take it to campus security?"

I asked the same thing of myself while standing in the middle of that empty hallway, wondering how she'd managed to vanish so quickly. I'm going to sound crazy, and maybe I need to be told that without sugarcoating.

"Something about it"—*everything about it*—"spoke to me somehow." Holy shit, I do sound like a moron. But there's no turning back now. "It's not exactly something she picked up on Rodeo Drive or snagged from the VIP suite at an awards show."

A full breath expels from me as I run the pad of my thumb over the sharp metal molding of the wolf. Holding on to the piece wasn't a conscious choice, and neither are the words that emerge next. "And for a family that radiates young and trendy, why does this feel like it was made a century ago?"

"More than one," Jesse murmurs. "Definitely," he adds once he's holding the earring up. "This thing must weigh as much as she does."

I force my thoughts away from Kara's enticing little figure as he rambles on.

"The clasp is probably solid gold, but the hinge is loose. Probably why it slipped off," Jesse says. The rubies and diamonds glint in the light as he holds it up and twists it from side to side. "This design . . . it's . . . wow."

"Right?" I say no more. I don't have to. This isn't something to be dropped off with a rent-a-cop at the security desk. There's more than just physical weight and ageless bling in the thing. There's history. Stories. Meaning. They're tangible in just the feel of the gold and gems together.

After scrutinizing the piece for the better part of a minute, Jesse finally murmurs, "Cerberus."

"Stick to star trivia, North. Cerberus is a hound with three heads, not one."

"Also used to not be a hound at all," he shoots back.

I push my laptop to the side and lean forward. "Says who?" It's not a throwdown. It's a legitimate information request. I can tell Jesse's switched into Professor North mode, and I'm grateful for it.

"Guy named Hevelius," he supplies. "Seventeenth-century astronomer. Seven out of the ten constellations he identified are still acknowledged today. Of the three that aren't, one was known as Cerberus—a three-headed snake that was held by Hercules. The gems in this earring are arranged in that constellation's pattern."

Why that revelation has my pulse revving, I have no idea.

"How do you know all that? Last time I checked"—and I know this from Jesse himself—"astronomy isn't astrology."

"The constellations straddle both," he explains. "Which means I also have a passing knowledge of Latin, though that lettering on the earring would take the eyesight of a hawk."

"*Ex ignes*," I supply from memory, as I've already spent far too much time inspecting it. "That's the top part. The bottom says *victoria*."

"From the fires, victory," he translates. "Probably a

family motto borrowed from their heraldry." He hands the earring back to me. "I'll admit, it's all a little strange, but not in the worst ways. After looking at this and having graded my first pop-quiz essay from Miss Kell Valari, this family has really begun to fascinate me."

I halt, the earring halfway back to my satchel. "It was that bad?"

"It was that *good*." He leans back and steeples his fingers. "I've been crazy about space since we were kids, but the girl talks about the Milky Way like she's already flown across it." He laughs wistfully. "And I thought the only stars she cared about were the ones she followed on social media."

I arch both brows. "That *is* fascinating."

"Right? Those Valaris are opening my eyes in ways I never imagined."

"Same, my friend." *Very much the same.*

The longer I sit here, holding this age-old heirloom in my hand, the deeper that truth seems to clamor at me. Call to me.

Which is pretty fucking crazy.

In my line of work, I'm accustomed to finding allegorical meaning, not truth, in things like ancient star systems, mythological beasts, and Latin phrases that sound like vengeful promises. Or, for that matter, battle cries.

An insight that leads to yet another.

None of this information is matching up. Hollywood and glitter with Old Latin and old constellations. Red carpets and golden fashion runways with antique gemstones and solid-gold earring clasps.

There are disconnects here. Lots of them. But when I think of the most vast disparity of them all—the difference between what the rest of the world sees in Kara Valari and the dark angst I've seen in her eyes—nothing feels off-balance at all. Everything about her—and me—feels completely right. Exactly where it should be.

Now I just need to know ... Why?

CHAPTER 9

I PRESS MY HAND against the metal door. It warms under the heat of my touch. I give myself a few more seconds to change my mind. If he's not home, all I've wasted is an hour on the internet and a nail-biting drive here to demonstrate what I'm willing to do to chase the forbidden mystery he's become.

The muffled sound of people talking on the other side sends me a step back. I can make out the deep timbre of Maximus's voice, then someone laughing. Another male.

Shit.

This was a stupid idea. I need to leave before—

The door opens with a soft whoosh of air, the metal hinges whining faintly, removing the barrier between us. Maximus leans on the edge of the door casually, unaware of my presence.

His dark-haired friend notices me first, his eyes taking on a glimmer of intrigue. "Well, then."

He looks vaguely familiar, but I can't figure out why. The wonderment doesn't last long, shoved aside by my nervousness. I wasn't expecting Maximus to have company. That he does could make this confrontation so much worse.

Finally, Maximus sees me. He pushes back from the door a fraction, like someone's just delivered bad news to his doorstep. "Kara. What—"

His friend quickly cuts between us, whipping his hand from the chrome wheels of his chair to reach for mine. "I'm Jesse."

I force a smile and meet the gesture. "I'm—"

"Kara. I know. I've got Kell in one of my classes. I'm Professor North."

I close my eyes briefly, internalizing the slew of curses I want to hurl at myself. That's how I know his face. Unfortunately, the revelation adds a new layer to my growing anxiety. Of all the people to run into . . .

"What are you doing here?" Maximus's pointed question sounds like an accusation.

Inwardly, I repeat it. What *am* I doing here? While my mind knows that answer, my nervous system is having trouble keeping up. I force myself to persist. This feels too important.

I jog my chin, ordering myself to meet his incisive blues. I didn't exactly leave him on a warm note last time, so I shouldn't be surprised that he's pissed I've now shown up at his door. On a Saturday no less.

"I'm sorry, but I think you might have something of mine."

Jesse's eyes light up. "Ah. The earring."

"Yes," I reply, though the edge in my tone is *How the hell do you know?*

"Max and I were checking it out earlier. Pretty cool piece. What did it say? *Ex ignes victoria?*"

I manage to respond even though my teeth are clamped together. "That's right."

He tilts his head. "Family heirloom?"

"Something like that."

He nods, but I can see more questions swimming in his amused expression. In that moment, he seems to be the mirth to Maximus's brood. After another chance to look up at the professor who is still glowering at me, I almost appreciate it.

"I was just leaving. I'll let you two catch up." Jesse winks at me before swinging his gaze back to Maximus and lifting his eyebrows suggestively. "Later."

Great. Fucking fantastic.

I step back to let Jesse pass over the threshold. He whips down the corridor toward the elevator at the end. Which means I'm forced to face the man I'm not so sure I want to see anymore. Maximus takes up the whole of the doorway, an unreadable expression on his face.

"I'm sorry," I say again.

He lifts an eyebrow. "Why are you sorry?"

He says it the way a teacher speaks to an incorrigible student. Like he wants me to write all the reasons on a chalkboard a few dozen times until I learn my lesson.

I will not show up at my professor's apartment uninvited.

I will not show up at my professor's apartment uninvited.

I tug the inside of my lip between my teeth and decide the pain of apologizing again can be tolerated, all things considered.

"I'm sorry for showing up out of the blue. I checked campus security and no one turned it in. I figured you might have found it after…" *After you tugged on my hair like you couldn't stop yourself.* "I just figured you might have it."

We share a silent stare that devolves into my shameless pass over his body. He's in jeans and a flimsy white T-shirt today. His hair is loose and messy, and I'm too eager to have my fingers get better acquainted with it.

"Come in," he finally says, turning into the apartment.

I follow him inside and shut the door behind us. The loft is spacious but modest. The simple exposed brick walls and vaulted ceilings make the one-room studio feel open and airy, even for someone of its owner's stature. My survey of the space snags on the bed in the corner. Its puffy white duvet is rumpled on one side. I'm riveted on it longer than I probably should be. But even now, there's lingering energy from that area. A warmth that's common to bedrooms, where secret dreams live—but a heat that's also unique to him. To this man…

If that's all he is. Because right now, more than ever, I'm starting to wonder.

When I look away from the bed, he's watching me. Intensely. I have to grab the edge of the kitchen table to stay upright from the force of his feelings. There are so many, all at once, and I feel my cheeks color before siphoning away some of it.

"There are two kinds of people in this world, you know."

"Yeah?" He crosses his arms.

I smirk. "People who make their beds in the morning . . . and those who never do."

He can't seem to resist an answering grin. "And what kind of person are you?"

I hear the answer play in my mind first. "I'm like you," I echo. By the time the words leave my lips, the meaning has changed and I'm reminded why I came. At least one of the reasons . . . "More than I think you realize."

Seemingly immune to the subtext, he strolls toward the kitchen table and reaches into the side of his carrier bag hanging on one of the chairs. "I guess academics can be a type." When he returns, the earring is dangling from his long, elegant fingers. "Here you go."

I hold out my palm, and he drops it there without touching me. His careful avoidance bothers me.

"Thanks."

His lips twitch to the side. "It seems like an expensive piece, so I held on to it thinking I'd see you Friday. But I didn't."

I look down at the sparkling gems against my palm, knowing I should respond to him with something more than *thanks*, especially because I've been spared from telling my mother that I lost it. But nothing springs to my lips.

"You only have two excused absences for the class," he adds.

My nostrils flare as I meet what I suspect is the practiced

look of a disappointed professor. I register only slight guilt for missing the class. I read the assigned cantos, wondering where he'd put the inflections and how his energy would change when he recited it in class. It was almost enough to make me show up despite other plans.

"Not to worry, professor. I did my homework." I whip out a stapled assignment from my purse and shove it into the space between us. "I came for the earring, but I also came to talk. It seemed to me that the lecture hall maybe isn't the best place for us to do that."

He shifts his jaw. "And my apartment is?"

A frustrated growl vibrates deep in my chest, inaudible but a marker of emotion that's been pent up for too long. "At least this way you won't be at risk of destroying school property if things get too intense."

He releases a long, quiet breath before moving into the kitchen and retrieving a bottle of water from the refrigerator. "What exactly do you think is going to happen here?"

I can't tell if his tone is mocking or hopeful. Does he crave these moments between us, or am I being ridiculous for insisting they exist at all? I pull in a deep breath, reminding myself to trust my instincts above all else.

"Whatever it is, I'm not going to pretend it isn't happening."

Another beat. A long one. Too long.

"You shouldn't be here, Kara."

I hold my ground. "Why? Because you can't control yourself around me?"

He sucks down nearly the whole bottle. "Maybe."

"Maybe it's the same for me too. Did that ever occur to you?"

"All the more reason to keep our distance. I'm not getting involved with a student, regardless of how tempting you are." He pauses, raking his gaze over me too quickly. "Please, just go, Kara."

"What if I don't want to?"

He tosses the empty bottle and walks toward me slowly.

"I'm asking you for the last time. *Go.*"

He might intimidate other people, but there's a kind of agony in his eyes as he stares down at me. I don't fear him or feel sorry for him. The idea of weakening his defenses or poking his ire only spurs me on. And I know the best way to do it.

"Make me," I whisper.

His voice drops low. "Stop this."

"I'm serious, Maximus. I've watched you mold metal like putty in your hands. Kicking me out of your apartment should be no problem."

"That's exactly why ..."

When the last of his thought seems to fizzle in the air between us, something snaps inside me. I take a fistful of his T-shirt and yank down, lifting myself to reach his mouth as I do. Everything happens fast. Searing and inevitable, the way lightning chooses a single blinding moment to strike.

It starts with the crash of lips. My fingers in his hair. Then the race to get into his arms. His strong hands cup my thighs at the fringes of my shorts, guiding my urgent climb until my legs are cinched around his hips. The full-body contact inspires a needy moan that I bury in our kiss.

I open my lips, an invitation for more. He takes it, giving me his taste and more of his bruising grip as he yanks us tighter. I relinquish my need to breathe to stay inside the kiss as long as I can. Eternity this way would be fine, I think, inside the chaos of my mind.

When I finally drag myself away for air, I lift my gaze to the ceiling so he can kiss my neck. The bristle of his facial hair along my sensitive skin has me closing my eyes. Sucking in another fevered breath along with his masculine scent. Digging my fingernails into the meaty flesh of his muscular shoulder.

He growls and walks me backward until my back hits the wall. Hard.

I lower my gaze to the fire in his. I don't have to guess that he's both angry and every ounce as turned on as I am. I feel it spilling out of his pores, saturating the particles of air around us, seeping into me where we're connected.

His chest moves with ragged breath. I think he's going to kiss me again, but he surprises me by taking my wrist and yanking my grip loose. He threads our hands and slams them into the exposed brick above my head. The bite of friction, stone against skin, is surpassed when he takes my mouth in another consuming kiss.

I'm on fire. Fully consumed. I hardly notice when he repeats the motion with my other hand, pinning me with the force of his massive magnificent body. But it's the weight of his desire that keeps me here. It's too good. Too heady. I whimper against his mouth because I know the last of my control is slipping away. And I'm sending it off without a shred of remorse.

I thought I knew about temptation until this moment.

When he suddenly pulls away, the separation feels like a thousand nails tearing at me. His grip stays firm until he lowers me to my feet and stumbles back a step. We're both catching our breath, but what gives me pause is the look in his eyes. Like he just committed a murder.

"What's wrong? Why are you looking at me that way?"

He shakes his head, his gaze darting all around me and to the floor. I start to pick up on the little details. The brick dust around my feet. Then the reddish-pink scrapes along the tops of my hands. I lift my gaze to his.

"It's nothing, Maximus."

"*Nothing?*" The word tears from him.

"What's the difference?"

I take a stride forward and yank up the sleeve of his T-shirt, where tiny red blood stains mark what I created moments before. Except nothing is there but smooth skin.

He brushes me away and takes another step back. "You need to go, Kara."

"No." It falls out before I can stop it, but it's more a sound of astonishment than rebellion.

"*Kara.*"

"No," I repeat. "Not until you tell me—"

"Don't," he snaps. "Don't even start—"

"You . . . healed."

He averts his eyes. "And you haven't. Another reason this needs to stop."

The storm inside me is raging. The lingering physical desire is going to war with the need to know more about him.

"You can't hurt me," I insist.

"Seems like I can."

"Not the way you think." I turn and size up the Kara-sized imprint indented into the brick. True enough, a human my size might not have fared so well. I face him again. "Are you going to tell me what's going on with you? What's *really* going on with you?"

He's quiet. His back is to me, his frame both impressive and intimidating, even as his breathing evens out. My purse has fallen to the floor, and he bends down to pick it up before slowly pivoting to me. He hands it to me. I take it even though it's a call for me to leave.

More tense seconds pass before he finally speaks. His posture is rigid, his expression too. "You want to know what's going on with me?"

The low and ominous tone sends a shiver of dread through me. Then I notice his hands are shaking.

"Yes," I whisper, though suddenly I'm not sure I do.

"When I was eight years old, I paralyzed my best friend because I didn't know what I was capable of . . . what kind of violence is inside me. It didn't stop there." He closes his eyes briefly—long enough for a deep V to form between his brows. "Every day of my life is about control. And that control doesn't exist when I'm this close to you. I'll never make that mistake again. If I unleash that shit on you, I'll never be able to live with myself. So please, Kara. For both of our sakes, please, just go."

CHAPTER 10

Maximus

AFTER DEFYING ME AGAIN and again, she did exactly what I wanted. That doesn't mean, in the six hours since, that I'm any happier about it. The essays I have yet to grade are still glaring at me, courtesy of the blinking cursor on my laptop, waiting for my digital red pen. Any attempts to distract myself have failed miserably—from books, my soul's true escape, or even the sight of the slightly smashed bricks in my wall, bearing a disturbingly familiar outline.

Instead, I've been pacing. From one end of my apartment to the other. I stopped counting the laps at around a hundred. Why does it even matter?

Around midnight, I quit long enough to wipe out the last two slices of pizza. I'd debated whether to take the pizza downstairs to Jesse, a pathetic excuse to seek advice I'm not sure I need. He always gets the last piece. It's tradition with us. But when Kara showed up, he rolled out of here like his chair had rockets. Didn't stop him from flinging me a zinger of a smirk as he did. Can't say I blame him. Not with Kara appearing like she did, freshly tanned and smelling like sunshine and cinnamon. In two seconds, the guy's look had conveyed a thousand direct messages.

You know where to find me when you're done, dude.

But you'd better not be done until tomorrow morning.

Just a reminder: I'm only three floors down from you.

Kara's parting look was far more devastating. She left without a word, as if she knew her sad silence would wreck me. I almost wonder if she could foresee my restless pacing and fighting as I deal with what I told her—what, in her eyes, amounted to a crap excuse for a confusing condition.

A confusion I'm still struggling with. Still reaching for answers that aren't there ... that have never been there. Long ago, I resigned myself to not ever knowing. To hiding the monster inside for the rest of my life.

So why the hell am I still so conflicted about it? And, down to this second, pacing over it? I already have my answer. Kara's woken up all the instincts. The fire. Even the violence. Except she isn't horrified. Not by any of it. She doesn't think I'm a monster. She's not pushing back with fear. She's shoving back with questions.

With that, she's opening the door to things that are harder to accept. Feelings I've long buried. My own curiosity. The deep-seated need to find answers.

The conflicting thoughts are a skirmish in my skull. They brim over, electrifying the air with palpable energy.

It's now three a.m., and I've officially declared sleep

my enemy tonight. After changing and running the eight blocks to my twenty-four-hour gym, I push myself through a workout that has the three other lunatics in there with me—film stuntmen keeping up their game—openly gawking. Other days I might care. This morning I don't.

By the time I jog back home and shower, it's time for Recto Verso to open. When I go, I'm often the first one in the door—usually for the exact reason Sarah cites as the brass doorbell jingles over my head.

"Bad dreams?"

A fine dust swirls through morning rays illuminating the front half of the store. She turns away from me to whip up my daily latte and then hands it to me. After accepting it, I reach over the long bar into the syrup well and add a shot of cinnamon flavoring to the savory brown liquid.

One of her brows jumps. "All right, then?"

I blow some of the foam off the top of my drink. "How about you let me get at least halfway through this before you start the interrogation?"

She answers with nothing but a soft chuckle. Probably a wise move considering I'm this jittery *before* the caffeine hits.

At last I mutter, "Why did you instantly go there? I mean, about the dreams?"

At first, that earns me nothing but a subtle smile. With Sarah, the look could mean anything from "take out the trash" to "I know the path to world peace." Right now, I sincerely hope it's neither.

"You have the look," she offers at last.

"The look?" I narrow my gaze and twist my lips. "Like what?"

"The look you always get." She shrugs, but not very convincingly. The movement causes the sequins on her classic Bowie tee to flash in the Tiffany-style lighting. The coffee bar has more muted light than the store's reading areas, for which I'm grateful at the moment. Dimness is good for downplaying confusion—though I'm likely not very effective at it either. "Like you haven't just been dreaming."

"Oh?"

The word is all she needs. Like Reg, Sarah knows not to play with small talk when I've been pacing instead of sleeping. "Like you had a dream, woke up, and then decided to act it all out for your stuffed animals."

I don't know whether to laugh or swear. I settle for a weird mix of the two beneath my breath before responding, "I never had any stuffed animals, Sarah."

"I know."

Just like that, the lights seem even dimmer. Too damn dark. I straighten on my stool and smack my hands together, appointing myself official mood lifter. Seems only fair. "So. What's new around here?"

A weighted silence—resulting in my new misgivings. Unlike Reg, Sarah's usually the first one to jump on the bandwagon for lightening the conversation. She has serious game at it too. The woman is up-to-date on every speck of pop culture gossip there is, from the top of the pop charts to the bottom of the fashion faux pas.

"Well," she finally murmurs, "I reckon that's what *I*

should be asking *you* now, yes?"

"Hmm." I take another sip of my latte, assessing her over the rim of the cup. The woman can be the queen of neutral composure and is out to prove it with irritating thoroughness.

"You 'reckon,' eh?"

She solidifies her stance, though the posture thing is only a backup for the resolve in her stare. "Aha. Now I get it." She jabs up her chin. "You didn't dream last night because you didn't *sleep* last night."

I set down my mug with an equally purposeful *clunk*. "Not a statement I'll be able to deny."

"Bollocks," she mutters. "I was hoping to be wrong."

"But you pretty much knew you'd be right." I arch a brow. "Right?"

She frowns, readjusting her stance again. "But you're only a few days into the new semester. What gives?"

The uptick of concern in her tone is weirdly comforting. And greatly needed. I'm off-balance. I have been for hours. Probably longer. When a dam has a crack, it's easy enough to ignore. But the crack is becoming a fissure, making me realize how much pressure has really built up behind it.

I take another second to sip my cinnamon brew. The taste alone lends me courage to say my next words.

"Tell me what you know, Sarah."

I'm prepared for her reaction, which is not much of one. After several long beats, she finally replies, "Uhhh... what I know? About what?"

"Me," I counter. "Any of it. Christ, even all of it, if you

have that much. And I don't mean a rerun of all the details I already have. I need the other stuff, okay? The shit Mom won't ever talk about."

Before I'm even done, her lips compress. She leans over and wipes at dirt that doesn't exist on the counter. "Your mother has never been the sort to drink with the hens and spill about her past, Max."

"I'm aware of that, but are you seriously saying she's never let anything slip, even inadvertently, over all these years?"

"I'm sorry." The new tightness at the corners of her eyes shows me her sincerity. "On the few occasions I've asked, she's answered by just shutting me down. And with…" She shakes her head slowly. "Well, with the kind of torment you hate inflicting on someone simply by asking. That probably sounds strange, but—"

"No." I stare into my cup. I experience the same thing every time I see Jesse struggle. Times that are few and far between, thankfully. But when they come, they remind me all over again of what I am and what I'm capable of. "Not strange at all." I heave a frustrated sigh, wishing to God my latte would turn into whiskey. "Forget I asked."

Before I'm even done with the grousing, Sarah sprints to my side of the counter, hitching onto the stool next to me. "Maximus. My word. What's going on?"

The concern in her rasp has doubled. The same energy comes through with her hand on my shoulder. But how do I answer? How do I tell her that if this were Kara touching me, my blood would be filled with sparks, my mind consumed with awakening? How do I tell her that I can't push aside that sensation anymore? That I can't keep patching the dam?

"I just need some answers," I snap, wanting to take back the harsh tone when her gaze flares. "Does anyone get that? I crippled Jesse when we were eight. That was less than a year after Mom and I moved here, but I don't remember anything about where we were or what we were doing before then. Not a single recollection or even a hazy memory."

"Maybe that's the place your dreams take you to."

"Well, that's comforting."

I turn to face the back of the store. The shadows there are a perfect match for the darkness clamoring inside me. All but possessing me.

"I need to know, Sarah. Christ, I deserve to know."

The brass doorbell jangles loudly, jarring me from our conversation. I turn and blink at the brightness of the sun pouring in the open door.

Sarah winces too before whooshing out, "Oh, thank God."

The answering laughter, issued from the middle of that invasive sunburst, instantly—but not shockingly—soothes me.

"Do I need to be amused or afraid by that?" My mother folds her arms, tugging at the sleeves of her thick work sweater, halfway covering her pink nursing uniform pants and flower-printed Crocs.

"If I say the latter but comp your chamomile, will you still stay?" Sarah answers.

"Uh-oh," Mom murmurs, fastening her stare on me.

The brilliance of her blues has my gut twinging with guilt. Nobody should look so ready to help someone else, even their own son, after doing the same thing for twelve hours.

But I shove the feeling aside for another day. That "day" has become years, and those years now exceed a decade. And I have to find out what lurks inside me. What scratches to get out whenever Kara Valari's within reach.

"Does somebody need to talk?" Mom prompts, earning her a grateful smile and a small tea tray from Sarah. There's a ball of chamomile ready to go in the cup and steam wafting out of the small pot at its side.

I don't bother voicing an affirmation. Nancy Kane has read me like a proverbial book for as long as I can remember, which isn't as long as I'd like.

"Let's go to the back," I suggest. "We can have some privacy."

"Ooh, this requires *privacy*, huh?" Mom tugs free the thick tie that's held her hair in a tight ponytail. "Oh God, that feels good." She adds a groan, shaking out her thick blond waves. Though she gets the roots touched up every few weeks these days, the brushed gold color is definitely where my predominant shade comes from. But what about the umber that's mixed into my mane? And the separate blue ring in my eyes?

And the fact that I can warp metal—or break anything else that gets in my path—without thinking about it?

"I guess this was a fortunate coincidence," she says a few minutes later, as we settle together onto the contemporary couch that Reg has installed into this new annex of the store. There's a long black coffee table in front of us, with a pair of mismatched papasan chairs on the other side.

"Coincidence is God's way of staying anonymous."

"Well, thank you, Albert Einstein," she teases before lifting her teacup and taking a sip. After letting her Crocs drop to the floor, she curls her legs up and leans a shoulder into the couch. "So now do I get a few Maximus Kane originals? Like an explanation for why you're here a good couple of hours earlier than usual? I thought you and Jesse were doing a grading marathon last night. You should be exhausted and sleeping right now."

She's not done. I get that already. Still, I attempt to cut in. "Mom—"

"Oh, my word. You *are* exhausted." She rubs a thumb beneath one of my eyes. "So dark already. This shallow into the semester. What's your course load this time? Did they finally talk you into adding the intensive Shakespeare class?"

"No. Mom—"

"Wait." She pauses, her gaze seeming to sear right past my tired features. "Wait a damn second." She sets down her cup absently. "Max. Is this about . . . a girl? Are you seeing someone?"

I pull in a long breath. "At my age, they're usually called women."

She grabs my hands with eager glee. "Tell me about her. Tell me everything."

"No." I twist out of her grip. "Everything is what *I* need from *you* right now."

Her face contorts with confusion.

"Mom...I need you to tell me the truth. The *truth*. About me. About why I'm like . . . this?" With that last word, I turn my palms heavenward. Except I'm settling for anything but surrender now. I'm lost, yes, but no longer content to be that way.

Suddenly she's on her feet again. She whirls from me but tries to make it look breezy—the same way she brushes at small tears streaming her cheeks, expecting me to believe she's just clearing off stray hair strands. It's her trademark casual-but-not-casual move that she *thinks* she's perfected. But I see through her thin act. All of it. She's desperately trying, and failing, to hide her quiet grief.

"There's nothing to tell, Max," she rasps. "You were born different."

"You're lying." I coil my fists atop my thighs, not trusting them to leave the new couch's cushions unharmed. I've spent so long—too long—ordering myself to stay controlled, collected . . . concealed. For the first time in my existence, someone has given me permission to ignore all of that.

To seek out answers.

"This isn't just about Jesse." How long have I longed to blurt out those words? They're cathartic but agonizing. "You have to know that I've been fighting against it ever since then. My strength. This . . . curse."

"Stop." She drops her hands. Her face is twisted with fresh anger. "It's not a curse. *You* are not a curse!"

"Then tell me what I *am*," I shout as I stand too. I don't want to. Being in this state means I'm a step closer to hollowing a wall or wrecking one of Reg's fancy new bookcases. But fury and impatience brew too hot in my veins.

Mom expels a long sigh. "Why now, Max? Why do you want to—"

"Was my father ever there?" It's a question I've asked before. I ask it again—I have to—with the desperate hope of getting an answer. Maybe this time. *God, please. This time.* "Was he *ever* there, Mom? Does he even know about me? Is he alive?"

She turns and braces her hands against a bookcase. Her knuckles are white. Her shoulders are hunched.

"I've already told you. We met when I was in Egypt, volunteering for Healers with Heart. Your father was there too. He was... unlike anyone I'd ever met. Larger than life. He could sweep a woman off her feet with a well-timed look." When she turns back around, there's a tear-streaked smile at the edges of her lips. "And that's exactly what he did. I fell in love with him, but it was fleeting. He was gone in a few weeks, before I even knew we'd created you."

"And you never figured out where he went? Or where he came from?"

Her smile fades. "It was a whirlwind affair. There wasn't time to share a lot about our pasts. I'm not proud of having to tell you that, but things sometimes... happen... in the heat of the moment, at the pace of mindless passion. That doesn't mean I wasn't thrilled when they told me you were on the way. Before I even felt you kick in my belly or held you in my arms, I was utterly in love with you."

"I know, Mom."

I finish it by clenching my jaw—not because I don't believe her. Because I really do. The woman does love me. Would do anything for me. If burglars blew in through Recto Verso's front door with guns, she'd take a bullet in my place. But I can't understand the bizarre cosmic force that holds her back from giving me every detail of my identity. The gigantic missing chunk of my truth.

I right my stance and plant my feet, tucking my hands in my back pockets. "Things happen. You were a long way from home. Falling for a stranger in a strange place."

"Alexandria," she whispers with a note of wistfulness.

As soon as the word falls out of her mouth, the bottom falls out of my world. I go still. Very, very still.

"Cairo. The last time, you told me it was Cairo."

A gulp moves down her throat. "It was so long ago."

"Was it even Egypt?"

She stops and juts her chin. "You're peppering me with questions, Max. You're not being fair."

"*Sabah al-kheir*," I growl.

She searches my face. "What? What are you—"

"*Sabah al-kheir*," I repeat. "It means 'good morning' in Egyptian Arabic. If you'd spent any amount of time there, you'd know that."

Her eyes flare. "Why are you doing this? Why are you pushing me like this?"

"Why are you making it necessary to push?"

I'm back to a shout, and I don't care. There's no one else in the store or at the coffee bar—Sarah's made herself conveniently scarce—so I let it fly with the same volume Mom's gone to. We've never fought like this before, but nothing's ever felt more important to me. Especially now. Especially seeing her escalate into an outright fume.

I'm getting ready to royally hate myself for the new sheen of tears in her eyes, but with a couple of her hard blinks, they're gone. Her jaw falls. A strange huff escapes her.

"Who?" she demands.

"Who . . . what?"

"Who. Is. It?"

"Who is *what*?"

"Whoever's putting these demands back in your head. Somebody's got to be doing this to you. Making you reopen this wound. A wound I can assure you I share. In more ways than you can possibly imagine."

I shake my head, wanting to tell her my imagination's vaster than she thinks. Instead I say, "It's never healed. Because I've never known the whole truth." I can hear the sadness beneath my declaration, despite how my senses are oddly detached from it. If I let those synapses connect right now, I'll lose my thin thread of control.

"Just tell me who it is," she presses.

"Nobody."

Shit. If Mom wants to continue keeping her truth locked away, I'm justified in doing the same. On top of that, everything about Kara—her status in my professional life, her dominance of my inner life—feels too much like my metaphorical thread right now. Fragile. Special. And strung too tight for comfort.

"Nobody, huh?" Mom tilts her head and folds her arms. "That's a lot of floor gazing for 'nobody,' son."

"Okay, tell you what. You give me all the truth I'm asking for, and I'll show you the same courtesy."

"This has nothing to do with *courtesy*!" Her punctuation is an angry sob. "And everything to do with keeping you—"

She cuts in on herself with another sigh. It stems from places even deeper inside her. It sounds almost . . . panicked.

"Keeping me what, Mom? Just tell me!"

She sways in place for a long beat. Her breaths are like hurricanes of emotion. As I force my stare to fully meet hers again, I fight to discern the meaning behind her frantic expression.

Holy crap. She's really terrified.

"I—I have to go."

"Where?" I blurt. "Why? Mom?"

"I'm sorry, Max," she rasps. "I'm so sorry . . . if I've failed you."

"Failed me?" The words sound preposterous, even now. I'm furious, to be sure, but no way do I consider her a failure.

But I don't get the chance to say that. Not when she turns and sets a direct course for the front door. Part of me still yearns to run and stop her, but another part knows that won't make a difference. We both need to cool off, yet that's not happening when neither of us will surrender ground— or information.

Right now, maybe that's for the better. At least from where I'm standing.

I have no idea how to talk about Kara, especially to

my mother. When I contemplate doing so, there are either too many words or not enough. All of them are abysmally inadequate for describing the woman's cosmic-level force over me.

But how? *Why?*

I still barely know this girl. Even now, after I've tasted every inch of her tongue and groped her lithe little body like my life depended on it, that certainty is like a knell in my mind. A toll that grows even louder after Mom pushes her way outside and the store's bell stops jingling...

Leaving me alone with the chaos of my anger. The black holes of my memory. The ongoing obsession with a woman who keeps defying me with her fire, her honesty, and her truth... even when she's not in the same room with me.

I jack my head back and close my eyes. With any luck, a few minutes of exhausted sleep will finally hit me. But something tells me that's wishful thinking. Something attached to the fresh image of Kara that blooms behind my eyelids.

I guess I can call this conclusion official.

I'm pretty much fucked.

CHAPTER 11

Kara

SITTING IN THE FRONT row may have been a mistake. The murmurs and whispers throughout the lecture hall are more relentless than ever. Am I really surprised, though? The answer, from deep in my gut, is a resounding and disappointing no.

What's more distracting is how hard Maximus tries not to look at me. When he does, the force of his gaze is an assault on my senses. It nearly matches his passion for the cantos as he reads, his fingers flowing over the air once more. And his silent turmoil when he asks a question and passes over me. Again and again and again.

I quell a rise of frustration. Why would he push for me to come out of the shadows in the back just to ignore me? Half the class passes this way until I resign myself to being as invisible as he seems to wish. He's lobbing easy questions and getting easy answers.

"The souls who've been relegated to the second circle

of hell betrayed reason to their appetites. Their sin was giving in to their passions. Now they're doomed to an eternity in this whirlwind. What does the great gale symbolize?"

No one volunteers to answer this time, likely because the answer is sexual. I roll my eyes and raise my hand.

He clears his throat after a pregnant pause. "Kara."

"Lust," I answer flatly.

A few people snicker behind me.

He purses his lips with a nod. "Correct. Of course Dante recognizes several key residents. Semiramis, Dido, Helen, Paris. Finally, Paolo and Francesca, who find just enough reprieve from the endless storm to tell their sad tale. Some of these are familiar stories to most of you. Some not. On first glance, they all seem to carry the same thread, right? Passionate love affairs gone wrong." He pauses, dragging his fingertips down his beard until they join at the tip. "Did anyone notice one wasn't like the others?"

The room falls silent. I scan through all the characters' histories in my mind. Adultery, betrayal, passion, lust, war, a very dramatic suicide on a self-made funeral pyre.

Oh, that's it.

I shoot my hand up. Maximus makes a show of surveying the rest of the hall for any other takers. Not a chance in hell someone is going to figure this one out, though. Finally he returns to me, his lips tight. His nostrils flare slightly before he calls on me again.

"Dido."

He pauses. I know I'm right, but I wonder if he's silently

hoping I'm wrong one of these times. The challenge feeds something in me. A dormant instinct, perhaps . . . or maybe something deeper. I just know I like having it stoked. A lot.

"Why Dido?"

"She's a suicide," I say. "She had an affair, but when Aeneas left her, she killed herself."

"Which means?"

I shrug. "I guess Minos got it wrong when he assigned her soul to eternal torment. Otherwise she got off on the wrong floor. Suicides go to seven." I smirk when I see him struggle not to.

"Or maybe Dante just has a soft spot for lovers." His gaze fixes on my mouth, then my eyes. Finally. "We haven't gotten to the seventh circle yet. Did you read ahead?"

I tuck my hair behind my ear and lean forward on my elbow. "No. I studied the map."

"Of course she did," someone calls out in a nasty tone.

Maximus shoots a pissed-off glare in the general direction of the heckler, but I can tell from the darting shifts of his eyes that he can't figure out who said the offending words. He may as well get used to it. Though I'm not exactly sold on the first-row seating yet, so maybe he won't have to.

He circles the podium and picks up a thick stack of papers. I sink back into my seat with a sense of relief as he begins distributing his printed critiques for the assignments collected from the class I missed.

I catch a few outraged gasps from around the room and smile. I guess Maximus is a hard grader after all.

"As most of you can tell, there's some room for

expanding your view of the work and improving your grade. I'd suggest reading through my comments several times. Nobody enjoys being edited, but my purpose is to make you all better critical thinkers. It's a life skill worth developing. These summaries are due weekly, every Friday. Late delivery is an automatic incomplete. No exceptions. If you have any questions, I'm happy to discuss them during office hours."

Then he dismisses the class. My smug smile fades because I don't have mine. I thought delivering it in person might make up for the fact that I delivered it late, but I guess not.

When the hall empties of people, I walk down to him. "Maximus?"

There's no answer from him. Not even a nod.

"Professor?" I prod. "I didn't get my assignment back."

He avoids eye contact, shoving his copy of the *Comedy* and some other papers into his leather satchel. "I said any questions about the assignments can be addressed during office hours."

I let out a dry laugh. "And office hours start right after this class. What's the difference?"

He looks up. "The difference is you're not my only student, Kara. And office hours take place in my *office*." He arches his eyebrow, like I'm clearly an idiot for thinking I can demand answers from him the way I have been.

I lock my jaw and force a smile. "Very well, Professor. I guess we can walk over together."

He releases a tense sigh and strides past me. I struggle

to keep up with his pace as we make our way to the Archer Building. When we finally arrive at his office on the fourth floor, I'm delighted to find the plastic chair next to the door empty.

"Wow," I say, following him into the little office. "I really thought the line would be longer."

He drops into the chair behind his desk. "Close the door."

I do as he asks, trying not to think about all the things I'd rather do behind closed doors than interrogate him about my missing assignment.

When I turn back, he's looking out the window, absently dragging his thumb along his lower lip. That quickly, I'm launched into a vivid memory of those lips. The way they felt against mine. The way I'd sought them out again. The way they'd sought mine . . .

I take the seat opposite him. "So what is this about?"

"I'm dropping you from the class."

My heart falls to my stomach. "Excuse me?"

"You missed an important class, and you already have a zero for the summary that was due Friday."

My jaw falls open, but he's speaking again before I can.

"And even if you hadn't turned it in late, it was . . ." He picks up a pen and starts clicking it rapidly. "Subpar."

I launch upright. "Bullshit."

"You're not a lit major, Kara. It's clear in the way you craft your thoughts. You're better suited to sticking with a seminar in your major. I'm sure your GPA is stellar. There's no point in taking a hit this late in the game."

I circle the desk. My skin feels like it's on fire, for entirely different reasons than the last time we were this close. He spins in his chair to face me.

"You're lying." I shove my finger at him accusingly. "Besides that, I've been waiting to take this class for three years. You can't just pull me out of it for no good reason."

He clicks his pen a dozen more times before I tear it out of his hand and throw it across the room. He closes his eyes briefly like he might be reaching for his Zen place after my little outburst.

"This isn't going to work," he utters quietly. "You know all the reasons why. I don't need to spell them out for you."

"You've been patronizing me for ten minutes. Why stop now?"

"Kara . . . This has to stop before we both do things we regret."

"Like what?"

His eyes darken, transforming my spike of anger into something equally intense. Something that might land me in the second circle of hell if I weren't already bound for worse. I take in a calming breath, cross my arms, and lean my hip against the edge of his desk.

"You're attracted to me," I say.

"Obviously." The retort is low and clipped.

"Fine." I suck in a long breath. For some reason, I didn't anticipate his reply. The word itself, sure, but not his bluntness. "I'm attracted to you too. And that's not exactly . . . normal for me."

He frowns.

"I'm not immune to attraction," I say. "But it's easy for me to ignore it most of the time. This physical pull between us is stronger than anything I've ever felt with anyone else, but it's more than that. There's something special about you that I can't figure out. Even though it's dangerous and driving both of us a little crazy right now, I can't let it go until I know what that is."

For a long time, he simply breathes and stares, like he's deciding what to do with me. I brace myself for him to insist we keep our distance again. But hopefully he's figured out that's just not going to work on me.

"I know I'm different," he finally says.

The small admission stuns me. I'm afraid to say anything that will keep him from sharing more, so I stay quiet and wait.

"I just don't know why. And until you started shoving your way into my personal space the way you have been, I was content not to know."

"What are you afraid of?"

"Who said I was afraid?"

I unfold my arms and slowly glide my fingertips across the back of his hand. I expect him to recoil from my touch, but he doesn't, which makes me bolder still.

"I'm different too, Maximus. Even if I couldn't read the fear in your eyes when you pulled away from me the other night, I could feel it." When he tenses, I decide to let him into my world a little more, even though I know I shouldn't. "Humans..." *Bad start.* "Human beings give off vibrations. It's like the way people read body language or smell pheromones and inherently *know* something about someone else. The way I feel it is more like a vibration. Which can be kind of overwhelming when I'm around a lot of people. Or around people with really powerful emotions." I lick my lips, worried I've said too much. "People like you."

"You sound crazy. You know that, right?"

I resist the urge to throw something at him.

"Well, if you went around telling people you could twist metal like a bendy straw, they might call you crazy too. How about we establish a judgment-free zone here, all things considered?"

He sighs. "Fine. I don't know. Saying any of this out loud makes it seem…"

"Real?"

"Maybe. I shouldn't be able to do the things I do."

"And I shouldn't be able to feel the things I feel. But here we are."

"So what do we do now? Dedicate office hours to reveling in our shared weirdness? That doesn't feel too constructive to me."

I tilt my head. "I was thinking dinner."

His eyes widen slightly. "If we so much as think about sharing a meal in public together—"

"The paparazzi will have a field day with it and your face will get splashed on trashy magazines far and wide. I know. This is my normal, remember? I have ways to get around these things."

He eyes me warily.

I lean over him to grab another pen and scribble an

address on the top margin of my ungraded assignment.

"Meet me here at six. I'll work out dinner."

His eyes light up, bringing me a new frisson of excitement. "Hmm. A woman with a plan."

"Maybe." I kick up the corner of my mouth. "Okay, probably. Just wear comfortable clothes."

I'm ready to leave, but he grabs my hand, keeping me from moving farther away from him. Our gazes lock.

"Are you sure about this?"

I lift my brows. "About dinner?"

"No."

He runs his thumb up and down my wrist. The gesture is gentle and sweet, and I have to restrain myself from crawling into his lap and dedicating the next hour to re-exploring his mouth, his touch, everything . . .

"You're determined to figure me out. Has it ever occurred to you that you might not like what you find?"

"It hasn't." *Not a single time.*

"Shouldn't that worry you?"

I shake my head. "If I only wanted to see the best of you, I wouldn't be here."

"But what if—"

"I can handle it, Maximus." Also not a lie. I show him as much with the steady surety of my eyes as our gazes tangle once more. "I can handle *you.*"

All of you.

I'm not sure when I've yearned for a challenge more. I hope he sees that truth in my eyes, but I'm not sure. Because this time, when I pull away, he lets me go.

CHAPTER 12

MAXIMUS

"THIS IS... *WOW.*"

I'm not looking at Kara as I declare it, but her soft hum tells me she's heard me. "Well, it doesn't seem as overwhelming from up here. That's for sure."

I don't miss the bleak notes in her reply as we look out over the trendy sprawl of Los Feliz and Hollywood. The downtown skyline, several miles away, is drenched in the hues of a sultry September sunset. From up here, the huge buildings look like miniatures constructed on a movie's special-effects set.

After a quiet moment, she steps across the packed dirt of the Griffith Park Firebreak Trail to stand a little closer to me. She's near enough to touch, serving up temptation I don't try to ignore. For once, it feels right to give in. To pull her close and tuck her against my side. It feels even more right as she settles there, splaying her touch affectionately across my stomach. I wrap my hand around her shoulder and stretch my fingers in, gently fingering the wisps of hair that have escaped her cute ponytail.

Everything about the moment is more connective than seductive, if a little heavy with the anticipation I've been holding on to all day about meeting her here. But now we're just...together. As if we've been this way for a lot longer than eight days.

She leans her cheek against my shoulder. "I had a hunch you'd like it."

"A 'hunch,' eh?"

I utter every syllable with deliberate intention. Maybe her gifts are more intuitive than psychic, but I haven't forgotten what she confessed this morning in my office. The vibrations she feels. The way she feels them from *me*. The way I overwhelm her. I still can't unpack everything that I'm experiencing in return.

"This trail is usually a little lighter with foot traffic," she goes on, sidestepping my comment. "People opt for the easier route rather than trying to plow straight up the side of the hill on this one."

"I don't mind the tougher way," I assure her with a chuckle. While her answering laugh spreads warmth that rivals the sunset, I add, "But you had a hunch about that too, didn't you?"

Kara tilts her head up, tossing me a soft smile. "Some things about you are easier to understand than others."

"Meaning what?" I'm only half kidding. I manage to keep my tone light before realizing the effort is useless. The emotions percolating under the surface have likely already given me away. My energy. My enchantment with her. My sheer and happy surprise that she's chosen dirt and trees over some stiff, stuffy restaurant.

Sure enough, Kara words her reply with obvious care. "Your propensity for physicality isn't exactly a well-kept secret." She swallows before gliding her touch up to my chest. "Not that I'm complaining."

At once, there's a fresh glow in my blood. "Kara Valari," I tease in a low rumble. "Are you flirting with me?"

Her head darts back up when she laughs. Her velvety browns are sprinkled with gold flecks. Her lower lip disappears beneath her teeth. All too quickly, she interrupts my fascination with the move by answering me. "Do you . . . want me to be?"

With gruff scuffs in the dirt, I turn to fully face her. "Can't you tell?"

Again, with intimacy that feels so natural, I move one hand to grip her hip. I'm so goddamned tempted to roam that palm farther down, not that she's helped the matter by dressing in a pair of denim shorts that would make Daisy Duke blush. I'm grateful when Kara keeps her own touch planted at the center of my chest, a small anchor helping me control my physical lust.

But no force on this earth can stop what's going on with the rest of me.

It's happening all over again. The awakening to her. The awareness of her. That burst of fire and light and color, racing between her blood and mine, as brilliant as the gilded sunlight all around us . . .

Sunlight that's suddenly alive with swirling stars.

I keep the quixotic impression to myself. It's a thought, not a feeling, so it should be safe from her. The early twilight breeze turns into a full gust and pries feathery tufts away from the nearby fescue bushes, and Kara giggles as the little buggers cling to us.

"You've got stars in your hair, Professor."

"So do you, Miss Valari." I can't help the smile that brims as I flick one away from her eyebrow. "And here. And . . . here."

But once I finish thumbing one off her bottom lip, I don't move my touch.

I revel in the snag of her breath. Then the flicker of the sunlight and the need in her gaze. While pressing my thumb to the corner of her mouth, I stretch my fingers across her cheek.

"Stars," I repeat, letting my feelings match my words. I know she gets it. I know she feels me. She's getting off on my adrenaline and my wonder, and I accept the flow of hers in return. It's like we're becoming junkies for each other— and for the first time, I don't resist being higher than a kite.

"You think they're guiding us somewhere?" she asks in a whisper as warm as the wind.

I mold my body closer to hers. "If the destination's heaven, I'm halfway there."

The words, warm and husky on my lips, feel perfect for the moment—until Kara steps away, nearly tripping over her own feet.

What the hell?

"Sun's going to be down in just a few minutes," she hurries to say. "Race me up to the observatory? We can keep talking over dinner." She tilts her head and winks, an obvious play to lighten the suddenly weird air that's fallen like a lead balloon between us.

I want to push her on the whiplash response, but my intuition already reins me back. Pressing her to reveal anything more than she wants, especially in the middle of this trail, is going to be an exercise in futility.

I'll have to be sneakier about the whole thing. Smoother. A task completely outside my wheelhouse. That means I'll have to ask myself the unaskable question.

What would Jesse do?

Unbelievably, the query becomes my lifeline as I follow her up the rest of the hill. The final part of the trail also proves to be one of its steepest, meaning Kara's having to show off the flex of her glutes in all their well-honed glory—and those ruthlessly sexy shorts.

The only thing that saves me from rocking a full-blown hard-on once we get to the top is focusing on my conjecture of how Jesse would do this. It's fate's cruel joke on the pair of us. I've got the legs that work but the small-talk game that doesn't. Jesse's stuck in a wheelchair for the rest of his days but can charm a nun out of her panties.

I'm pretty damn sure Kara Valari's not wearing any panties.

Not that charming her out of them would be my intention here.

I just need to figure out how to get her to open up to me. Because for the first time, in the absence of my own fear, I'm starting to think she may have plenty of secrets of her own.

I sit back and survey what's left of the decadent food spread we've demolished. "I can't believe you arranged all this in a few hours. Okay, scratch that. I can't believe you arranged all this, period."

While her cute ponytail allows me to view every enticing inch of the blush staining her cheeks, I tamp the fiftieth urge to tug at the tight elastic tie and set her thick waves free. It's not the only temptation I've been fighting the last hour.

"I'm really glad you're having fun," she says with a sweet smile that turns my throat into sandpaper and my senses into mush. But the good kind. *A lot* of the good kind. While our view from the small table she's somehow set up on the terrace is even better than the view from the trail, I can't take my eyes off the beauty in front of me.

"Fun?" I scoff. "Fun is a run on the beach or a Sunday matinee. But this is…"

Romantic. Meaningful. The best night I've had in a long time.

But I don't say any of that.

Kara quirks a curious smile. "This is … what?"

Again, I think about speaking the truth of my soul out loud—but her reaction to when I did it the first time tonight, out on the trail, is still a lingering sting in my memory. Instead, I pop an olive into my mouth and gaze out at the skyline once more.

"This is fun on crack."

Her melodic laughter draws my attention back to her.

"So how did you do this?"

Her answering smile is a little coquettish and a lot captivating. "Do what?"

"You know what," I return. "This place is closed on Mondays. Jesse and I used to get so mad when we had a Monday off school because we had to find some other kind of fun. Those alternatives rarely beat the observatory."

"Let's just say I know a guy who knows a guy," she answers with a coy smile. She reaches across the table and threads her fingers through mine. "So you and Jesse came here a lot?"

"You could say that. Free admission, air-conditioning, and kick-ass displays about space. To a couple of downtown kids who already knew more about the subject than our teachers, with moms who couldn't afford to skip work, there were few things better."

"That truly does sound like fun on crack."

Her lighthearted jest gets her an answering hand squeeze.

"Even getting here was a blast. I'd load Jesse and his chair onto the number two bus, and then we'd transfer onto the Observatory Dash." The memories have me smiling and shaking my head. "Some of the characters on that bus... I mean, damn... you wouldn't believe me if I told you."

"I dare you to say that after an hour at one of my

mother's parties."

"Is it that bad?" My tender tone is a response to the dark desolation in hers. "Life as a Valari?" I clarify. "I mean, the glamour has to be overstated a little, which is where you get the haters. But behind that huge exterior, there's got to be the truth, right? The reality?"

Kara disconnects our grasp and rests back in her chair. Her eyes are as luminous as the moon rising against the dusky sky just above the observatory's dome.

"Sorry. I'm prying." I run a frustrated hand through my hair, worried I'm already screwing up an otherwise perfect night. "You probably get this all the time. People trying to get information out of you. Shit—"

"That's not it." Her expression is taut but sincere. "Honestly, it's just that I don't think I've ever been asked about my life by someone who might actually . . . *care*."

I lean forward, resting my elbows on the table. "I do care." *Probably too damn much.* "If you want to talk about anything, I'm here. Whatever it is . . ."

She laughs weakly. "All the spectacle and the glory of my fabulous life, eh?"

"I said whatever it is." I stress my sincerity by reaching for her again, stretching my fingertips out and lightly grazing her knuckles. I slide my touch across the top of her wrist. And then around it.

She sighs heavily. "My family is . . . complicated."

"Most are."

"It probably seems like every detail of our life is splashed across the media. Talk about false realities. Very little is as it seems. Beyond all that, we're a study in contradictions. We're really private, but we're not. We're close, but . . . we're not."

I frown. "What about Kell? You seem close with her."

She nods. "I am. I mean, more than anyone else, that's for sure."

"Jesse has her in one of his classes." I smirk, remembering the way he spoke of her. "He was surprised that she had more depth than her social media presence might suggest."

She chuckles. "She does. It's . . ." She circles her hand through the air like she can summon the truth of the matter that way. "Everything about the Valaris eventually funnels down to image. Most of it, anyway."

"I can't begin to imagine a life in the public eye like that." When she doesn't answer, I press on, sensing she wants to share more, even if the subject matter is stressing her out. "You seem to be the sole Valari who doesn't want the whole world to know it."

"You're not wrong." She averts her stare and forces a tight smile. "So what made you want to become a literature professor?"

Since my gaze hasn't left her face, I'm well aware that she's deliberately trying to sidetrack me. But she also probably thinks she's shared more with me than she should have. While she still keeps a lot of herself tucked away from me, I'm able to detect her nervousness when she bites her lip. I'm barely more than a stranger—a stranger who could sell her confessions for the right price.

I'm determined to prove I'm not. If it takes baring more of myself to her as collateral, I can work with that.

"Becoming Professor Maximus wasn't a childhood dream or anything," I answer. "I'm not complaining, though. I enjoy the work."

"So you sort of fell into it? That kind of thing?" She blinks and studies me harder, like she's determined to excavate a better answer from me.

"As much as you can fall into a life of academia. I suppose it happens by default when you realize the only thing you're really passionate about is reading."

Something hardens in her gaze, but I can't decipher it. She fidgets with her napkin. Here's my opening to volley the subject back onto her, but something tells me that's not the right course here. Quite a few somethings, as a matter of fact.

I exhale a deep breath. "When I was younger...after Jesse's accident...I threw myself into books. They were safe." I pause. "I couldn't hurt anyone turning pages, you know?"

She nods. Not with pity but quiet understanding.

"I'd quit sports and needed something to kill the time. At least something to compete with all the shit going on in my head. So I spent a lot of time at the store."

"Recto Verso?"

"Yeah. Reg and Sarah took me in when Mom was busy. They pretty much let me turn the place into my personal library. Good thing, since I devoured books like most kids consumed video games."

"And?" Something glitters in her eyes, like she knows there's more to it.

"And...I guess there was something about these old classic stories that pulled me in. Figuring out all the subtext. Riddling out all those little hidden gems that I try to stump you guys with in class."

"There's always a story under the story," she adds.

"Exactly!" It feels so damn good to let it out with a full rasp of fervor. "And past that, no matter how messed up everything can get, the hero always finds a way to pull through. Every time." I rein myself in with help from a contemplative gaze out to the horizon, taking in the fading colors before they melt away completely. When I finally look back, Kara's attention is still fixed on me. "After everything that happened, I needed that. I needed to believe that I could pull through. And that..."

"What?" she prompts between my hesitant taps against the tabletop.

"That...Jesse would too."

She takes a long sip of her wine. "So I take it you're a fan of happily ever afters."

I smirk. "Who wouldn't be?"

"Hmm. Maybe a few very serious academic types."

"I take the texts seriously. I've never been much of a literary snob, though."

"Those blazers you wear with the elbow patches suggest otherwise."

I laugh again, throwing my head back this time, and her answering smile is officially the best thing I've experienced all night. Suddenly I wish I could stop time and hold this moment a little longer. Taking in the soft blush on her cheeks.

The way the wind flutters wisps of her hair across her face. This quiet escape—just us—away from all the prying eyes.

As if she can read my thoughts, her blush deepens, and she looks down. "Do you want to go inside?"

"Sure."

We get up, leaving dinner behind. I beat her to the door into the Hall of the Sky, holding it open for her. Together we step inside and walk through to the rotunda and the colorful displays that lie beyond.

"Can I tell you a secret?" Her voice bounces around the smooth walls and tiled floors that surround us now.

The seductive taunt causes me to stop so hard that my athletic soles chirp on the marble. I take her hand and tug her back to me. When we're chest to chest, I almost forget about her lingering question. I'm too dazed by the visual of her. The proud poise of her slender shoulders. The generous swell of her breasts, tapering to the sweet nip of her waist. And then—God help me—the flare that accommodates everything below. The parts I've refused to think about. The flesh I can't help obsessing over . . .

Her expression seems to match mine. A little lost. Dark with longing.

"What is it?" I murmur. "All your secrets are safe with me."

She pauses a moment, seeming to take in my promise—one I mean with all of me.

"I've never actually been in here before. Inside the observatory."

My eyes widen. "Are you shitting—I mean kidding—me?"

She slants a stare of warning. "Safety zone for all the secrets, Mr. Kane. You promised."

"And I'm still your lockbox," I return. "But how have you grown up here and not experienced all this?"

That alone seems to prompt her next move. She tilts her head back, casting her gaze heavenward. "Oh, wow."

I don't have to follow her focus to know the cause of her exclamation. "The ceiling in here does that to a lot of people," I assure her. "And actually, seeing as we have this place to ourselves…"

I lower myself to the floor, taking her down with me, until we're both sprawled and share a perfect view of the rotunda's mural.

"Talk about spectacle and glory," she mutters with no small amount of awe.

"All the panels were painted back in the thirties by a guy named Hugo Ballin. The big circle in the middle illustrates the gods and goddesses of the zodiac signs, wielded in the sky by Atlas." I point up to the different places on the mural as I speak. "The Pleiades are also there, and then he's got Jupiter—or Zeus, depending on whether you're feeling Greek or Roman."

"Zeus. Huh." Her thoughtful murmur seems layered with new meaning. Or is that just my heightened senses working overtime? A misplaced interpretation of her rasp on the still air? The battle I'm still waging, now more than ever, not to clutch her close, kiss her senseless, and give her whispered promises of more?

As a result, I default to Professor Maximus mode. When the occasion fits…

121

"Ballin wasn't exactly shattering boxes with the concept," I explain. "Many of the constellations were named after the gods because the ancients believed the gods moved among them. Each god and goddess was given a place in the sky to honor them and to therefore appease them. The bigger the deity, the larger the constellation." I gaze up at the huge dome dominated by the cathedral-like art. "No less of a crazy theory than gods walking the earth and conspiring with humans, I guess."

Kara shifts her weight, lifting herself to gaze down at me. "Crazy? Why?" she prompts. "Just because the theory belongs to an ancient civilization? Because it's all called mythology and not literature? Because science and facts don't directly support it as proven history?"

I don't answer her at first. I think I'm waiting for her to crack a just-kidding grin. When she doesn't budge, I challenge her. "What are you saying? That you believe there's a bunch of superbeings cavorting around in the sky when they're not snacking on nectar on Mount Olympus?"

"I'm saying that there are lots of things in the world—in the universe—that you can't begin to understand or explain away."

"All right," I drawl. "I'll bite. Like what?"

"Like the Bermuda Triangle," she says at once. "And the Nazca Lines and Bigfoot and déjà vu." And then she's leaning over, reworking our hands so they're entwined again, so that the energy, so bizarre and insane but bright and beautiful, flares between us again. "Like us, Maximus," she whispers. "Like . . . this."

Too late, I realize that I'm not breathing. There's something bizarre and forbidden and different about Kara Valari. But something warm and familiar and right too.

So damn right...

Whoever she really is, sharing this time together has only sharpened the yearning to figure her out. To know all her secrets, even as she helps me discover all of mine. But before that, there's a much more urgent purpose. I need to kiss the hell out of her. No matter how thoroughly I'm terrified to.

I reach up and pull her ponytail free, then sift my fingers through the silky strands until I'm cupping the back of her head. Slowly, I guide her down to me. I'm too eager for the lips that have just formed those words. In this moment, they resound in my mind like a declaration of freedom and in my heart like a manifesto of truth.

Because something tells me, as she forms her mouth over mine, that the two of us really are barely scratching at the first layer of a deeper truth. Terrified to go any further—but more terrified of what will happen if we don't.

CHAPTER 13

KISSING MAXIMUS IS A thought-robbing endeavor. For all the way he stimulates my mind, being this close to him makes me quickly forget about the other ways we match. Seconds ago, my thoughts were weaving through the constellations, deep in myth and mystery—all things I've spent my academic life contemplating along with the truths I already know.

Now I'm all blood and hot skin and clawing need. Human. Demon. Possibly a dangerous combination of both. Emboldened, I skim my hand down the front of his shirt and tease my fingertips under the hem. His muscles jump and clench the higher I go. Our mouths unlock just enough that his moaning exhale warms my lips. I wonder if it's the kiss or the small touch that's undoing him. Then his free hand shifts me over him so my thigh slips between his.

His arousal is unmistakable, pressing against my hip. It might be a little awkward if it weren't so damn intoxicating to know how I affect him. I should move away. Ease the pressure between us. But I'm driven to test his control the way he tests mine, so I deepen our kiss and drag my torso a little higher as I do, adding to the friction.

Maximus reaches to where my shorts have ridden high and takes two firm handfuls of the flesh there. The possessive motion creates a surge of pressure between our bodies. It's a blinding blaze through my system. Too much too fast.

Oh, but I love it. I moan against his lips and curl my fingers against his pectoral.

"Goddamn, you're killing me with these shorts." He exhales in a ragged breath. "We should stop. Kara, tell me to stop."

"Stop" sounds like the worst word I've ever heard, so I kiss him harder, making it quite clear that I'm not on board with that plan. At all.

"Kara." His voice is a desperate rasp between us, rough with his worry and longing.

"I don't want to stop. I want you to keep touching me. Kissing me." The rest of my pleas echo silently through my mind. The ones that involve him doing more than kissing and touching. But I'll never be able to share that experience with him, no matter how badly I may want to.

It's a sobering thought.

I should stop this. Revving the attraction a little is one thing, but this is a high-speed chase down a road I have no business traveling. At least with Maximus.

I break the kiss, but before I can come up with a good excuse to stop things, he switches our positions so I'm lying on the floor. He cradles the back of my head, protecting me from the hard tiles as he hovers over me.

He brushes his lips gently across mine. I bow my body toward him, eager for more full contact. He takes the invitation and lowers, taking care not to crush me. Not that I'd mind. I'm already fully obsessed with the feel of him. The weight of him. His heat and the way he smells like the rain when we're this close.

He brushes his fingers along my jaw and follows the journey with his mouth until his next breath tickles my ear. "I don't want to stop either. I don't think I'll ever want to. Not with you, Kara."

The confession is enough to kill any refusals forming in my brain. More, it transcends the physical frenzy that's seized my senses. Heat and awe swirl behind his eyes when our gazes meet again.

When he kisses me, somewhere in the deepest recesses of my mind, I think I could fall in love this way. With his tortured whispers, heated looks, and the worshiping way he trails his lips over all the skin he can reach.

I thread my fingers in his hair and blink up at the ceiling. The only witnesses to this intimate moment are the figures painted into the sky. They're not my gods, but somehow I can still feel them watching. Judging me.

Maximus keeps moving down my body, nipping my breasts through my cropped top. Then dragging hot kisses across my bare stomach. I can barely breathe. I've never wanted anyone this way. I don't think I ever will. But we can't. I can't . . .

Still, our sighs and moans keep echoing off the walls. Then the pop of my top button on my shorts coming loose. His name on my lips like a prayer.

Then the thunder. A quiet rumble that's easy to ignore until the booming cracks of a fast-approaching storm have us both silent and still. My eyes fly open when Maximus shifts over me.

The question in his blue eyes mirrors the one in my head. Should we get out of here before the sky opens up? *Or keep doing sexy things on the observatory floor to the sound of the rain?*

A gray-pallored Zeus stares at me over Maximus's shoulder. The god of thunder himself. I'm not sure whether to thank the man in the mural or hate him right now.

"Should we go?"

I shift my attention an inch to the left to the beautiful man staring down at me who could easily pass for a god himself. I reach for him, already regretting the end of our night. The second my fingertips meet his cheek, the sky erupts with another angry clap of thunder.

He lifts to his knees and then hauls me up to stand as he does. "Come on. Let's get out of here before it gets bad out there." He turns toward the terrace. "Shit. The food."

"Don't worry about it."

"Are you sure?"

"I know people who know people. Remember?"

His smile is a bloom of relief in my chest. I'm so messed up right now. I haven't recovered from where my head was five minutes ago, and I might not ever. More relief comes when he takes my hand and leads us out of the building. Wordlessly we hurry toward the east trail—one that hopefully will get us down before the rain starts.

We make the descent quickly, but we're not fast enough to outrun the rain. Drops begin pelting us just before we get to the bottom. The full deluge of the storm arrives as we make the last dash to his truck. We jump in and catch our breath. The rain creates a white noise around us and obscures the view out his windshield.

When I shiver, he turns on the engine and switches on the heat. I don't miss the way his attention snags on my rain-drenched clothes. I'm just as guilty. He looks impossibly gorgeous with the fabric of his T-shirt clinging to his well-defined torso.

"Thank you," I say, rubbing some warmth back into my arms.

"No problem." He rests his head on the neck rest with a heavy sigh. "Thanks, Dad. Impeccable timing."

I lift my eyebrows. "Dad?"

He turns to me with a smirk curling up the corner of his lips. "That's just my personal joke. Pretending that the god of thunder is my dad." He points his finger to the sky.

"Zeus?"

He laughs quietly. "It's dumb. I guess it's better than thinking about what happened with the real one, though."

My brain rushes to catch up to what he's saying. "What happened with the real one?"

"That's an excellent question. I have no idea, and my mother refuses to tell me. Not ideal when you're trying to figure out who you are, you know?"

I'm quiet for a long moment, struggling with how suddenly and deeply my heart aches for him. I'm also fighting to understand why someone would keep that information from their own grown child. My lineage is an ugly tree of betrayals and deceit, but at least I know what it looks like. Living in the dark would be so much worse. At least I think so.

"That seems unfair."

He beams his stare forward like he can somehow see through the rain-drenched window. "I had to come to terms with unfair a long time ago." He switches on the windshield wipers. "Speaking of unfair, let's drive you home so you can get dry."

I cover the top of his hand with mine as he puts the vehicle into gear. He pauses to look at me.

"I had a really nice time with you. I'm glad you said yes."

"Me too." His eyes are unreadable. They hold too much. Or maybe we're both feeling too much of everything right now. I can't figure him out.

Worried that he's already regretting the whole night, I release some tension when he captures my hand. He keeps it tight in his during the rest of the drive home.

Almost an hour later, he pulls up to my house and idles behind Kell's Bentley.

"I guess I'll see you Wednesday," I offer, even though I wish I could see him sooner.

Maybe he'll want that too. But he's not looking at me, and I hate it.

"See you Wednesday," he utters quietly.

Despite his sudden coolness, I lean across the front seat and kiss his cheek. I pull back before the moment can turn into more and then run through the rain to the front gate.

Once I'm inside, I hurry to my room and take a hot shower. Chasing the chill from my bones is a relief. But my vision is flooded with Maximus. Our perfect dinner. His tender touches. His bold ones. I groan with frustration as I towel off and throw on a T-shirt and some comfortable sweats.

Kell is standing on the deck with a glass of wine. I grab one of my own and join her. The night has grown dark, but the rain has stopped. Not a cloud in the sky, actually.

"What are you doing out here? Everything's wet," I say, closing the sliding door behind me.

"The storm knocked the internet out. I'm bored as fuck. How about you? Where have you been?"

"Just stayed late at the library," I lie.

She shoots me an unimpressed look. "Is that why your car has been in the garage all night?"

"I got a ride."

She lifts an eyebrow and brings her glass to her lips. "You're a bad liar, Kara. If you're going to keep sneaking around with your professor, you might think about boning up on your bullshitting skills. Or you could just tell me the truth."

I take a big gulp of my wine in lieu of answering her.

"Well?" she presses when I don't give her a response.

"I think I'll stick with omission if it's all the same to you."

She turns toward me, leaning her back against the railing. "I suppose it would be if I didn't feel like it was up to me to change your mind. I'm just trying to give you some sisterly advice. We both know it's just a matter of time."

"Until what?"

She cocks her head. "Until they send someone for you. Then playtime is over. It's a black cloud following me everywhere too. Trust me, I get it."

"Then why are you on me about it?"

"Because I care about you. I don't exactly know where they send rebellious demon girls who don't save themselves for the right person, but I really don't want to see you go there."

"I'm pretty sure it's hell. That's where we're all going to end up anyway."

She chews on her lip and looks out toward the glittering lights of the city. "Yeah, but we're not there yet. I know you hate this life and everything Mom's trying to do, but it could be a lot worse. It could be, you know, actual *hell*."

"We're living in a delusion. None of this is real."

She straightens and throws her arms out to the side, causing her wine to slosh onto the decking. "*I'm* real. *You're* real. Isn't that worth protecting?"

I'm tempted to keep arguing with her, but I can sense her growing frustration. More, I sense it comes from a better place than anyone else in my family is capable of. The bond we have, as thin as it seems sometimes, is still a bond.

"All we're doing is inspiring people to be as vapid and self-involved as we all seem to be. That's what it means to be a Valari. Sorry if I'm dragging my feet on my way to that party."

"You don't want to go to the party at all. That's the problem. And…" She closes her eyes and exhales tensely. "Kara, I just don't want to lose you."

I tip some of my wine into her nearly empty glass. "You're not going to lose me," I say lightly, even if the dread in my chest is heavier than before.

She sighs dramatically. "Are you falling for this guy or what?"

"What do you want me to say?"

"Just tell me the truth."

I lift my chin and search my soul for the answer. Before tonight, I could have been indecisive. Now Maximus is in my blood. A full-blown addiction. Books have always been my only addiction, but Maximus is his own story. A living, breathing mystery. The most fascinating hero I've ever met. And I don't ever want the story to end. Ever.

Kell cocks her head, bringing her wine-stained lips together tightly. She's waiting for my honest answer, even though it's not the one she wants to hear.

"Yes," I finally say. "I'm falling for him."

CHAPTER 14

MAXIMUS

"MY, MY, MY. IT'S a beautiful day in the neighborhood, indeed."

Jesse's comment—like so many he makes—has me debating whether to groan or chuckle. I follow the line of his gaze across the lawn below his office window to the trio of females lazing in the midafternoon sun.

"You're a hopeless cause, Professor North."

But the mirth beneath my mutter isn't so easy to maintain once I open my phone. Today my social media feed is filled with nothing but shots of Kara Valari. She's dressed in a trendy blouse and red denim pants and is beaming her way through a charity luncheon for a local animal rescue center.

Fucking great.

Because every effort I've made to push her out of my mind since last night, including two cold showers, a run on the Santa Monica berm, and a two-hour lunch with my best friend, have been splintered by twenty seconds of puppies, kittens, and that woman's backside in skintight red denim.

And I thought she'd never best the Daisy Dukes from last night.

Jesus. Christ.

Last. Night.

"Yo! Earth to Maximus Kane."

I'm grateful for the chance to snap my head up. "Huh? What?"

"Now who's the hopeless cause?" While I'm focusing on his words, he flings out a length of super-elastic rubber that latches on to my phone with a loud *thwop*. Before I can blink, the device is yanked out of my grip and handily caught in his thanks to his little gizmo. "Well, look at all *this*."

"Goddammit, Jesse."

"And this . . . and this . . . Why, Maximus Kane. Are you cyber-drooling over Kara Valari?"

"Give me my phone back."

He holds it up and out of the way, as if we're kids quibbling over who gets to be player one on the game system. "Not until you give me the scoop about what happened with this little cutie."

"*Don't* call her that." Protective rage is a strange invader in my senses.

"Make you a deal." He raises a brow. "I'll stop talking when you start. Let's start with the other night . . . at your place."

I scrape a hand through my hair. "What's going on here? You've never pulled this with anyone else I've been seeing."

"Because none of them have showed up at your front door on a Sunday night before."

"And that changes...what, exactly?"

As a maddening answer, he simply wiggles the phone over his head. "No details for Jesse, no phone for Max." He doesn't relent his pose, knowing I won't breach his personal space unless I'm lifting him for practical purposes. "Come on, man. Humor me with a few juicy details. Don't leave me holding your phone and my dick here."

"Thanks for the terrifying visual."

"Know what's even more terrifying? The fact that in the three years we've lived at that building, I can't recall any woman in your doorway except for your cleaning girl and old Mrs. Worthington with her brownies."

I take a turn with the brow cocking. "Do you have brownie envy? Is that what this is about?"

Jesse narrows his glare. "This is about you and healthy human companionship. Well, besides me. The kind of companions who might *like* the idea of your manly scruffstache between their silky—"

"Okay, hold up." I surge out of my favorite wingback chair and start marching around the end of his desk. "Damn it, Jesse. Why are you pushing this?"

He tilts his head, his expression sobering. "Because part of me is worried about you, man."

"I've dated, okay?" I turn and brace my ass to the desk's edge. "You know there have been a few...exceptional ladies...in my past."

"Sure," Jesse drawls. "But Wendy from college, Therese

from the staff retreat, and 'Recto Verso Renee' don't count."

"Why not?"

"Because they're all ancient history." He huffs. "Dude, Wendy is married, Therese has *kids*, and Renee moved back to Britain."

"Okay, fine." I rub my knuckles through my beard. "So I've been busy."

"No," Jesse counters. "You've been fucking picky."

"You know, there's this term that a few guys in this world still live by, Mr. North. It's called being a *gentleman*."

For extra fun, I overenunciate every syllable of the term. As revenge, Jesse exaggerates his new laugh. I grit my teeth. He's so gleefully certain about all this, seeing through my rhetoric and down to my most agonizing truth. That I haven't pursued a woman for such a long time because there's been nothing inside to pursue her with. A void I've filled with a thousand other things besides what's really me. A me I know nothing about. Because chasing it results in exactly what happened at the shop with Mom.

Anger. Confusion. Frustration. Disappointment. A deeper dive into a darker void.

"Okay, just for giggles, let me get this absolutely straight." Jesse's interjection is a needed slice into my moroseness. "Are you telling me you had Kara Valari at your front door, looking like sin and smelling like the ocean, and you were a *gentleman* about the whole thing?"

I drop my gaze and abandon the quest for my phone. At the moment, there's a bigger concern in front of me— like controlling how much of the truth I feel okay about revealing here. No way do I want to lie to him, but what Kara and I share is still too new and special in my mind—and other places of me. It feels too vulnerable.

"I didn't say that."

"Ah! Yesss." Jesse pumps a fist. "And here I thought that extra bounce in your step might just be from caffeine."

"It *is* just from caffeine."

"Which means what?"

"Exactly what I said." I move back to the chair and drop into it. "I'm a gentleman, not some horny hellhound."

"You ever think she might *want* a horny hellhound?"

"She didn't leave disappointed." *All right, maybe a little.* "But it was just a kiss." *And groping. And stroking. And caressing. And gazing into her huge, dark eyes until my soul wanted to swim in hers for hours.* "That's all it's really been so far."

"So far?" Apparently, Jesse deems the disclosure worthy of handing my phone back over. He slides the device back across the desk. "That's a pair of loaded words, my friend."

It doesn't take me long to lift my head. "Yeah. I guess so."

A deeper interrogation brews in his gaze, then across his whole demeanor—but before he can act on it, there's a stir of movement in his office doorway. I join him in looking up, to where a dark-haired, kohl-eyed beauty awaits his acknowledgment with unnerving stillness.

On paper, Kell Valari is a year younger than Kara—but looking at her now, I'd guess the opposite as truth, by more than that gap. It's not just the force of the woman's outward appearance, which is as scrubbed and styled as the rest of the Valari royalty. It's everything else that informs her arrival. The authority in her stance. The regality of her posture. The confidence in the sole step she ventures toward Jesse.

"Is this a bad time, Professor North?"

Her words sound so much like Kara but not. Where Kara's voice still wavers in places, sounding uncertain— maybe hopeful?—Kell's is more assured, as if she already knows the answer to her question. For that matter, every other question in the world too.

In short, she's spun of everything my best friend craves in a woman. A truth that's now stamped across his too-beautiful-for-a-man features.

Still, Jesse gamely replies, "It's a fine time, Miss Valari. What can I do for you?"

The moment would normally be my cue to fake interest in my phone, but the notion is fleeting in light of my fascination with Kara's sister. Her smoky eyes are now locked on my friend. She pulls in a defined breath through her flared nostrils and then lifts the corner of her mouth. But only by a fraction.

"Well, I'm not here for official reasons," she confesses. "There's just something I'm curious about, and you seemed like the best person to consult." While she talks, she withdraws her cell from the side pouch of her trendy satchel.

"Uhhh . . . great." Jesse spreads his hands, looking every inch a flummoxed dork. "I'm all yours. I mean, I'm all ears. Consult away."

"I took this picture in the middle of that freak storm last

night," she says, moving over to stand next to him. "There was lightning, thunder, and gallons of rain coming out of the sky—but then this."

Jesse's stare is confused at first but bugs out as he focuses on her screen. "Is that a—"

"A full constellation, right?" Kell returns quickly. "But I can't identify it and thought maybe you could."

Jesse zooms in on the image by spreading his fingers across the screen. "I'm not sure I've seen anything like it."

"I didn't even notice it until I looked back through my photos this morning," she says. "I don't remember seeing it last night when I was taking the shots. It looks like it's right on top of the clouds. Or maybe . . . in them?"

"Perhaps it's just a trick of light. Your phone reflection on the glass, maybe?"

"I was on the balcony of my bedroom," she explains. "I slid open the door to take the pictures."

As the two of them huddle over her device's screen, strange needles in my bloodstream multiply. It's not just the sight of my best friend getting cozy with a woman so physically similar to the woman I'm crazy about. It's what they're talking about. The storm last night. Which pivots my thoughts to everything I was doing during it. Everything I was feeling during it. The sensations that coursed through me, even hours after I dropped Kara at her place. Stirrings that were hot and new but bizarrely familiar.

Like they are now.

"I'm going to leave you two to the spectral sleuthing," I assert, rising once more. "My office hours start in fifteen minutes, so . . ."

"Yeah, yeah. Talk to you tonight, man."

Jesse's reply is more a distracted rote than a thought, and he doesn't look up from the image casting an electronic glow across his captivated face. Kell is another story, though. As soon as I clear the threshold of Jesse's office, she's not more than three steps behind me.

"Professor Maximus. Do you have a second?"

The pricks in my blood, now feeling more like daggers, encourage me to pretend deafness and keep moving. But my respect for Kara, and the love she no doubt bears for her sister, have me scuffing to a stop.

"Miss Valari." I conduct half a pivot. "How can I help you?"

She steps up, sending a pair of forceful *clacks* down the hall courtesy of her elegant high heels. The rest of her outfit is decidedly casual, though her jeans have Italian detailing and there's a three-carat ruby on a glistening gold chain around her neck.

"Listen." Her voice is surprisingly quiet, even gentle. "I care deeply about my sister, okay?"

That makes two of us.

Outwardly, all I do is clear my throat. Her decorum deserves the same in return. "Thank you for sharing."

She folds her arms. "Well, she did a little sharing of her own with me last night."

"Regarding?"

"You."

Thank God I expected that part. I'm ready with my sham of nonchalant surprise. "Me? In what sense?"

She ticks her head to the side and leans in to calmly scope me out. "I think you already know."

I square my jaw along with my shoulders. "I know that I'm your sister's literature professor. Whatever else you're intimating—"

"Stop."

"Stop . . . what?"

"Just stop." She steps back and takes in a sharp, deep breath. "And let me be clear about this part. I'm not asking you to stop these denials, which are kind of hilarious now that I've smelled the proverbial roses." She gestures up and down with one hand, figuratively painting the air in front of my form. "Maybe pretending to the rest of the world will make it easier for you to put on the brakes with Kara behind the scenes too."

A lead brick thuds its way down my throat. "Theoretically speaking, if I were seeing Kara . . . socially . . . why would I choose to 'put on the brakes' with her? Last time I checked, your big sister was a grown woman with impressive control of her own mind."

"Her mind? Sure. I'll give you that much." She's not vehement about it now. Her voice cracks with a new emotion. Resignation? Sorrow? "It's just the rest of her she's got to worry about."

The brick's now in my gut. "What the hell does that mean?"

Kell shakes her head as if I've jarred her from a trance. "Listen. I'm begging you here, okay? Just . . . let her go. And do it soon. The longer you let her think there's any kind of viable choice, the worse—so much worse—it'll be for her in the long run."

Against my will, my jaw clenches. The stabs in my blood are now blinding flashes behind my eyes. I haven't had a migraine since the early days of middle school, but damn it, I recognize the approach of one now.

"Choice?" I growl it out but swear my utterance sounds like thunder. Or is that the sound of the sky outside? "She's a bright woman. Whatever she elects to do with her life, there'll be plenty of choices."

"Right." The woman's bitter laugh is hollow as she casts a bleak look at the darkening day outside. "Choices galore. That's the life of a Valari woman, all right."

I blink hard, struggling to keep focus on her profile. At this angle and in the dimming light, she reminds me even more of Kara. The proud chin. The petite triangle of a nose. The smooth, high forehead.

"Bitter subtext is one of my favorite themes," I confess. "What, in all this universe, are you talking about? I imagine your lives can often be burdens you haven't asked for, but you're grown adults. You and Kara have the ability to write your own fates."

At first, Kell's answer consists of nothing but a long laugh. But this time, there's no acrid undertone to it. "Our own fates?" she counters. "Sure. I'll give you that one too. Fate will have a field day with all of us." She looks up at me with an even darker grimace, her eyes full of anguished flames. "But Maximus Kane, you are not part of my sister's fate. You never can be. And the sooner you get that through your thick skull, the better."

The fire in her declaration matches the heat of her eyes, now intense enough to scorch me like a flamethrower. But I don't look away. I can't. Every buzzing cell of my blood, battering every inch of my veins, orders me not to stand down. To fight everything she's just said with all the fiber of my being.

Thunder that now booms in support of me ... in every inch of the sky outside this building.

CHAPTER 15

Kara

DALTON OPENS THE FRONT door as I pull up the drive. He welcomes me with a graceful, sweeping gesture. "Good evening, Miss Valari."

I stride up to him. "Hey. Is Mom home?"

"I'm sorry, she isn't. She's having dinner at Nobu."

Without Kell here to distract my mother, I'm relieved to learn that the house is free of her.

"Who's she bending to her will now?" I mutter it nearly beneath my breath, half-suspecting the palm trees themselves are rigged with listening devices. "Let me guess. Jaden's new director?"

"I didn't recognize the gentleman," he offers coolly, following me inside the foyer.

I spin around, widening my gaze. "You saw him?"

"They met in her office, briefly, before leaving together."

I'm tempted to interrogate him more, but staying out of my mother's affairs is safer. She already has an entourage to obsess over all the details surrounding her—an entourage that's mercifully absent tonight, as well.

Still, I'm curious what kind of "gentleman" would be collecting her from the house and taking her out to dinner. My father—if he can be called that—only stayed in town long enough to produce the three of us. My memories of him are few and unremarkable. He was an incubus who disappeared as abruptly as he arrived after having done his duty. No more, no less. Exactly according to tradition.

A tradition that I cling to now, with at least a small sense of consolation, when contemplating my own fate. One day, I'll have some semblance of freedom again.

One day...

That's not coming anytime soon.

After a heavy sigh, I glance toward the back of the house and then turn my attention back to Dalton.

"I'm going to see if Gramps is up."

He simply nods in response. I leave him to the mansion that's emptier in more ways than one.

I journey across the tropical-landscaped backyard to the modest guesthouse. Flickering light from the television reflects across the glass. Through the window, I catch my grandfather's figure in the kitchen. I open the door, and he turns from the stove, a wooden spoon in his hand. His eyes light up when he sees me.

"Kara."

I smile and go to hug him. "Hey, Gramps. What's for dinner?"

Then I spot the empty soup tin on the counter, and the

answer is obvious. I cringe. "Canned soup? I think we can afford at least some better takeout for you."

"Nonsense." He snorts. "Chicken noodle is my favorite. No complaints here."

Not convinced, I take the spoon from him and swirl the soup around the small saucepan. "Smells good at least."

"It's delicious."

I laugh. "I'm pretty sure it's the MSG."

"Ah"—he waves his hand dismissively—"here, there's enough for two. You can judge for yourself."

He nudges me away so he can fill two bowls. We bring them to the little kitchen table that's a few steps away.

"What brings you tonight, my sweet girl?"

I take a tentative spoonful of the salty soup. He's not wrong. It is tasty. Its warmth fills me with the same comforting calm as his loving stare. "Just checking on you."

He hums a response, which doesn't sound quite like an affirmative. When I look up, one bushy white eyebrow has gone crooked.

"What?"

He slurps down another spoonful. "I appreciate you checking on me, ladybug. But I'm wondering if maybe there's something else on your mind, that's all."

"Like what?"

"Like maybe your mysterious friend, if we're still calling him that."

I let my spoon rest against the bowl with a small clink.

"Have you seen him again?" His tone is light, but I don't miss the seriousness lingering behind his words.

"I've seen him. Not sure I can call him a friend anymore, though." As soon as I say it, I recognize it as fact. My irrefutable truth. Maximus is rapidly becoming more to me. So much more.

"Did you argue?"

I sigh. "We argue plenty." Like when he pretends he can cut me from his class.

"And?"

"And that doesn't really seem to keep us apart." Sometimes—many times—it accomplishes the opposite. In electric, indelible ways . . .

As my mind fills with a string of hot Maximus-centered memories, my grandfather is discernibly quiet. I don't search for meaning in the silence. I have more questions than answers when it comes to Maximus, especially now. But talking about how mixed up I am about him with anyone feels dangerous. Even if it's Gramps. And especially when it's Kell, who's barely said a word to me since I admitted to falling for my mesmerizing professor.

"Have you learned any more about him?" he presses.

Gramps's expression is more taut than when I arrived, matching the new mood in the air. Apprehension that probably has everything to do with me dancing with a dangerous prospect—a man who isn't the demon I've been saving myself for.

"He doesn't know who his father is," I say, remembering the anguish it seems to cause—a wound that isn't any less painful for how long Maximus has endured it. "He has questions too. He knows he's not like everyone else."

"Does he know about *you*?"

"Of course not." I rear back defensively. "I'd never tell him about the family."

Somehow admitting to Maximus that I'm a demon— he'd never believe me anyway—seems a lot worse than falling into bed with him. Which would be all wrong. On so many levels.

Dangerous levels.

Which means a few casual fantasies are worth forgiving myself for. It's not like Maximus will ever find out. He'll never know enough about me to understand what it truly means to be a Valari. No one outside our closed circle ever will. But being vague about it just makes me sound like a poor little rich girl—entitled and pouty. From what little he's shared, I can tell his childhood wasn't without its struggles, financially and otherwise, that would make mine look like spilled chocolate milk in comparison.

But still, I want to know more about him. *All* about him.

Every time he shares a little morsel from his personal life, I find myself driven to uncover more. Maybe it's the same for him. Maybe he wants to find my truth the way I'm preoccupied with finding his.

"What are you going to do, Kara?"

My grandfather's question is the same one that's plagued me from nearly the minute I met Maximus. What do I do about this impossible temptation? The addictive possibility of Maximus . . .

"I can't stop seeing him," I finally say.

Gramps is strangely neutral about his answering regard. Finally he murmurs, "You're pretty sure about that."

"I am." I stamp everything I am into the statement. "Even if I wanted to, at this point my fascination far exceeds my willpower to stay away."

Another heavy pause. He pushes his empty bowl away, and the wooden chair squeaks when he rests back against it. "You sensed he was more than he seemed to be. What makes him so different?"

"Some of it is just really difficult to ignore," I say. "For starters, he's . . . enormous. A god among men."

"You can chalk that up to exceptional genetics."

This time I'm quirking the eyebrow. "Can't we all?"

He grins. "That's not what I meant."

"It's not just that. I've seen what he's capable of. I've never witnessed his kind of strength before. I've seen him heal too. He tried to brush it off as nothing, but there was nothing human about it."

He hums again. This time it's more thoughtful, like maybe he's trying to unravel the mystery of Maximus too. "His mother must have some answers."

"Maximus is sure she knows more than she's telling him."

"Maximus?"

I blink as I realize I've never uttered his name to Gramps before.

"Maximus Kane." I let go of another tense sigh. "You might as well know now. He's a literature professor at Alameda."

He holds my stare for a long moment. "You're playing with fire."

I shift in my chair, suddenly feeling uncomfortable... on the brink of unnerved. The intensity in Gramps's stare... they're not like anything I've witnessed from him before. And the energy behind them, hitting me like zaps of fire in a snowdrift, make me alternately hot and cold.

"I know."

"Do you? Really?"

"What does that mean?" I snap defensively.

"You're risking everything, Kara."

I scoff, but it's a rickety sound. Whatever is building with Maximus is becoming so much stronger than the fear my grandfather's warnings should elicit. How can I explain that Maximus is everything I never knew I wanted? How he doesn't look at me the way everyone else does? How I feel every time he does? How I might never, ever grow tired of it?

"Maybe I'm willing to sacrifice a life of lies to live a moment of truth."

I don't know that I can or will, but saying the words out loud almost makes me feel brave enough to act on them.

He closes his eyes and draws his hand across his face. "Kara... You don't know what you're saying."

"I'm saying I don't know if I can accept the life that's been handed to me. It's not fair."

"It isn't. But you have no choice in the matter if—"

"If what? You said it yourself. Everyone has a choice."

"Not when it comes to this."

"Why?" There's anger in my demand, but it's scratching the surface of what I really feel. "Why is *this* the exception?"

"In our world, decisions carry consequences," Gramps says tightly. "Consequences that follow you. I've spent my life enduring mine, sweetheart. I don't want to see you make the same mistakes."

The fervency in his voice gives me pause. He's always been my advocate. A quiet cheerleader for the good in me. But tonight something's changed. I worry it's his own fear at play. We've never spoken about the circumstances that brought such darkness into his life. Like many family stories, everyone seems to know the broad strokes, but too many of the details are missing.

"Gramps?"

"What?" he grates.

"What really happened to you?" I whisper. "I don't understand how anyone could think you deserve all this."

"You know enough, Kara. I'm not dredging up the gory details for you."

"But I *want* to know. Maybe I even need to."

"It's a long story."

Part of it the rest of the world already knows. That Giovani Valari should have died forty years ago when Malcolm Caulfield, husband of one of the most successful starlets of the time, shot him in cold blood before turning the gun on his wife and himself. Gio clung to life, drifted into a short coma, and eventually flatlined before he miraculously pulled through. Malcolm and Penelope Caulfield weren't so lucky.

In the weeks after, rumors circulated that Caulfield's violence was due to an affair between Gio and Penelope, but with no one to speak to the truth but him, the rumors stayed rumors. None of it explained why my grandfather was able to escape the grip of death *and* an eternity in hell, or why he ended up in the underworld to begin with.

"Gramps?" I prompt again. "Please. You keep saying that I don't know and I don't understand. So help me to do that." I reach for his hands. "Help me see."

My fingers barely brush his before the man rises sharply and starts tidying the kitchen with haste. "Has it occurred to you that I'm not especially proud of the reasons that brought me into all this to begin with?"

I contemplate that for a moment. "Considering I've been raised in a family of demons, I'm not confident that any confession could color my opinion of you."

He wipes down the already clean counter vigorously. "I was not a saint. Pride. Envy. Greed. You name it. You might think looking into the mouth of hell and getting a second chance could change a man. Apparently your grandmother was the only one who could do that. Whoever's calling the shots down there must know what they're doing."

"Okay, they were determined to make an example out of you. I got that part. What I want to know is why."

He turns toward me, his lips pulled tight. "Because I earned my ticket there, and I still managed to hitch a way out. There's nothing they hate more than a stolen soul." His soft eyes swim with pain. "Sometimes I wonder what's worse. An eternity down there or living every day knowing this is all my fault. That my freedom, if we can even call it that, robbed you of yours."

I try to absorb the blow of that hard truth. He's my grandfather. I wouldn't exist without him. But was I really brought into the world with no other purpose than to be a pawn in his punishment? As much as I love him, his misdeeds inked my own fate. I know that as a crushing certainty now.

He exhales a ragged sigh. "I'm sorry, Kara. I'm not much good for visiting right now. Why don't you come by in a week or two, ladybug? I haven't felt like myself lately." He steps closer to give my shoulder an affectionate squeeze. "Good night."

Before I can argue for him to stay, he's already climbed the stairs to his bedroom. I don't want to leave, but I feel awkward lingering. I can at least attempt to sort out my thoughts on my way home, though I'm not confident I will.

I internally berate myself for putting Gramps in such a conflicting position. He loves me, I'm sure. All the more reason to want to shield me from a fate he knows too well. A penance with which he's already been tortured.

I walk through the main house, but before I can reach the front door, Dalton is there. With a smooth swoosh, he swings it open for my mother's entrance.

She shoots me a gleaming smile when she sees me. "Kara! You're here! How perfect!"

She saunters toward me, and I meet her for a brief hug. Over her shoulder, I can see another figure following behind. She pulls back and gestures toward the man who must have been her date for the evening.

"Arden. Come and meet Kara. Kara, this is Arden Prieto."

Arden is tall enough that he reaches me in two graceful strides. He extends his hand for mine. I reach out, expecting a handshake until he lifts my fingers to his lips, forcing my stare up and into his.

At once, I gasp—but not from any kind of pleasure. His eyes are coal gray, if assigning a color to them is even possible. The orbs are dark and intense, like perhaps they're not just irises and scleras and corneas but two mysterious tunnels that lead someplace deeper. They match his slick black hair and the stylish scruff on his jaw. It's the kind of five o'clock shadow that's completely intentional, not a result of being overworked and short on time.

"Enchanted," he murmurs as he drags his lips off my skin.

I can tell from the heat of him and every molecule of energy radiating between us that he's one of us.

The second his grasp loosens, I pull back. "Nice to meet you," I offer tightly, grateful for the chance to be free of his forward touch and merciless stare.

My mother's eyes are wide. Her mouth seems frozen in a perpetual smile that small children reserve for theme park experiences.

"I am *so* thrilled you're here, Kara. I was going to have you join us for dinner later this week to talk about Arden's work."

"His work?"

She laughs and touches his shoulder like they're old

friends. "Yes, he works with antiquities. I promised myself that we'd get serious about our collections this year."

"Collections?"

She laughs again, but it's more strained this time. "Our collections, dear. Heirlooms and ..." She flits her hand rapidly as she searches for the right words.

"Art and artifacts of special significance," Arden supplies smoothly. "The market for relics is stronger than ever and very competitive. I can help navigate those waters and ensure quality acquisitions."

"Oh. Great." I respond like I don't have a pulse anymore, which might just be the case. Seriously, kill me now. If the Valaris need anything less, it's another room of overpriced things that will make my mother feel superior to everyone else around her.

"And you *must* help, Kara," she says. "I don't know a thing about it, and I don't have nearly enough time to wrap my head around it properly."

I frown. "And I would?"

She meets my exasperated look with one of her own. "For all the time you've spent with your nose in dusty old books, now's the time to make some use of it."

Even if Arden wasn't standing witness to our exchange, I'm not sure I would argue with her. I can tell that my mother has already decided to involve me in this new project of hers, whether I like it or not.

Kill. Me. Now.

Few of my broodings bear repeating more.

"Come, let's have some wine, and Arden can tell you more."

The steady look in Arden's eyes tells me he has no qualms about Veronica's plan to extend the evening's festivities. Unfortunately, I'm nowhere ready to participate in them.

"I'd love to, but I have an early class in the morning," I say quickly. "It was a pleasure to meet you, but I really should be heading home."

My mother pouts a little, her annoyance plain. "Fine. We'll figure out dinner this week. Yes?" She lifts a hopeful smile to Arden.

"Dinner would be perfect," he says, finally tearing his gaze from me to placate my mother.

"Fabulous. I'll send you Kara's information. I can't wait to start."

CHAPTER 16

MAXIMUS

O N A LAST-MINUTE WHIM a few years back, I decided to try running the LA Marathon. I ended up carrying another guy for the last five miles, since he'd promised his girlfriend he'd see her at the finish line despite the lung disease kicking his ass. His name was Montague. He insisted I call him Monty. And the grin on his face never vanished, despite how he'd hardly been able to breathe.

Right now, I feel like changing my name to Monty.

Because somehow I've made it through the last hour talking about the pitfalls of primitivity, lust, and unbridled appetites without giving in to a single one of mine. And without casting so much as a glance toward the woman who's still searing me with her simple presence.

I can do this. Already *have* done it. Mostly.

Only three minutes left...

Screw it.

"I say no more to you, answer no more."

As soon as I'm done reciting the line from Canto VI, I close my leather-bound book with a one-handed *whomp*. "That seems like a serendipitous place to stop for the day, yes?"

I'm answered with a collective groan of relief from across the room. I raise my voice so my follow-up cuts through the din of rustling backpacks and reactivated phones.

"To be clear, ladies and gentlemen, my leniency extends no further than this early dismissal. Your term project proposals are still due by five p.m. today. That's a printed version, bound in proper format, on my desk in the Archer Building. This project is worth fifty percent of your grade."

By the time I conclude the speech, it's clear I've been tuned out in favor of chattering about tonight's events. The Conquistador Crush is one of the highlights of the school year at Alameda, a ten-day whirlwind kicked off by a formal fundraiser ball, a rock concert on the campus green, and then a four-day weekend carnival.

Tonight I have to don a monkey suit and make an obligatory appearance at the formal bash. The fact that they're staging this year's event in the library courtyard, literally steps from my office door, is little consolation. At least I'll have a good excuse for escaping the throng. There should be a good-sized stack of papers on my desk before the afternoon has waned.

The emptied hall should give me some relief. But as long as Kara remains, I can't erase the visceral awareness of her. Pretending to ignore her through the hour hasn't stopped every drop of my blood from percolating for her—

especially in this moment, when her stubborn stillness forces me to raise my stare to her.

"God*damn*."

The word escapes me, primal and guttural, as I fully take her in. The dark gleam of her loose-braided hair. The enticing pearl buttons of her silky white blouse, and the matching zipper pulls of her pristine ankle boots.

But most of all, another pair of sleek and sinful jeans—black this time—hugging every line below the waist as she rises up and crosses the short distance between us.

"Kara."

"Maximus," she replies in an equally icy tone.

I compress my lips. Her censure is pure frostbite, though I should be grateful for every freezing syllable. My composure needs it. "What can I do for you today?"

"Hmm. How about starting with acknowledging that I exist?" she snaps.

She strikes a determined pose, killing all thoughts of ice-covered landscapes. I swear to God, real flames are whorling in the depths of her eyes. It's got to be just a play of my imagination, but I swear by everything that's holy, it's the most captivating sight I've ever seen.

Except I'm even more conflicted now.

"Kara. *Damn it*."

"Are you really going there? Right now? With this weird pretense that I've offended you?"

"You haven't offended me, okay? It's just—" I stop and drag a hand through my hair. "You're more of a distraction to me here than I think you realize. Does that make sense?"

She rocks back on a heel and drags in a long breath. "So if I sit in the back again, your ice-out will be less obvious?"

I don't answer, because I crave her closeness as much as I recognize the dangerousness of it.

"What changed in two days that you can't even look at me?" Her voice is softer now, more vulnerable. And the kindle in her eyes has simmered into a sheen of hurt that rips my fucking heart out.

More than that. I'm torn to the foundations of whatever is beyond that.

I have no easy labels for it because I've spent my whole life pretending none of it exists. That there are parts of me best left unexplored. A wide tundra of my spirit covered by my self-imposed frost, now melting beneath her singular, stunning fire. Even if that heat manifests as her fury. Maybe because of it. *Maddening temptress.* She's not letting me duck and run—which should have me snarling at her like a trapped dragon—but instead, I'm letting the tundra burn. Worse, I'm secretly yearning for more kerosene on these flames.

A kerosene called Kara. A wildfire I can't possibly fight. Not even with all the mental resources I've amassed over the years. None of it—the self-control, the discipline, the fear, the inner forewarnings—feels like enough. So why am I even trying?

The answer pounds the perimeter of my skull. Clamors at the confines of my chest.

"Fuck," I mutter while circling behind the podium. I pretend to be busy closing the presentation program on my laptop. Gliding my fingers across the touchpad brings a welcome dose of cool control. My prolonged silence has her heaving an angry huff.

"Look. I'm not trying to be clingy here. I don't need your tongue down my throat for personal validation. But if you're still going for the excuse of maintaining professional appearances, I'm not the only one who isn't buying it. I'm the student who knows this material the best—but in the last hour, you barely acknowledged I was breathing, let alone thinking. You know what that looks like to anyone observing us with half a brain, right?"

Instead of answering her, I funnel my frustration into slamming my computer shut. The resultant sparks and smell of fried fuses have me adding a trip to the electronics store on my trip home.

"Remarkably, a few of us mere mortals outside the Valari universe are aware of what 'optics' are." From the second I bite out the words, I long to take them back. The yearning grows as Kara steps back like I've daggered her.

Returning to her seat, she hastily stuffs her belongings into her red leather backpack. The mortification on my face probably matches the hue by now.

"Kara."

"I'll get out of your hair now." She's stuttering in time to my goddamned heartbeat. I'm losing her. Fast.

"*Kara.*"

As she starts up the steps, I realize I only have one hope here. The truth.

"Kell came and talked to me," I call out at last.

When she stops and turns, my lungs expel what feels like three days of air. Except she looks like my confession is the equivalent of another knife through her middle.

"She . . . what?"

"Yesterday. We bumped into each other outside Jesse's office. Apparently she had some things she wanted to say." I drag a hand through my hair again. It does little to ease the awkward moment. Though it's little consolation, her reaction answers my curiosity about whether Kell told her anything about our chat.

"Why does this even shock me?" Despite her bitter mutter, the news impacts her hard. She plunks down on her ass, stretching her legs out along the adjoining step.

"But you're not actually shocked," I return. "Right?"

"I suppose not."

Her defeated tone is like a sheep hook around me. At once, I put down my destroyed laptop and clear the handful of steps to reach her side. I lower down beside her and loop my arm around her shoulders.

She settles in, notching her head against me and pressing a hand to the center of my chest. And just like that, I'm complete again. As complete as I can feel these days. So much of me has been splintered into so many pieces. More astounding is how it's all happened so fast.

Because of her?

I don't want to answer that, even to myself. Part of my mind scrambles for other excuses, but they're all lame. This is the truth, as unreal and unexpected as it seems. I'm fissuring, and she's the chisel.

But chisels are meant for sculpting as well as fracturing. As thoroughly as Kara has split me open, so much of me believes she's a key to the answers. The healer of my open wounds. Her warmth drenches me as if the roof's been cut back and the sun's shining directly in on us. It's as perfect as the fire in her eyes, the electricity of her touch, and the connection I feel to both. I don't know how she's even real, but I'm damn glad I'm the one who's holding her close right now—and getting clutched so possessively in return.

She frees a heavy sigh into my pectoral. "Let me guess. Kell told you to stay away from me. That you *have* to stay away."

"In so many words."

"But she didn't tell you why."

An odd certainty underscores her tone. I replay the conversation with Kell in my mind, unable to latch on to anything other than the memory of her concern.

"Whatever her reasons are for not wanting you to see me, they're probably valid."

I'm not sure I mean that. Not completely. Learning the specifics behind Kell's warning might not change anything besides deepening my determination to prove her wrong in every way. Or maybe it'd make me hate myself even more for ultimately not being the guy Kara truly deserves. Because I care enough about her now to recognize that fact. She deserves a hell of a lot better than me.

"So you believed her," she finally rasps, curling her fingers into a tight fist against my chest. "When she said... whatever she said."

"I believed that *she* believed it," I reply. "And that she was confronting me out of her love for you." I pause for another moment. "I also think our connection frightens her."

Kara gulps hard. "It does."

"You're sure of it?"

"I am."

"Why?"

"My family…" She drops her gaze to where she's sneaked a fingertip between the buttons of my shirt, grazing the skin beneath. "I've told you. Things are complicated."

"Kara?" I prompt, squeezing the ball of her shoulder. "What is it?"

Two seconds into her weighted silence, I can already tell that answer won't be forthcoming. Not even as she tugs away far enough to link her gaze directly with mine again. To let me see all the somber meaning in hers. But this time, without those glorious flames.

I'm thankful she's showing me what's behind them instead. Her earnestness. Her nervousness. Her…fear. An emotion I fully recognize as it brews inside me too.

I slide my hand up the side of her neck to where it can flatten to the side of her face. Beneath my palm, her skin is a collection of warm, strong angles—so unlike the bleak, desperate smoke in the backs of her eyes.

Give me more, little temptress. Something. Anything.

I'm about to say all of that when Kara darts her dark stare back up to me. "Does it frighten you, Maximus? This… us. Does it frighten you?"

I work my fingertips around a few loose wisps of her hair. I tug on them gently while dipping my face closer to hers. "Not all the time. But sometimes...like here and now, looking at you like this, holding you like this..." I push in tighter, not stopping until our lips are grazing and our breaths are mingling. "Yeah. It scares the crap out of me."

For a long moment, Kara's only response is the tripled pace of her breaths—then the second finger she adds to that sizzling touch atop my heart. The organ underneath pounds at the wall of my chest like a prisoner declaring mutiny, clamoring to throw itself right into her waiting hand.

"You feel that?" I push more of her hand against my wild, bucking sternum. "You do, don't you?"

She jerks her way through a nod.

"Then you understand. You know that I'm scared because I don't understand so much of this. Nobody's ever done this to me before. Had this kind of crazy power over me. I don't know how it's you or why it's you. I only know I'm so damn glad it's you."

She blinks slowly. "You are?"

"Yeah. And God fucking help me, I want to know more of it. I'm burning to give *you* more."

"And I'll take it." Her lips, tasting like cinnamon, brush at the edges of mine. Her skin, smelling of roses, heats beneath my touch. She turns and presses tighter against me, delving her hands into my hair. "Everything this is, everything we are...I need it, Maximus. I need you."

"Then open up for me." My croak is desperate, and I don't give a shit. I secure a hand at her nape, holding her steady for my equally imploring stare. "Kara, please. Whatever these ridiculous Valari secrets are, I can handle it. *All* of it. Just trust—"

My insistence is swallowed by the *thrunk* of the door that's opened at the top of the stairs. A half-dozen students barge into the lecture hall. Kara scrambles to her feet, inviting the snickering stares the new arrivals shoot her way.

I answer them with a quietly lethal glower as I rise, but their presence already has Kara racing to leave. I'm there behind her, following in her immediate shadow.

At the top of the stairs, she stops. There's a cramped audio and lighting control booth to the right. She takes my hand and tugs me into the enclosure. I have to admit, even with our small but curious audience, I'm fond of the new accommodations. It's darker in here. And warm. I like having her this close. A lot.

I'm mesmerized by what the fresh wash of shadows does to her beauty. Rather than subduing her glory, the dimness enhances every stunning feature, every entrancing curve. I dare to slide a palm to her waist, hiding the move between her body and the foam-lined wall. At once, our blazing connection flares to brighter intensity.

"Listen," she rasps. "These secrets you seem to think are so ridiculous? They're not. They're exactly the opposite. They're . . . dangerous."

I smirk. "You could tell me, but then you'd have to kill me?"

"Don't. Joke," she spits.

I pause, intrigued by her new claim. "Then stop evading."

"I'm not evading!"

"You are. And I'm not giving up just because you said 'dangerous.'" I tighten my hold on her hip, punctuating my newfound fervor on the matter.

As she rakes her hand up my arm, her breath hitches. "Maximus... In spite of all your jaw-dropping, wow-inducing—well, you get the idea—but in spite of it, you're still flesh and blood underneath. A mortal man."

I hike one brow. "As opposed to being what other kind of man?"

She tightens her clench on my shoulder. "Just say you get the point."

I curl my hand until it's wrapped around hers. "I get the point that underneath all of *your* jaw-dropping, wow-inducing, you-get-the-idea-ness, you're still flesh and blood too." I hold my next breath until I'm forced to exhale the raw truth. "And I'm invested in all of it, Kara. So whoever you are besides all that, you need to understand that I'm in this for *you*. And I want more, damn it. A lot more." I stretch my thumb in, pressing it to the middle of her palm, which gives me what I crave most. Her gaze, lifting again to meet mine. "I'll treasure it, okay? I'll keep it safe. I'll keep *you* safe."

She blinks up at me. Once, twice. In those two seconds, so many deliberations war across the sleek angles of her gorgeous face. I hate that I've caused her such confusion, but I could stand and watch the effects of it all day long.

"Thank you." She lets her touch descend, releasing more currents up and down my arm, and then wraps her fingers over my forearms. "Your words mean more than you could possibly imagine."

I drop my head until my forehead is less than an inch from hers. "Then why do you look like I'm asking you to cut off a limb?"

"Because losing you will feel that way." She confesses the last of it on a quivering breath. "And if I give you the truth, that's probably what will happen."

"Why don't you let me be the judge of that?"

Another shaky sigh from her. "Max—"

"Do you really think that little of me?" I push in closer, yearning to slam that allegation into her with a kiss. But more students are filtering into the lecture hall now, as well as the ethics professor. While the woman isn't a close friend, she knows me well enough to pick me out of a police lineup. Or a dim tech control booth.

"Whatever it is," I say, "none of it changes you. What I already see in you—and feel about you."

Kara gives me another long silence. She bites her lower lip, giving away her pensive conflict, before dropping her hands. "I—I have to think about this." She moves back by a sizable step. "Besides, we can't talk here."

"Then where?" I growl.

She retrieves her backpack from the floor. "You're going to the fundraiser tonight, right? In the library?"

"Yes." I thread my fresh confusion into the word. "Are you?"

"They're christening the Veronica Valari Wing at eight. What do you think?" She steps close again. "That also means that by eight thirty, everyone in my family will be in limousines, heading back to the Hills for the after-party.

And nobody else at the event will be caring about what's happening in the older stacks."

My attempt at sobering my smile is a lost cause. "A rendezvous in the old library? Do you know how many new ways I just fell for you?"

She fights her own smirk. I lean against the wall in a casual stance to dodge my true desire here. To grab her, complete with her well-bitten lips and her sexy-smart brain, and kiss her senseless, the social media explosion be damned. I'm soaring too high with satisfaction and anticipation to care about it right now.

In a few hours, I'll have more pieces of the puzzle. A few more truths about the person consuming more of my mind, my spirit, and my heart every hour.

And maybe, just maybe, she'll lead me to more pieces of my own puzzle. The core of my own truths.

The reasons why I am . . . the way I am. And just what the hell I'm supposed to do with it.

CHAPTER 17

Kara

" A ND WITHOUT FURTHER ADO, let's give a warm and gracious welcome to an outstanding icon of our community, the woman who has turned this library wing from dream to reality, the inimitable Veronica Valari."

I join in the swell of applause as my mother glides across the courtyard toward the riser in front of the building that bears her name. The university president, who's spent the past ten minutes singing the woman's praises, greets her with a pair of air kisses and an affectionate embrace. My mother takes the microphone and swishes the long train of her satin gown behind her, greeting the crowd with her pearly smile and a smoky laugh.

"Thank you, President McCarthy. I am so honored to be here."

The cafe lights swaying gently in the evening breeze cast a warm glow on the rest of the crowd gathered around cocktail tables covered in Alameda's school colors, crimson and gray. Many in the throng are here out of obligation, like Maximus, who I've yet to spot. But I suspect more are here for an opportunity to rub shoulders with a Valari or the handful of celebrities attaching themselves to the event for PR opportunities.

As my mother launches into her prepared speech, a warm hand brushes against my lower back. My heart lurches in a blur of hope, anticipation, and excitement—though every shred of the euphoria falls away when Arden, not Maximus, slides up beside me. The man's eyes are blacker than the sky beyond the spotlights, and his smile is a smooth show of confident assumption.

"Lovely to see you again, Kara," he murmurs silkily. He lifts his cocktail to his mouth. The way he beams his gaze over the rim of the glass is unsettling, like a hunter who won't take his eyes off his prey.

"Mr. Prieto. I didn't know you were coming tonight."

"Please, call me Arden. We're going to be spending quite a bit of time together after all. No point in carrying on with the formalities."

The crowd titters at something my mother's saying. Probably a humblebrag disguised as an attempt at self-deprecating humor. But the wealthy client under the spotlight fails to distract Arden. He's all about looking at me now. Endlessly. Excruciatingly. Long seconds drag by as he keeps raking his gaze over me.

"That's an exquisite dress."

I wish I couldn't feel his palpable appreciation of it,

but the oily energy is rolling off him. I contemplate cutting through the heaviness of his admiration and confessing that I chose the scarlet gown with the provocative cuts for someone else. But as charming as demons can be, they can turn equally vicious with very little prodding. I'm not in the mood to test this one.

"Thank you."

He sets his empty glass on the table, edging closer to me as he does. I try not to visibly bristle at his intimate—or at least very friendly—proximity.

"I have some friends at the college," he says, his tone cool and confident, exactly the way he carries himself. "I don't usually come to these things, but when I heard you'd be here, I thought I'd drop by and say hello."

I answer with an awkward shrug. "Hello then, I guess."

He smirks at that. "Your mother tells me you're quite the passionate academic. This is your last year at Alameda, right?"

"It is. I'll be sad to leave."

"And what will you do after?"

My heart falls as I contemplate the truth ahead of me. The fate that looms closer with every passing day. "I'd love to continue on with graduate studies, but I think my mother's patience has worn thin waiting for me to get more involved in family affairs. She has a lot of projects in the works."

He nods with a quiet hum. "I suppose I'm one of those projects." Something glimmers in his eyes that matches the secretive smile he wears. "She's quite determined to build a collection that will stamp the Valari name on the world of art and antiquities. It's inspiring. I'd be lying if I said I wasn't eager to start."

"Who could tire of spending someone else's money so glamorously?" I manage to hide some of the sarcasm beneath the words.

But the look he levels at me makes me wonder if I succeeded.

"I think we both know it's about more than money. Not like it has any value in other realms."

At his reference to the underworld, I'm quietly curious how well he knows it.

"Then what *is* it about? Enlighten me."

He cants his head, a curious frown pulling his dark brows together. To a lot of other females, human *or* demon, I suppose he'd be found beautiful. His features are carved and sleek, finished with a strong jaw, an expressive mouth, and a dazzling smile—though his scrutinizing stare holds no warmth or admiration. It has me wishing I could look away, but something about his energy makes me want to hold my ground.

"Establishing dominance," he finally says, his voice sharpening.

Of course it is.

I blink my way clear of the barely veiled challenge he's seemingly issued. I don't like it, nor how he's issued it, but that's a secondary point right now. "I suppose that's my mother's department." I'm more sad than resentful about having to admit that fact. We've always been so different, and I fear that will never change.

Just like that, the edges in his tone mellow into a softer cadence. "You do still have so much of your humanity." That tone even takes on a hint of awe—one I find as troubling as his confrontational side. He doesn't help by gliding the backs of his fingers down my bare arm, following the motion with an appreciative gaze over the rest of me. "I have to say, you wear it almost as beautifully as you wear this dress."

"Kara."

My senses don't need a single second to react. The deep timbre of Maximus's voice sends me back a full step away from Arden and his weird touch. One glance up at the towering man, proud and gorgeous in his all-black tuxedo, has my breath catching. But what really has me reeling is the equally dark look in his eyes.

"Maximus." I clear my throat and quickly correct the blunder. "I mean... This is Professor Maximus Kane. He's my instructor for—"

"And you are?" Maximus cuts off the rest of my introduction and squares his body with Arden, who's tall and lean but a fraction of the professor in stature.

After they size each other up for a long, tense moment, Arden extends his hand.

"Arden Prieto," he answers coolly. "A friend."

"A friend," Maximus repeats, like the words have a bitter taste.

I open my mouth to explain, but I'm momentarily lost for a better way to explain Arden's presence here tonight. He's a demon fine arts broker with a weakness for humanity, it would seem, but none of that sounds sane.

Maximus pivots back to me, so many questions swimming in his gaze. "You didn't turn in your term paper proposal."

My jaw unhinges again while my brain tries to catch up. Because I definitely did turn it in, and my first defensive instinct is to say so.

But that's not what this is really about.

"Oh wow." I laugh nervously, rushing to play along. "I can't believe I forgot. I was so focused on getting ready for tonight, it must have slipped my mind."

"No worries," he replies tightly, like pretending to go easy on me is painful for him right now. "You're not the only one who got caught up in the excitement, so I'm extending the deadline a bit."

"Thank you, Professor."

Maximus answers with a soft grunt. "You can drop it by tomorrow. You know where to find me."

"Of course. Thank you again."

Without any other acknowledgment, he faces Arden once more. "Pleasure to meet you. Sorry for the intrusion."

Before Arden can reply, Maximus pivots and makes his way out of the courtyard. I watch every move he makes, unsure whether to be thankful or wrathful. Is he really leaving like this? Without another word?

Not that I'd hear him anyway. The crowd begins to clap loudly over my mother's final utterings of gushy gratitude into the mic.

"We should go rescue her," Arden says. "They'll have her standing for photos for hours with this many people."

"She has a way of gracefully exiting when she wants to."

Speaking of...

"If you'll excuse me, I'm going to let our drivers know she'll be ready soon. She probably won't be staying much longer."

He eyes me carefully, like maybe he knows I'm hiding something. Or even worse, lying through my teeth. "When can we meet to discuss the acquisitions for Veronica?"

I stifle the frustrated sigh that wants to break free.

"Dinner Friday?" he offers.

I don't give myself a moment to mentally draw up my calendar. All I care about right now is how the distance between Maximus and me is growing by the second.

"Sounds perfect." I force a smile to smooth the air— and my departure. "Text me the details."

Without a backward glance, I turn and follow Maximus's exit from the party. The crowd thins the farther I get from the heart of the event, but Maximus is nowhere to be found.

"Damn it," I rasp. I've lost him.

Stepping out to the library's front entrance, I chance a look at the adjacent building. The windows are all dark in Archer, save one that's dimly lit and achingly familiar. On the fourth floor.

By the time I scale the stairs and reach Maximus's office, I'm breathless but hopeful. The door is cracked when I arrive. Through it I can see him, one hand pressed high on the window, the other clutching a glass of amber liquid.

As I push the door open, its soft creak hits the building's

silence like a lightning crack. Maximus starts and turns at the sound.

I lean against the jamb, allowing myself a moment to truly drink him in. He's ditched the tuxedo jacket and loosened his satiny tie. His hair is still collected in a bun, making the emotions he wears all the more prominent.

"I thought I lost you," I say softly.

He empties the tumbler and turns back to the window.

"You're upset." I fully enter the room and shut the door behind me. "Because of Arden."

"Your friend, right?" I don't miss the icy emphasis on the noun.

"He's not my friend. I'm not sure why he introduced himself that way. He's doing some work for my mother. That's all."

"Right," he mutters.

I take another step toward him. "I'm telling you the truth."

"Is that why you came here tonight? To tell me the truth?" He's still talking to the window, and the avoidance is driving me crazier than his insinuations.

I come closer. Close enough to touch him. "I came here to see you."

After a long moment, he tilts his head, giving me the full weight of his stare. I lift my palm to the wall, letting it buffer the impact of all the longing and frustration collected in his blues. They're the color of midnight in a graveyard, and my senses rail with matching desolation. But with speed I've gained from years of focus and experience, I shove back the feelings and straighten my posture.

After pulling in a cleansing breath, I pull my hand from the wall and reach out for him instead. Another wave of emotional tumult threatens my composure, but I'm tender about running my fingertip over the pretty silver cuff link at his wrist.

"I like this formal look on you."

"Do you like the jealous look too?"

I blink up at him, schooling my features. I didn't chase after him to get into a fight. His bait isn't going to work. "I'm learning to appreciate all of you, actually. Even the pieces of you that are unexpected."

He inhales a deep breath and releases it slowly. "Kara …"

"Maximus?" I embrace the gift of saying his name again. Right now, because it's just us, I can pretend it's an offering to him. A prayer of adoration. "I'm serious about this. What will it take to prove it to you?"

His gaze narrows, giving away his inner debate before I can even sense it. "All right, then. Tell me something about you. Anything. I want to know you better than a random stranger off the street who reads about you in the headlines."

"You already do." It's the truth, but I already know it's not enough. It won't satisfy him. Not this time. "Who's the person in your life you're closest to?"

He blinks in confusion. "Jesse, I guess."

"Because of what happened when you were little?"

"Not necessarily. We were friends before the accident. I'd like to think if it never happened, we'd still be."

I smile, recognizing little tendrils of my own jealousy

forming. The person I'm closest to is forbidden. The same way Maximus will be if anyone finds out we're flirting with a relationship together.

"Why are you asking me? We're supposed to be talking about you, remember?"

"I know." I close my eyes with a sigh. "My grandfather is that person for me."

"Giovani Valari? The screenwriter?"

I nod. "He lives in my mother's guesthouse in Beverly Hills. No one's allowed to talk to him. I spent years figuring out ways to see him without getting into trouble. I still do."

He winces. "He's your family, though. Why on earth would they do that?"

"We were really close when I was little. Then things changed. I never understood why. It's just the way it is now."

"And you just accept it?" He shakes his head, and I know there's nothing more I can say to help him make sense of it. But he deserves to know what we're up against.

"Just know that it'll be the same with you. If they find out about us, they won't just cluck their tongues and then come around. They'll forbid it. Kell's already told you as much."

His jaw tightens. "Because I'm not a rich celebrity? I can't whisk you away on my yacht and play the red carpet charades?"

The defensiveness in his words tears at my heart. "No," I protest at once. "That has nothing to do with it, I promise. The Valaris already have more money than they know what to do with. To the point where it has less value than other things."

"Like what?"

"Like ... tradition ... control ... power."

"I don't understand what any of that has to do with you. With us."

It has everything to do with it.

But I can't say that out loud. He doesn't understand, and he never will. He can never be allowed to.

I reach up and rake my fingertips through his beard gently. "When we're together, I don't think about it. Alameda has always been my escape from that world. But you're ... well, you've become more than an escape."

So much more ...

In the deepest recesses of my soul, I know that falling for Maximus will be my ruin. Nothing good can come from these moments together except the bliss I feel under his touch. The solace of his companionship.

This bliss.

This solace.

This complete heaven, banishing the hell for which I've been groomed. The fate for which I was conceived.

"What am I, then?"

With him, I feel like I'm more.

And even if it's not forever ... I'll take it.

I bite my lip and fiddle with his cuff link absently. "Lately I'm beginning to think that being with you is where I'm supposed to be. At least right now." *A minute. An hour. However long we have.* "And I can't stay away."

At first, Maximus does nothing. Then without a single word, he joins our hands and turns his body to mine. "My life has always been about restraint. I can't remember a time when it wasn't. And when it comes to you..." He winces slightly. "Honestly, I've never felt so powerless. The minute you walk into the room, restraint isn't a word I even understand anymore."

I draw my hand up his chest, enjoying the feel of his heartbeat. "You can let go with me."

When he draws me against him, I'm grateful that we're done with words. The sweet and slow melding of our mouths is forgiveness and reassurance. Acceptance of this growing connection between us. Defiance against whatever or whoever threatens it. More, it's a heart-swelling reminder of how right it feels to surrender to the moment with him.

With an effortless sweep, he lifts me onto the deep windowsill, shoving a stack of books away to give us more room. One of them falls onto the floor with a thud, but his hands don't stop. He strokes his fingers over every bare inch of my skin until he's skating his incredible touch up my arms. Then inwardly, so exquisitely and slowly, over the silky panels that cover my breasts. Then lower again, palming his way along my thighs, thanks to the high slits of the gown. He leans in, pressing my legs wide to accommodate him.

I sigh. I soften. I surrender.

For all the twisting and aching my heart's done tonight, the thing feels like a balloon in my chest now, taking up space I need to breathe. He nips at my jaw, kissing and caressing his way to my shoulder, where he's shifted the fabric to kiss the flesh underneath. I cover his hand with mine, coaxing the panel free. Then the other. I'm bared to him, and it feels so good.

He doesn't move, barely breathes. Seconds bleed away with only his eyes passing over me in silent worship. "You're the most gorgeous creature I've ever laid eyes on."

My skin tightens at his words, but I ache for more. I'm dizzy to have this man's hands on me. His mouth. Anything that will feed or ease this frenzy that's taken hold of me.

"Touch me," I beg softly.

He gifts me with the barest touch, dragging his thumb along the outer curve of my breast, circling in slowly. I'm ready to beg him again when he dips his head and sucks my nipple into his mouth, lashing the tip with his tongue.

I suck in a sharp breath. "Oh!"

His low rumble is filled with matching lust as I tangle my fingers in his hair. My desire unleashes more of his own, and he dips back in to lavish the same tantalizing treatment to my other breast. He nips and sucks and licks, tempting the balloon in my chest to nearly burst.

Never mind that the pulse between my thighs is shredding all my reasons to stop. I tighten around his waist, instinct driving me to create more friction there. A little voice in my head tells me that this is all too much, too fast—but a louder voice is screaming it's not fast enough. The danger is quickly swallowed up by the lust that's burning through me. The flames are consuming, and I don't care.

I don't want to stop. I never want to stop.

He lifts his head to take my mouth in another kiss. This one is more brutal than the others. Like maybe he's getting close to the edge of his control. It should worry me, but it doesn't. I trust him. I trust whatever this is between us.

"Kara..."

My name breaks on his lips.

"I don't want to stop," I answer in a fevered whisper.

"Good. Because I want to taste more of you. So much more."

He inches his hands higher until the tips of his fingers reach the straps of my thong.

"I want to make you come, Kara. I feel like I'm going to lose my mind if I can't taste you."

Our gazes lock. There's so much asking and hunger in his blue depths. I'm robbed of any uncertainty about where he's taking this. He strokes his thumb along the front of my panties. I shudder against him at the hint of the orgasm he's promising me.

"Say yes," he murmurs, stroking me once more.

I answer with a moan, which he must take as a yes, because he lifts me away from the window and sets me down on the edge of his desk.

Without breaking eye contact, he slides my panties down my legs and tosses them away. Then he's on his knees, dragging his tongue and hot kisses along my inner thighs. I'm trembling. Somehow in this delicious chaos, I recognize it's not just lust. It's fear and anticipation and everything Maximus makes me feel that I shouldn't. Everything we're doing that's forbidden and wrong but feels so incredibly right. Unbelievably perfect...

He looks up at me with that intense gaze again. "Kara, you're shaking."

"Just nerves." The words come out too breathy and light.

I swear he can see through it to everything I'm not saying. Maybe he's even figuring out what kind of line I'm crossing here. A line I've never crossed with anyone before. Just the idea of it has always been too dangerous. And nobody has ever felt worth the risk.

When he stills, the vibration between us changes. Thickens. It's more real now. More significant.

"We can stop. If you're not sure ..."

I shake my head. He pauses a moment, like maybe he's weighing my words—or the truth in them.

"I'm okay," I promise. "I'm sure."

He brings his hand to my stomach, then my sternum. His brows knit from the moment his palm presses on the spot where my heart is flying beneath my ribs. For another agonizing second, I think my trepidation may stop him ...

"Lie down for me, beautiful."

Thank the stars it doesn't.

The sexy murmur and possessive push he gives me does something to my insides. A fresh hit of desire makes my head buzz to new levels as my back hits the broad wooden surface. Then I'm launched into another dimension when his lips and tongue sweep against my most sensitive flesh. I bow off the desk with a thready cry. My hips take on a mind of their own. And we're quickly caught up in an erotic game of push and pull. A test of strength and will. Patience and hunger.

Even as he manages to keep me spread and pinned and climbing with every lash of his tongue, I feel my world tilting. The pressure in my chest is everywhere now. Pulsing down every limb. Hooking deep in my belly.

"Maximu—*ah*!" My hands fly from his hair to the mess of papers above my head, finally grasping the smooth edge of the wood.

All too quickly, the orgasm hits me. It's painful but wonderful in its intensity. The tortured groan that erupts from Maximus sets off more of my own untethered cries. I hang on through the violent throbs of pleasure. When the last ribbons of delirium taper off, all I can do is whimper.

"Come here," he rasps.

He lifts me so our mouths and torsos clash once more. Another soft moan vibrates between us. He tunnels his hands in my hair, angling me until we have to tear away to breathe.

But his features change the second we pull apart. His eyes widen as he scans over my face.

"Kara ... Your eyes."

I suck in a sharp breath, turn my head, and cast my gaze downward. If rapture looks anything like fury does on me, Maximus has just witnessed the fire in my eyes. Another inconvenient symptom of my biology that I've learned to hide. One I should have considered before going this far with him.

"What's wrong?" he presses. "Kara?"

"Everything," I mumble.

"What? Why?"

I don't answer. I'm too damn close to spilling everything as it is.

What the hell was I thinking? What the hell *am* I thinking?

He brushes his hand across mine, but the moment he does, the deep grooves I've left in his desk come into focus.

And he was worried about hurting me in the throes of passion?

With that question, I've answered my first one.

I'm not thinking here at all. And that's the problem.

"I'm sorry," I whisper. "I should go."

I right my dress, slip out of his grasp, and grab my clutch from the shelf by the window.

I can't even look at him. I can't say goodbye. All I can do is run away.

CHAPTER 18

Maximus

IT'S NOT THE FACT that she's bolted from me—again—and left me with more questions than ever before.

It's not even the lust I've been battling all night because of her, or how she's made me believe, more than ever, the color red was created just for her.

It's more than that. Because now, *we're* more.

I've seen more than just her bare skin and her slick arousal. More than her succulent mouth parting for the hungry invasion of mine. More than the heat of her breathtaking body as she opened for me, waiting for me to taste her rich depths.

I've seen her secrets.

Some willingly given. But others, including the revelation that made her flee, not so much. So as the sun crests over Alameda's campus and I finish grading the last term project proposal on my desk, I'm as frustrated and furious as I was eight hours ago when I watched her tear out of here like she was on fire.

Fuck. Me.

Was she on fire?

What really happened last night?

I've replayed it all in my head. The perfect minutes that won't stop tormenting me, threatening to punch a hole through the slacks of my wrinkled tux. The parts that have me restlessly pacing through the morning sunbeams, wishing they were moonlight all over again. Burning for a chance to relive it all—but with the knowledge I have now.

Which is what, exactly?

The taunt of my brain has me stopping with a sharp jerk. I'm done with this pathetic mooning. There's a truth here as glaring as the sunlight in my eyes and the charcoaled dents in my desk. Getting to Kara's secrets won't be as easy as unveiling her passion. But I'm not a stranger to challenges. I've faced a huge one called self-control every day of my life.

And now I've got a major clue to jump-start my quest.

An hour later, bearing a stack of every screenplay Giovani Valari ever wrote, I make my way toward the farthest corner of the second floor in Alameda's library. The building is as quiet as a tomb right now, due no doubt to a lot of people still sleeping off hangovers. Fine by me. There's enough noise in my head from all the questions still burning through it.

What's the core of my connection with this woman? This pull that seems to defy biology, chemistry, rationality?

Why does she keep acknowledging the bond—only to run when I plead for more ties to keep it together? Why does her family keep emerging as a logical explanation for that, and how deep do their hooks extend into her?

What's the explanation for the fire—literally—in her eyes?

Why does she keep hiding? *What* is she hiding?

It's time to start yanking every thread I have here. Hard.

The second-floor research corner is my special hideaway in this place, rejected by most of the students because there are now brighter, newer spaces. With the opening of the new wing—which reflects Veronica Valari's tastes in every shiny social media–ready way—I suspect that'll be even more the case. I'm not complaining. Now I have even more space to spread out and—

"What the hell?"

My grumble has my best friend lifting his head and flashing his trademark smirk. "Well, isn't this a pleasant surprise," Jesse drawls. "I thought you'd be waist-deep in a stack of term project proposals by now."

"And I thought you'd still be in coffee-and-cuddles mode with the redhead who couldn't keep her tongue out of your ear during last night's festivities."

"There are advantages to sleepovers with girls, you know."

"I'll take your word for it."

"Or maybe you don't have to?" He shoots a knowing glance at my worn-out formalwear. "Still had working eyes in my head, Professor, even with that sweet gal's tongue knocking on my tympanum. You bugged out from the gala fast. And—surprise, surprise—Kara Valari was hot on your heels, even in those red stilts she was rocking."

My stare narrows before I can help it. "Did you really just get scientific Latin-y on me while referencing your sexual foreplay *and* Kara's shoes?"

"Few things finer than a combination of human biology and well-made stilettos, my friend."

"I can probably think of a few."

"Just tell me you weren't contemplating any of them last night." He yanks a thick book off the stack that's piled on his side of the table, opening it to a dazzling rendering of the solar system. "Don't let me down, man. Do *not* tell me you turned that woman down when she was dressed like that and had eyes only for you."

I scrub a slow hand down my face. "All right. I'm not telling you that."

"Thank fuck." He dips his head and raises his brows. "So?"

I compress my lips. "It's complicated."

"Buddy, the stock market is complicated. Rush hour traffic on Pico? Complicated. But recognizing when a stunning woman is into you and doing something about it? Maximus Kane, that's not complicated. That's a blessing from the gods."

As he finishes with a flourish worthy of some profound philosopher, I permit a smile—a small one—to spread across my lips. Kara's taste still lingers faintly on their surface. I silently pray for the effect to be permanent.

"Well, the gods don't have to worry about their efforts being wasted," I finally murmur and then jab a pointed finger across the table. "But that's all you're getting about that. End of discussion."

He pumps his arm like a train conductor sounding a whistle. "Well, because it bears repeating. Thank fuck."

I won't get a better opportunity to change the subject. I peer closer at the titles he's pulled for his own stack of books. All of them are thicker research tomes, so valuable that they can't be checked out of the library.

"And what's brought *you* to the corner of musty and quiet today, Professor North? More importantly, did you leave any astronomy research books for the kids to access?"

"I'm on a mission." He squares his shoulders. "A mission for some damn answers." Then looks toward the ceiling. "Anyone listening up there? *Answers*, please!"

I crunch my brows. "Answers for what?"

"Explaining the star formation that Kell Valari caught on her camera the other night." His features tighten as he pulls out an enlarged version of the image from Kell's phone, now printed on photo paper. "I'm going to go ahead and say it. I'm past stumped about this shit."

"Which must have you wanting to take someone's head off."

"Yeah. Mine." He tosses the photo back down, and it glides a few inches along the tabletop. "But this constellation—if that's what it is—makes no sense. Not just for the eastern sky at this time of year. For *any* sky, at *any* time of year. Damn thing is too big to be a drone, and it doesn't fit the MO for a plane, even military grade."

"Well, that sucks." I don't need Kara-like perception

to feel Jesse's vexation. Since the day he was parked permanently in that wheelchair, the guy has known his advantage in life would come from his mind. And it's a brilliant mind. When he doesn't know something, Jesse is unrelenting in his quest to resolve it.

"Hmm." He grunts. "Not sure I'd say that."

"Meaning?"

"That at this point, I almost hope I don't find a plausible explanation for this thing."

I narrow my gaze even tighter. "Why?"

"Because then I can pose the theory that this might be a brand-new constellation."

I halt my finger above the touchpad on my laptop. The spreadsheet I'm working on is just a collection of blue squares right now, but I plan on filling them as quickly as I can get through each script.

"You're serious," I finally blurt.

Jesse nods. "Very."

"How's that possible?" My grasp of his special field is as truncated as his is of mine, but I know the basics. "There are eighty-eight constellations, right? That hasn't changed in nearly a hundred years."

"But that's what makes science cool, my friend. Making the impossible real." He scoops up Kell's photo again and wiggles it in the air. "Getting to find new stars in the sky."

I return his eager grin with an easy smile. "You're keeping in mind the other elements in the picture, right? The neighborhoods at the base of that hill? The urban sprawl on the *other* side of it? What if this is just the result of some kids playing with their flashlights?"

"In the middle of a freak thunderstorm and the downpour that came with it? I doubt it."

This is typical Jesse. *Making the impossible real.* His physical limitations have never stopped him from doing anything—but his favorite thing to do is to give me shit.

Like he does now, shooting a devilish smirk toward my stack of research material. "Has a certain lady in vintage red inspired you to become a classic film buff, Professor Kane?"

"Sure," I reply good-naturedly.

He scrutinizes my pile more carefully. "Wow. Are these all originals?"

"In one way or another, yeah. Some are just cast table-reading copies, but they're all from the same years Valari's scripts were produced into films."

"Wow. I didn't even know we had them up here. Guess they'll be moved over to the new wing soon."

"Guess again."

"Huh?"

"Giovani Valari is estranged from most of the clan. It's not exactly his choice, but given the circumstances of his past ..."

"Right." Jesse jogs his chin with a contemplative hum. "'Circumstances.' That's tactful at least. Just like 'estranged.'" He doesn't ask about Kara's relationship with her grandfather, for which I'm thankful.

He grabs a script off the stack, opens it, and starts flipping through pages. "You know, this one looks pretty intriguing. *Hell to Pay.* I don't remember the film but feel like I should. I always thought Valari was best at spy thrillers and mafia dramas, but this one has enough pathos for the art film crowd too."

"Jesse." I look up as I say it, though my throat caps it.

"You think the movie was just an indie release? Back in the day, independent films didn't have the same cachet as now. And this thing was written after all the drama with that starlet and her husband. Valari wasn't such a hot property anymore. His daughter is the one who's propelled the family name back up to—"

"*Jesse.*"

"What?"

"There are probably a few things you should know here."

He turns the script over on the table as a way of saving his place. "This sounds serious."

"Yeah." I push my hands together as if to pray—wondering if that might not have been the best way to start the day as a whole. I rest my chin on top of my pressed fingers. "You, more than anyone else on this planet, know all about me. Right?"

A frown takes over his face. "You mean the two tons of parmesan cheese you like on your pizza? Or the fact that you save all the crusts and feed them to the neighborhood strays on your way to the gym? Or the darker stuff, like your strange obsession with Garfield memes?"

"I mean the stuff that's a lot darker than that." I say it fast for fear of not getting it out at all. "The reason I was able to do what I did to you. The reason why I'm able to do other . . . weird . . . things."

He slides backward in his chair, leaving his sarcasm behind with the *Hell to Pay* script. "Why are you bringing this up now?"

"Because I think—I mean I'm pretty damn sure—that Kara might be like me." I raise my hands and tunnel them into my hair. "And yeah, I know how crazy that sounds. And while it's not completely the truth—"

"Then how much of the truth is it?"

He all but snarls the interruption. I don't blame him. The guy will be in a wheelchair for the rest of his life because of what my abnormality made me capable of, and now I've dropped the bomb that I may not be the only superhuman freak in this world. Hell, in this *city*.

I look up. Ruefully shake my head. "She's different, Jesse. She affects *me* differently. This can't be a complete shock to you. You noticed it from the first night you saw us together. You were the one encouraging me to see where things went with her."

"Because I thought she'd loosen you up a little, asshole. Get you out on a few real, normal dates. Walks on the beach. Miniature golf. Skydiving."

I shove my elbows onto the table, which hunches my shoulders over. "This already feels like a free fall." I cock my head back and palm my eye sockets. "And I don't know where I'm going to crash."

"Why don't you just ask Kara?" he drawls. "She might know, yeah?"

"Because if the answer were simple, she'd have told me instead of dancing around the subject. And I wouldn't be here reading movie scripts from forty years ago, praying for a single clue to the real answer."

The answer that lies deeper than all that. I know it already. Hell, I *see* it every time my gaze locks with Kara's. It's in every agonized shadow she lets me see in her huge brown eyes. And it's on full display when she's furious or passionate, flaring to life in all those amazing, entrancing flames...

"All right," Jesse says softly. "Let's hash this out, then. What exactly makes you think she's like you?"

"She's...intuitive."

He cocks a brow, giving me a long beat to say more. When I'm firm about my silence, he finally says, "Intuitive. That's it? Lots of people are intuitive, Maximus. Hell, Reg and Sarah know I've got the flu three days before *I* do."

I struggle for words. *Me.* Fighting to find words. "There's more to it than that, damn it."

"More like how? She can read your mind?"

"No. Not that either. Not exactly."

"Right. Just your...what? Your heart? Your soul?"

I push out a frustrated sigh. "A little of both, I guess." *Or maybe a lot of both.* "The best term for it might be... hyperempathetic. She picks up on emotional vibrations from people."

"Emotional...vibrations."

"Right. Energy waves. Except in more detail."

"Energy...waves."

"Yes."

"In what kind of detail? Can you be more specific?"

I curse under my breath. "I'm not sure why I expected you to believe this."

But I know damn well why. A few minutes ago, the guy was talking to me about the possibility of new stars, even an undiscovered constellation. If he believes the impossible can happen with collections of helium, hydrogen, and fucking angel tears, why doesn't he give my assertions half a chance?

"You want to break out any one-liners about the flames I saw in her eyes too?"

"Now *that* one, I half believe," he replies. "I mean, spontaneous human combustion has basically been debunked by science, but this isn't a head-to-toe occurrence where she's concerned. Unless one counts that dress from last night…"

"I'll thank you not to mention that dress with that smirk on your face, dickhead." I've never said anything so viciously to him before—but he earned it.

"Yeah, yeah. My apologies…"

He trails off, and I look back up just in time to take in his unblinking gaze, which is focused back on the script in his hands.

"Yo. Hey," I demand. "Earth to the North Star. The story can't be that good."

Jesse makes a lopsided figure-eight with his head in some bizarre cross between a nod and a shake. "It's…that *revealing*," he says. "I mean…I think…"

His voice is as strange as his demeanor. I'm glad when he spins the script around so I can read it at the correct aspect. He stabs a finger to the sheet and orders, "Start right there."

I dip my head, making sure I'm looking at the right spot, and I start skimming through the text. "*Anthony sits up, shaken from his nightmare. He looks up and jolts again. Visalia, crouched at the foot of the bed, is totally naked. Flames consume her eyes. Anthony begins to speak, but she cuts him off.*

"*It is time, Anthony,*" Jesse continues. He leans forward and reads the dialogue from his angle. "*Hell granted you life once more. This is the price of your renewal. By giving back the essence of your own life.*"

There's more of the scene left. A lot more. But the details are, in Jesse's words, revelatory—explaining why the film version of *Hell to Pay* might not have ever seen the light of day. At best, the movie probably had a limited release with a hard "R" rating. But I'm fairly certain even that didn't happen. An instinct as sure as my heartbeat is telling me the script never even got pitched to studios . . . that Giovani Valari's ostracization had already begun.

Because he'd written about his truth? Could this have been about . . . his *life*?

As the impact of that thought hits, I'm rocked back in my chair once more. I slam a hand to my chest, certain half the roof must've fallen in on it. And then the sky with it.

"God in fucking heaven," I grate.

"Try again, man," Jesse mutters. "This time, the other direction."

CHAPTER 19

Kara

"WE MADE OUR WAY across the sodden mess
of souls the rain beat down, and when our steps
fell on a body, they sank through emptiness.
All those illusions of being seemed to lie—"

A student's loud coughing interrupts him mid-sentence.
Instead of finishing the stanza, he holds the place in his copy
of the *Comedy* with his finger and clasps it closed in front
of him. Others look up from their own texts and follow his
slow pacing across the length of the hall.

"Indeed. *All those illusions of being seemed to lie.*"

He hums softly, like he's figuring something out even
though he's the one who's supposed to be enlightening us.

I'm fearful that's not how this lecture is going to go. Not
with the looks he's already been shooting my way. Looks
that could cut through glass with their intensity, despite the
fact that I've tucked myself into the back row again. After
everything we did the other night...after everything he saw

I was capable of, I couldn't bring myself to sit any closer.

I couldn't bring myself to skip class either. I guess masochism really must run in my veins along with the demonic DNA—and the other unique cells of my chemistry. The ones that need to be near this man, even if it's under these conditions.

So here I am. Here *we* are, our gazes locked once more, having a silent conversation for two in a room of fifty.

"Miss Valari," he says, his voice deep and clipped. "You're familiar with Cerberus, aren't you?"

He speaks with a degree of certainty that has a fresh bloom of heat creeping under my skin. Not the lust-inspired kind, but an aggravated flush that reminds me I need to keep all my emotions and reactions in check—something I failed to do after Maximus gave me that earthquake of an orgasm.

In hindsight, while I've beaten myself up for the slip, I'm not surprised by it. The intimate moment was a Richter-shaking blast, forever altering the landscape of my body, my mind, my senses. And I haven't thought of much else since.

I thrum my nails over my notebook, determined to banish all those thoughts for at least the duration of class, hard as it may be.

"Sure."

He smiles tightly. "I thought so. Why don't you tell us a little about this ravenous beast that Dante meets in the third circle?"

I stare down at my notebook and the random scribblings there. The storm in my bloodstream is overshadowed by dread. Of all the times I've sought his attention and the chance to prove myself right, this is one instance where I'd rather not. But the silence stretching through the room presses me to speak. I clear my throat and keep my gaze cast downward.

"Cerberus . . . is a three-headed wolf who guards the gate to the underworld."

"And what's his purpose there?"

I close my eyes. "He allows all to enter and none to escape."

"None to escape."

I lift my head at his statement. It definitely isn't a question. In fact, it feels oddly like a challenge, which his unflinching stare almost confirms.

I swallow over the tightness in my throat. "That's the general idea, yeah," I say, hoping I sound more unaffected than I am.

What the hell is he getting at? Or is he just singling me out in class as payback for running out on him? He may think he's playing some stupid mental games because his ego's wounded, but nothing about this is playtime. But how the hell do I tell him that without *telling* him?

He can never know how closely he's skirting my family's sick truth.

He purses his lips and answers with a quick nod before opening the book again.

"*His eyes are red, his beard is greased with phlegm,*
his belly is swollen, and his hands are claws
to rip the wretches and flay and mangle them."

He snaps the book loudly shut. "Dante describes

Cerberus as a bearded beast. That gives him a human quality, no?"

My hands start to shake. I grasp my pen and scribble more mindless designs along the margins of my notebook. "I don't know," I mumble.

"You don't know? I'm sorry. I didn't hear you."

Bastard.

Screw trying to save him from my family's savagery. I'm going to kill him myself.

In the space of two weeks, he's gone from protecting me in class, to trying to kick me out of it, to *this*.

The subtle snickers across the room are like gasoline on the flames of my fury. I lift my gaze up to his, not caring if it's searing with a blaze for all the class to see.

"I. Don't. Know." I all but growl the words, daring him to push me further, to test my knowledge on a subject he should be grateful to know so little about.

His lips part and his eyes soften—the first glimpse of remorse he's shown for tempting me into this spectacle. And that's about what it's become. I'm fully dressed, but I may as well be in my bra and underwear here. Or less. He's exposed me in return for protecting *him* from dark and dangerous truths.

He breaks our connection, swiftly returning to the text to pick up where he left off. For the rest of the class, he explores less exciting territory—one of Dante's political prophecies. I watch the clock, preparing myself to bolt the moment he dismisses us. But the hefty stack of term paper proposals he's holding is an unfortunate reminder that I'll have at least one more interaction with the man before escaping this unique circle of hell.

"Remember to collect your proposals before leaving," he says. "Any questions, you know where to find me."

Due to my spot at the back of the hall, I decide to wait for the others to collect theirs from Maximus. But by the time the crowd disperses, he's empty-handed.

I sling my backpack over my shoulder and walk slowly down the risers to where he's perched himself on the edge of the desk. I stop abruptly in front of him.

"You know, all you're missing are the circus hoops, Professor."

He winces. "Excuse me?"

"Are you going to give me my paper, or do you need to quiz me some more to make me earn it?"

His next words are equally biting. "Maybe if you were a little more forthcoming with the truth, I wouldn't have to put you on the spot."

I tense. "Listen, I don't know what that was all about, but—"

"*Hell to Pay.*"

I pause. "Huh?"

"It was the first screenplay Giovani Valari wrote after Malcolm Caulfield shot and nearly killed him. Have you read it?"

I press my lips together tightly. "I haven't."

"I have."

I attempt another swallow over the painful knot, willing it away. Willing this entire interaction into the past. Maybe

I can help things along. I step around him and glance at the table for my paper. Nothing. I cross my arms with a huff.

"Maximus, just give me my paper and let me leave."

"I don't think so."

"Damn it," I sputter. "Why?"

"We need to talk."

I scoff. "About what? Your theories about a screenplay my grandfather wrote over forty years ago?"

"Do you know what it's about?"

"Not a clue." I do my best to feign disinterest, channeling my best impression of Kell. He doesn't seem convinced as he squares his body with mine, giving me the full power of his attention.

"It's about a washed-up writer. Chewed up and spit out by Hollywood. Emotionally knocked down from all the wrong turns he took in life. All his sins. Then he kills himself, but he manages to escape the clutches of hell. Then he meets a beautiful woman who isn't who she seems—and he realizes his hell is just beginning."

My mouth drops open, but only a few frustrated rasps come out of my throat. Suddenly it's too much. Too real. I slam my lips shut, furious with my grandfather for putting pen to paper with all this truth. The awful, terrible truth.

I can't listen to a minute more of it. I turn and start up the stairs, but Maximus takes my arm and brings me back. I try to twist away, but he's stronger. Not a surprise, but not a revelation I want to accept right now. But as soon as our stares entwine, I go still. The look in his eyes—the desperation, determination, and need—tells me he needs me to stay more than I want to leave.

"You've been lying to me, Kara."

Damn it, how I want to scorch him with a new glare. Already I feel the danger of what else that will bring. Fresh tears. Instead, I bare my teeth. "I have never been more honest with anyone in my life than you. *Anyone.* How do you not see or know—"

"Then tell me why." He's not accusing. He's pleading. "*Why*, Kara?"

His anguish has me taking in a few ragged breaths. Have I been lying? Is that how he really sees it? Has my omission damned me in his eyes?

"Cerberus. The wolf in your earring," he presses.

"Wh-What about it?"

"It means something. Doesn't it?"

"No," I rush out. "It's nothing. An antique passed down to me, and—"

"Not your style."

"And what's your point? Are you a fashionista now?" I finally manage to tug myself away with some effort.

"You said I couldn't hurt you." He looks me over while barreling on, determined. "I'm wondering now if that could be true. You're a hell of a lot stronger than someone your size should be."

I compress my lips. I can't say anything to that. I haven't hidden my strength from him in the hopes of proving that he's not a physical threat to me.

"And your family," he continues, "exiling your grandfather the way they have. That adds up too, doesn't it?"

"You don't understand." I take a step back. "It's complicated."

"It sounds like it is. More than I could have ever imagined. But somehow it took one night with you in my arms to figure it out. All of it. The desk. The fire in your eyes. Hell, Kara ..."

I blink. Hard. So much for belying the emotion from my gaze. It's a hot, prickling invasion behind my eyes now. Through my whole head. Shit. *Shit*. He knows. He *can't* know. This is too crazy, too risky ... So much more than I bargained for.

"I think you've been reading too much Dante, Maximus." I attempt a little laugh. Massive fail. I sound more like a teakettle on half heat. "You're seeing things you want to see."

"And there's that. You, here in this seminar. Demanding to stay with a fascination for the material that rivals my own, which is saying a lot."

I close my eyes with a soft sigh. The moment I do, visions from our last night together assault me. Did I expect anything else? Why do I not even want to change the answers? How did I let myself fall so deep into so many feelings for this man?

"Tell me who you really are."

I raise my head up as soon as his soft demand breaches the air. Then I'm battling a fresh hit of confusion, frustration, fury, sorrow.

Would I tell him if I could? If I wasn't bound to three generations of this secret?

"I've told you more than I've ever told anyone. Now it feels like you're punishing me for it."

He lets go of a sigh and whips off his glasses to pinch the place where they bridged his nose.

"I'm not trying to punish you, Kara. I'm...fucking frustrated. By everything. You storm into my life and turn everything upside down just by being you. You claim we're both different than everyone else, which basically makes us the same—but the reality is that you're *not* like me. You can't hide behind a curtain of ignorance. You *have* the answers. You just won't let anyone in. And I'm—" He runs a hand through his tangled hair, fisting it briefly before letting go with another pained exhale. "I'm falling for you, so hard. Like, straight out of a plane without a parachute hard. Honestly, sometimes it feels exactly like that. And all I keep thinking is if I don't have all of you ..."

Something raw and vulnerable passes across his features, like maybe he's feeling it right now. That surrender. All the fear that goes along with that kind of jump.

He closes the space between us, tugging me gently to his chest. The tension inside me gives way to his towering warmth and thorough embrace. The security of his arms around me again feels like heaven. They feel like home. The incredible dichotomy of those two words together—*heaven, home*—delivers another hit of unexpected sadness as he tips my chin, guiding my gaze into his.

"I want all your secrets, Kara... All the little pieces of you no one ever sees, every wild dream and ugly truth. If I'm not the man who can earn all of it, nothing's going to feel right for me ever again. Because as crazy as you're making me right now, I don't want to go back to before. I'll take the free fall. Any damn day. But I need you to be real with me ..."

And just like that, he's unraveling my defenses with the new certainty that I'm not alone in this. He's asking me to jump with him. And I want to, but ...

"There's so much to explain." My whisper is jittery, frightened. Not because of what he's opening up in me, but because I'm terrified he'll change his mind and close me back up. "Things that are ... difficult ... to explain."

"I'm figuring it out anyway. Come clean and save me the research."

I smile a little, wishing it were that easy. Just blurting it out. Trusting that the second I mention I'm a demon, he won't change the way he feels about me. That *everything* won't change between us.

I bite my lower lip, then release it as he slides his touch in against my cheek and brings our faces close. "Remember when you said, 'If I only wanted to see the best of you, I wouldn't be here.' What makes you think I'd feel any differently about you?"

My breath clutches in my throat—just before a door in the back of the hall slams loudly, followed by the sounds of students chatting. I step out of our embrace, heavy with relief and regret.

The frown he's wearing seems to convey the same. "Let's go to my office so we can talk."

His office. No way can I step into that room again and

not relive the experience of being sprawled across his desk, writhing in pleasure beneath his fingers and velvet tongue. And if I get the sense he's reliving any of it too, I'm a goner.

"I . . . I can't today. I'm sorry." Weirdly, the last two words feel like confession for other things—for which I'm grateful despite the deepening grooves of his frown.

"Why?"

"I have plans." It's the truth, but still not one he'll want to hear about. After some back and forth, I managed to change my dinner plans with Arden to a meeting at his office instead. It might not be a candlelit rendezvous anymore, but the frosty way Maximus interacted with him at the fundraiser isn't making me eager to spill those details.

"When can I see you? You can come to my place this weekend if you want. Or I can come to you."

The idea of seeing him again off campus is tempting. It's what normal people do when they decide to be in a relationship. But Maximus Kane and me? We're far from normal. And I don't trust myself in a closed room with him right now.

He seems to sense my hesitation.

"How about we meet up at Recto Verso tomorrow. Just coffee. Okay?"

More students pour in. Their professor will be here next. We're already cutting it too close lately. People will be talking about us soon if they aren't already. We can't keep meeting this way. So I agree with a nod.

"Tomorrow. Coffee sounds perfect."

*⁺✳

Arden's office is tucked into a small but posh building at the edge of the Golden Triangle, close enough to that prestigious wedge of Beverly Hills to be relevant but not ancient. The building has an open-air atrium in the middle that looks like a set from *Casablanca*, with Moroccan lamps, lush landscaping, and a baby grand piano in a gazebo. I make my way into the waiting elevator, which takes me up to the third floor.

Arden's receptionist shows me into his corner office with picture windows flanked by the tops of palm trees.

He looks up from the huge cluttered desk, his smile gleaming bright white like his perfectly tailored Oxford shirt. "Kara."

The door whispers closed as he strides toward me. I think he'll reach for me, but his hands stay tucked into his slacks. His stare is more daring, roving over me boldly.

"How do you manage to look so perfectly edible with such little effort?"

Any reply I could possibly come up with lodges in my throat. I'm not typically self-conscious about my outfits, but suddenly I'm rethinking my jeans, boots, slouchy sweater combination. Of course I made every selection with Maximus in mind, not knowing how infuriating he was going to be all through class. I definitely wasn't thinking about Arden's approval, but I silently remind myself to test this new theory and dress as terribly as possible for him going forward.

"Sorry. You probably think I'm forward. I'm used to appreciating beautiful things all day long. It's hard to switch off. I hope you don't mind."

I manage a smile. "I'm used to being treated like a commodity. I'm a Valari, after all."

He seems to measure me with his dark stare for a long moment, breaking it with an amused grunt.

"Very well." He gestures toward his desk. "Your timing is flawless. I was just looking through some pieces for Veronica. Perhaps you'd like to chime in."

Several stacks of glossy listing photos cover the surface. He picks up a loose one. "This is a strong piece. It's listed with Christie's, but I happen to know the people who oversee this collection. I think we could probably coax some more out of them to round out ours if you like it."

I take the photo depicting a bronze bull-headed figure that can't be more than four inches tall. "It's a Minotaur."

"In bronze. Circa 500 B.C."

"It's almost two hundred thousand dollars," I counter.

He lifts an eyebrow. "Does Veronica's budget concern you?"

I let the photo float down to the desk. "Not in the least."

He chuckles once more, though I'm still boggled about his intent. A strange coil in my stomach sends me even weirder vibes, like he's laughing at something else. Like a grown-up getting the mature innuendo of a line in a kid's film.

"That makes two of us, then," he ensures. "Of course,

she's given me some basic parameters. But let's not worry about the figures right now. Let's focus on the bigger picture, shall we?"

"Which is?"

"Themes." He relaxes into the high-back leather seat across from his desk, gesturing for me to take the adjacent one. "I think we can easily land on some of your mother's favorites."

"Vanity? Power? Revenge?"

He laughs again, his eyes glistening as they fasten on me. "I'm so glad we're working on this together. I was worried you'd be dull."

"I do my best to be. I'm not a fan of the spotlight."

"So I've gathered. Why is that?"

I shrug. "I'm just interested in other things."

"Like what?"

I stifle an annoyed sigh. "Art. History. Literature. Language."

"All reasons why you're so perfect for this." His expression changes, returning to the same energy as before. Like he's measuring his stares out, carefully and quietly. But not timidly. He knows exactly what he's doing. Controlling every syllable of this narrative. "I say we start with your interests and fold in Veronica's as we go."

I hesitate. "I'm not sure that's fair. She's your client."

"And I don't think she'll be hard to satisfy. All I have to do is pick the shiniest, gaudiest, most expensive thing in the room, tell her how important it is, and she'll love it. I have a feeling you'll be harder to please, which gives this endeavor a little more...structure. Why not give ourselves some challenges and make it fun?" He leans in. "Tell me, Kara. What moves you? Give me a place to start. A theme."

He slants more of his weight into the space between us. I shift away by matching degrees.

"That's...um...a really broad question."

Not to mention a loaded one. Only one thing has really moved me recently. One man, rather. One exasperating, beautiful, tortured man. Over the past two weeks, somehow all of my thoughts, all of my being, have been magnetized to him. Even now, my mind is consumed by the blistering memories of him.

Arden tilts his head slightly, as if perhaps he might be able to figure out the answer simply by looking at me. "Come now, Kara. You have something in mind. I can see the wheels turning."

I gulp hard, really hoping that's all he can see. Because if anyone finds out what Maximus is beginning to mean to me, our days together would certainly be numbered. I hardly trust Kell with the information. I certainly don't trust Arden.

"What is it?" He reaches out and takes my hand, gliding his thumb along my wrist softly. "I can tell when people are lying to me, you know? It's one of those special little gifts that makes playing with humans so much fun."

I curse the fast beating of my heart now, with his thumb pushing into the pulsing echo of it. His persistent stare trips my efforts to mentally catalog all the times I've already lied to him in our brief acquaintance, which, even from a quick tally, is too many.

Still, though he may be able to spot a lie, it doesn't mean he can figure out the truth.

"So, tell me." He draws his hands back after a moment, clasping them comfortably on his lap. "What moves you? Or, perhaps *who*?"

And just like that, Maximus blazes over my thoughts again. Igniting everything. Consuming everything. His tenderness. His intellect. His passion. His fear. Everything he's shown me he's capable of, and everything I've yet to see.

But I have to supply another answer. Something that still feels like the truth.

"The hero," I finally say.

Arden lifts a dark brow. "The hero?" He makes a small sound. "Interesting. Epic? Tragic?"

"You choose," I say. "That should give you plenty to work with."

He looks me over again, his expression quietly amused. "I like it." He glances back to his desk. "Let's find some heroes then, shall we?"

CHAPTER 20

 # MAXIMUS

I SHOULDN'T FEEL HALF as good as I do when stepping into Recto Verso this morning. I've clocked no more than five hours of sleep in the last two days. Obsession with a certain old movie script and the research trips upon which it's guided me have seen to that. Those journeys have led me to some bizarre destinations. Confronted me with concepts I shouldn't have to wrap my mind around but have with disturbing speed.

It'll all start coming together—when I talk with Kara.

No. When she talks, and I listen.

I'm still jubilant that she agreed to this meeting, despite how she accused me of being too immersed in Dante to think straight. And yes, she was probably—okay, *likely*—right. I own that now.

But that was yesterday.

Today's going to be different. Today, Kara's going to tell me *her* story.

The resolution strengthens with every step I take toward the coffee bar, where Reg is singing along to a soft pop station. The song from the speakers is an awful auto-tuned version of "Holding Out for a Hero," making me prefer my friend's raspy rendition.

I slide onto one of the stools at the bar. "He's gotta be strong and he's gotta be fast, huh?"

Reg stops singing but continues her diligent wipe-up along the counter. "Since he's also got to be racing with the thunder and rising with the heat, I doubt the bloke even exists."

"I'm sure Sarah will be happy to hear that."

She cants half a smile my way. "Looks like you're sure about a lot of things this fine morning."

I lean over the counter, grab a ceramic mug, and then fill it from the large coffee urn. "I'm sure of the fact that it *is* a fine morning—and I plan on turning it into an even finer day."

"Well, happy Saturday to you too." She flings the dishrag over her shoulder and leans against the counter. "On your way to save the whales, secure world peace, or patch up the ozone layer?"

"Hmm." I take a contemplative sip of my brew. "Maybe all three." I'll probably feel capable of it after setting things right with Kara again. Breaking down the final barriers between us. Having her trust—and her truth. At last.

Reg finishes her long laugh. "All that, eh? By drinking only the Arabica?"

"Who needs caffeine when the day begins with proper motivation?"

"All right, then." A knowing purse of her lips. "And does this awesome new 'motivation' have a name?"

I get in my own astute head tilt. "Well, she *is* awesome. Just not new."

"Oh?"

Her smile widens, but not with the effort I'm expecting. It's the most forced cheer I've ever seen on the woman's features. I'm almost insulted she's trying to pass it off as authentic.

"And who's the not-so-new daisy we're referencing, exactly?" she adds tightly. "One of those lovelies you and Jesse brought to the Melora Hall party?"

"You remember my date disappearing with someone else that night, right?" I inch up a corner of my mouth, waiting for Reg to take full, sarcastic advantage of that truth. But I'm more unnerved when she doesn't.

Her reaction is more of what she's already given me. Her shoulders are still squared and tense. Her lips are still tight and twisted.

"Because you were mooning over Kara Valari in the classics section, yes?" Her expression flattens with sudden understanding. "It's her, isn't it?" she mutters. "Damn." She adds the oath beneath her breath, but I hear all the strained edges on the words. She pushes up her volume and asks, "Are you sure about hopping off this particular ledge, young man?"

I brace my elbows to the bar top. "I think I'm pretty much into the ravine now, Reg. But I'm also not a 'young man' anymore."

"Why, yes," she drawls. "You're positively ancient."

"And you're positively not excited about this." I search her with harder scrutiny. "Not by even half a good thought. Why?"

"I support you with plenty of good thoughts, Maximus. And I have done so for quite a long—"

"That's not an answer." I hold her with my stare. "You and Sarah care for me. I know that. I get that. What I don't get are your issues with me being involved with Kara."

"Hmm." She regards me with new focus but still manages to look aloof. "I didn't realize you'd become such a fan of the Valaris."

"She's a lot more than a family name, Reg." I'm somber about the words because I've never meant anything more. "Honestly, I haven't met any of them yet besides Kara and Kell. And unlike most of the world, I'm willing to withhold blanket judgments based on headlines that are built on marketing formulas."

"Is that what you think I'm doing now?"

"I only know that a couple of weeks ago, on this very roof"—I nod toward the ceiling—"you told me Kara isn't worthy of me. So that was either the kind of canned sentiment that comes from someone who cares, or you were drawing conclusions about a perfect stranger based on what the tabloids have told you. I can't imagine you got to that judgment by watching her across a crowded room for five minutes."

I'm calm about every word, but she goes painfully still, as if she's been shot from behind. "Then the best of your knowledge is wrong."

"Which means . . . what?"

She inhales with purpose. Releases the breath just as steadily. "Which means exactly what it implies."

I blink at her. Hard. "What it *implies* is that maybe you know more about the Valaris than you've let on."

Or hasn't she?

My scrutiny of her now is helpful in backtracking my mind to our conversation from two weeks ago. I needed to think. She needed to know I was okay. I attempted to sidestep the subject of Kara. But Reg hadn't.

You really are bound for better than her, you know.

Oh, no. She hadn't sidestepped a single damn thing. If I'd been watching for it, I would've seen it. But I wasn't. I couldn't. I was still spun out from my wild hit of touching Kara once more. And getting to press my body to hers, as well. Reg's subtexts had been lost in my addicted haze. The haze is still there now, but I've gotten better at pushing my mind past it. I've had to. Never more urgently than in this moment.

"Well?" I press.

I study her gaze, taking note of all its troubled shadows.

"I know more than I want to know," she says.

"Which means what, exactly?"

"When I first settled in LA, our paths crossed from time to time. For work."

"Work? Before the store?" I gesture to the shelves that line every visible wall. It's impossible to comprehend that the inviting ambiance, eclectic book mixture, and timeless coziness haven't been here for Angelenos since the city was built.

"Oh, yeah," she explains. "Even before I met Sarah."

I jump both eyebrows. "Wow."

"Interesting times." She dips a small nod. "I was on my own for a little while. And of course, starting a new business isn't easy or lucrative at first." Now her reply is surprisingly swift, reminding me of a kid who's memorized a rote excuse for responding to my exact question. "For a short time, I picked up extra gigs to pay the rent. Things got easier once Sarah came over for a visit and just never left."

I mirror her soft smile. "So . . . extra gigs like what?"

"This and that," she fills in. "Clerical temping mostly. Sometimes clients asked for bookkeeping or errand running too. Mostly jobs that are performed by full-time assistants, accountants, and managerial teams these days."

"*You* were a personal assistant for the Valaris?" At once, I jump to the more important question. "And you knew Kara when she was little?"

Reg pivots and wipes feverishly at the spotless tea leaf canisters. "I didn't say any of that."

"Then what *are* you saying?"

"Well, I wasn't at their beck and call, if that's your angle." She goes at the bean grinders—also shiny and pristine—next. "But I wasn't just there for a few hours of filing each day, either. And before you ask, spending all kinds of time with them wasn't round-the-clock glam, glitter, and champagne. And before you ask *again*, I hardly saw any of the children, much less spent meaningful time with them. They were beautiful and happy little things, though. Kara, especially, was the apple of her grandfather's eye. He was solid blinkered about caring for her himself."

As she continues to scrub at the grinders, I try imagining Kara as she must have been at that time. *Beautiful and happy* . . . And yes, already locking down her first smitten fan. Giovani Valari. The man to whom she's remained so loyal, in spite of her mother's disapproval.

And just how the hell had *that* happened? The family estrangement?

I don't press Reg for those answers. Hopefully, with the truths Kara is coming here to entrust to me, I'll learn them directly from the source.

At last, Reg tosses her cleaning rag into a laundry bin and then pins me with her refortified gaze. "Let's just say that I witnessed enough of the mire to know what I'm talking about here. Enough to know that up on that hill, behind those posh mansion walls, there's dirt and perfidy that will affect the Valaris for generations to come. I know enough to tell you now, if you insist on continuing to see Kara, then I shall insist on riding you to keep up your guard."

I lock my gaze to hers. "We're discreet."

"Discreet isn't enough. I mean it, Maximus. You need to be vigilant. Bloody hell. You need to be paranoid. At *all* times."

At first, all I do is glug my coffee. The bitter brew burns on its way down, but I welcome the sting. A brutal fusion to reality. Reg has said a whole lot without saying anything. It's overwhelming.

A mire for generations. Dirt and perfidy, stockpiled in a mansion. Vigilance and paranoia.

How do I tell the woman the total truth now? That every moment with Kara means getting to lower my guard? That no person on this planet has ever made me this free?

That answer is already clear. I won't tell her.

"At least you've been aware enough to be watchful," she goes on. "There'll be bloody hell to pay if your mother finds out about this."

I rear back. "My *mother*? Why would she care about—"

"And then there's Veronica," she interrupts and facepalms herself. "Oh, heaven help us, Nancy's fit will be dust in the wind if Veronica catches a sniff of this mess."

This mess.

Reg's assessment isn't technically wrong—because there are a lot of messy parts about how hard, far, and fast I've tumbled for Kara—but the inference that we're like a couple of kids who don't realize it . . . is just wrong. Neither of us asked for this, but neither of us is ignoring its impact. On everything. Sometimes, accepting fate's whiplash is the first step to recovering from it.

That's no help for my onslaught of feelings now.

My perplexity spirals into protective rage. My hand crushes into a fist, demolishing the ceramic mug from which I just drank. Thank fuck I was done with the contents. I'm not as grateful for everything I'm still feeling.

She steps over and reaches out—around the chunks of my shattered mug—for my hand. Her fingers are freezing talons. Her grip is shockingly brutal. "I assure you, if you take this any further with that woman's daughter, there will be consequences."

The ice in her clench is now a chill through my blood and fissures through my mind. Through those cracks, there's comprehension I don't want to see. Unfeeling light. A dawn of dread.

Still, I force myself to question her. "Consequences? Reg? What the *fuck* are you implying?"

"Maybe you already know." Her voice is suddenly soft and sad.

But I'm not sad. I'm damn near redlined with anger now, pegged-out to the point of sarcasm. "Sure. Right. Because I've totally loved getting hit with nothing but half-truths and symbolism for the last two weeks." I pull my hand free and drag it, nicked and bloody, through my hair. "Christ. Medieval poetry is clearer than you and Kara put together."

"No matter what this is between you two . . . no matter what you are both feeling . . . Maximus . . . you can never be with her."

I thought the conversation was excruciating before. This isn't like the woman scolding me for unfinished homework or not eating all my vegetables. This isn't an admonishment I can tune out. I have to hear it. I have to comprehend it. Yesterday, I promised Kara no less. My vow hasn't changed since then.

A high-pitched squeal pierces the tension between us.

The next second, Sarah rushes out from her office doorway wearing a Coldplay T-shirt and the biggest grin. "Oh, now, this is brilliant," she exclaims. "The king of the day, in the flesh. When were you planning on filling *us* in?"

I glance backward, ascertaining she isn't referring to

someone other than me. "Okay. What did I miss?" I ask warily. There's something about that mischief on her face, illuminated a little more by the glow from her phone, which she now swings over to show to Reg.

In return, Reg is painfully quiet. She looks ready to vomit on everything she's just cleaned. Instead, she wrests the phone from her wife, flips the screen toward me, and spits a single word.

"Discreet?"

Only then do I get my first horrified view of a photo at the top of *Star Passion*, a popular gossip blog.

Well . . . shit.

"Enlighten me, Professor. The definition of 'discreet' seems to have changed since the last time I checked."

Inwardly I echo my profanity, but the word never makes it to my lips. I take the device from Reg and scroll down the page. Nothing gets any easier to take in, including the salacious "breaking news" beneath the dim but clear photo of Kara and me, hands clasped and stares locked, from the tech booth at the back of the lecture hall. Farther down, there's another shot. Her hand is on my shoulder. I'm leaning down as if getting ready to kiss her.

Though I used Herculean effort and held back, not a soul who sees that picture will think that. The visits counter at the bottom of the page tallies the views at six digits—and climbing fast.

"Shit." I slide the phone back across the counter toward Sarah.

The woman barely notices. She's still ping-ponging a

dumbfounded look between Reg and me.

"Anyone care to enlighten the girl who just dropped a clanger here?" she finally demands. "Reg? Aren't we *happy* for our boy? Maximus? This is a good thing, right? This girl... I mean, look at how she looks at you. Oh yes, let's look..."

"No," Reg snaps. "Let's not."

"I don't understand. Maximus? You and this young woman...are *not* together?"

I release a pent-up breath through my nose. "I wouldn't call it 'together.'" I'd call it connected and captivated and riveted, but probably not *together*. We were meeting today to try to change that. Now, will Kara even show? If she does, will she even think about opening up to me anymore?

"Well then, let's not quibble semantics," Sarah says, brightening again. "Whatever you're calling it, you'll invite her over and we'll chill the bubbly to celebrate!"

"No." Reg practically barks the repeat. "No celebration. No bubbly either." After stabbing me with a fast glance, she mumbles, "I think I need something stronger."

Before Sarah can argue, the bell over the door jingles behind me. The vibrations from the clangs are barely finished on the air when my senses sizzle with even better tremors.

Better. And worse.

"Kara."

No crisis can ever steal the power of her name on my lips. I treasure its potency for another couple of seconds as she walks over in a long-skirted dress and matching fedora. Her dark hair tumbles loose and free over her shoulders, just like a bigger wave of adoration spills across every inch of my chest.

"Hi," she greets Reg and Sarah with a sweet smile before turning her gaze, wide and bright, up to me. "Good morning, Mr. Kane." She makes it a point to enunciate every syllable of her greeting, emphasizing her readiness to see me as more than just her teacher or even her friend.

She scoots up beside me and stands on her tiptoes to press a soft kiss to my jaw. I'm unable to hold back from clenching it beneath her caress. As much as I relish the intimate brush, it means she hasn't heard the news. The storm hasn't slammed her yet.

But it's about to.

I know it as soon as I clutch her hand, like I'm in quicksand and she's my salvation of a tree limb. I see it in the new tension bracketing her mouth and the deepened shadows in her eyes. I feel it in the restless shift of her body. She already senses it, like an oncoming storm rushing a defenseless shore.

"Maximus." There it is, in the unsteady rasp of her voice as well. "What is it? What's wrong?"

I battle for a reassuring smile. It's gone in less than a second. "Some photos have hit the media," I state slowly. At first, she's eerily still. Her clasp on my fingers turns into a vise-grip.

"Photos," she finally says. "Of us?"

I pull in a long breath, buying myself some seconds to navigate the chaos of my mind, searching for the best words to start with. But fate's got the last laugh on this one, because seconds are all that remain of our peaceful bubble—popped wide open by a blinding flash from the front door. Then another from the direction of the shop's service entrance. And a third from a window Reg must have rolled open earlier.

"Sixes and bloody sevens!" Sarah exclaims. "What on—"

"Out!" Reg cuts in with a virulent shout. She marches to the front door, throws it wide, and stabs her arm toward the sidewalk beyond. "This is private property, you leeches. I'm already calling LAPD. You'd better be good and gone before they show up."

As soon as the photographers are done clamoring over each other to leave, she slams the door with a biting curse.

Her wife looks on with a flushed face and wide stare. "Well, hasn't this turned into an interesting party."

Under normal circumstances, I'd be giving Sarah's droll line at least an appreciative chuckle. But laughter isn't a blip on my radar right now. The only obsession on my mind is the woman I've locked against my chest with a steeled armhold around her waist.

Fortunately, her hat's brim helps to hide her face, still twisting hard and desperately into the front of my T-shirt. I can feel wetness too. Not a lot of it. Her shoulders are collections of coiled muscles, giving away her effort to hold herself together. So much for the lame assumption that a girl like her would be seasoned at handling an onslaught like this. War zones shouldn't be a norm for anyone. The mob outside must be two dozen thick by now.

I dip my head in, pressing my mouth against her ear. "I've got you," I soothe with every inch of my spirit, every corner of my heart.

But she's far from all right. She's a ball of tension in my arms, which activates every protective bone in my body. I default to action. With a trio of forceful steps, I back her into a notch of space in the wall behind the bar. While my shoulders protrude from the crevice, it's deep enough to accommodate all of her and most of me.

I finally relent my hold, moving my hands to rub gently up and down her arms. "Once the cops get here, they'll get things under control. I can sneak you out the back and through the alley. Better yet, you can just stay here the whole day."

The new warmth of my voice gives away how I'd love nothing better, but Kara's still hunched in and shivering like she's caught on a washed-out bridge. Still, when she lifts her stare up at me, there's new hope in her eyes.

"You'd let me do that?" she whispers.

I lift a hand to her face. Press my forehead to hers. "That's like asking if I'd let myself glimpse heaven."

In a rush of sweet, sighing energy, she finally slackens a little. But not so much that she relents her hold on me. My senses heighten as she slides her arms around my neck, even shifting one hand into my hair. Her tentative smile ignites me ... pulls at me. Despite the din that continues outside, I'm going to kiss her. And she's going to let me. Nothing can break our bond. Nothing can hold back our heat.

Except the second my mouth brushes hers, a ruthless

sound blares from her dress's pocket. And in the space of that heartless hail, everything about Kara's composure is back to washed-out bridge mode.

No. Worse.

She pulls out her phone, which is still screaming like a tornado warning and buzzing like ten beehives, from her pocket. "It's my mother."

"I'm sure she's familiar with how voicemail works."

"You don't understand. Honestly, it's probably best that you don't."

She flattens a hand against my chest like the mere sound of her mother's ringtone is a call to flee. In that moment, recognition hits without mercy. If I don't block her from leaving, I'll lose her.

"Kara, don't leave. Neither of us expected this, but—"

"This is more important." Her voice wavers. "I'm sorry."

"So you're saying that those idiots with their cameras and whatever conclusions anyone wants to draw about the photos they snap is more important than everything I'm feeling for you . . . every goddamned way I'm drawn to you?"

"No. But this is my life. I didn't choose it. It's just the way it is." Her breath leaves her in harsh husks. "I'm sorry, Maximus. I'm so, *so* sorry—but I have to go."

"I'm not letting you leave this way." It's irrational and probably unfair, but the advantage of my strength is something I'm willing to use to keep her here a little longer.

"Please. If I don't go, she'll come here, and—"

"Then let her come."

"*Maximus.*"

Nothing about her shaky plea or the quivers in her fingertips prepares me for how she punctuates that. By shoving me with all the force in her arms. A force equal to that of a dozen full-grown men.

A force strong enough to set me back a few steps.

It's a new experience. No one's ever been able to budge me by an inch, let alone full steps, without me consciously allowing it. I'm not sure I like it. At all.

While my brain struggles to catch up with my shock, Kara deals an even harder blow. Her gaze, so full of torment and conflict, is worse than any physical blast she could ever unleash on me.

"I'm sorry," she says once more.

This time when she turns to leave, rushing out the back entrance, I'm struck with more than the ache of missing her. More than the torture of being left with her cinnamon spice in my senses and her pretty fedora at my feet.

For once, I wonder if the river between us has changed directions. Because the devastating force of the feelings she fled with is a cinder block in my chest now. The heartbreak in her eyes. The defeat in her withering energy, like she used the last of it to push me away.

And for the first time since she walked into my world, a new agony rips ruthlessly through me. The possibility that I might never get her back.

CHAPTER 21

Kara

"TELL ME THERE'S A good explanation for this, Kara."

My mother's displeasure fills the room like her too-strong perfume, pressing against the silk-covered walls of her office. I feel like I can't breathe in here, but I can't leave. She's been scrolling over the *Star Passion* article repeatedly for the past five minutes, as if the images or their impact on our family might change if she looks just a little longer.

When she finally turns back to me, it's almost a relief. Except her eyes are black with disappointment—like lava gone cold.

"Tell me this is part of a bigger plan to generate publicity for the family," she says, her voice too quiet. "Tell me you wouldn't intentionally jeopardize our position here over a childish romance. With your *professor!*"

Her voice climbs on the last word as she slaps her hand onto the desk, like that one particular detail is the last straw on the pile of my offenses that she just can't handle. I know she's past pissed off. But for the first time in my life, I'm less worried about her wrath than I am about everything I'm about to lose because of it. Not the clothes on my back, the roof over my head, or even the car I drove here. My heart is lodged in my throat because of the things that have no dollar signs attached or status to validate. The fallout of my carelessness will reach further than that. Because of me, Gramps is going to suffer. Probably Kell and Jaden too.

And Maximus.

Oh, God.

How deep into the fire will she throw Maximus for this?

It's impossible for me to even contemplate that answer. We haven't gotten to the specifics of those consequences yet, but I know they're coming. Veronica Valari might be a vicious bitch, but she's a woman with a plan first.

"Are you going to answer me?"

"If you want me to lie to you, I will." I lift my chin by a determined notch. "I'm guessing that's not what you really want, though."

She huffs a breath out through her nose. "So how long has this been going on?"

"Not long."

"Please..." She closes her eyes with a pained grimace. "Please tell me you haven't done anything foolish."

I glance out past the heavy curtains that frame her picture window. I wish I could jump through it and visit Gramps. Pretend like today never happened.

"I haven't slept with him, if that's what you mean."

She releases an audible sigh. "That may be the best news I've heard all day."

I look back to her, unable to share in any of her relief. Unable to do *anything*, really, except spear her with my quiet but fulminating fury.

Finally, I murmur, "It's a little ironic, don't you think?"

"I don't see anything ironic about this, Kara. This was a near disaster. Now that I know you haven't crossed any lines, I'll see if I can work it to our advantage with the media, but—"

"No." I'm not any louder about it, though I push out more anger from between my locked teeth. "The irony is that we're descendants of the fallen."

Her eyes seem frozen wide. "Yes, and …?"

"And they fell by choice. Don't you think it's awfully ironic now that I'm robbed of all my choices? When did the doctrine change, Mother? And why is my virginity so damn important? This is archaic—"

She slams her hand onto the table again. "Does a soldier have a choice when faced with duty?"

"I'm not a soldier, and neither are you."

"For being such a dedicated student, you can be extremely stupid, Kara. Can't you see this isn't about you?"

The insult stings—until I recognize it for what it really is. A sad attempt at manipulation. I refuse to let her succeed at it. I won't be stopped from at least saying my piece. I'm not going that quietly into this wrenching fate.

"I'm caught between two worlds. We both are. I'm just

233

trying to figure out who the hell I am. Don't you get that?"

My voice wavers at the end, and I hate myself for even that small weakness, but something softens in her at the same time. Under all her hyperfocus and manipulation, she's still my mother. Maybe she still cares, at least a little. Maybe because once upon a time she was robbed of her choice and wasn't entirely thrilled about it either.

"We may be caught between two worlds, Kara, but we only serve one kingdom." Her voice is more measured than ever. "And we may not be soldiers, but we're loyal. We don't reign below, but we can live like kings here as long as we serve well. And the minute you give your body to someone else before you've fulfilled your obligations, you're turning away from that promise. Every one of us will suffer. Not just you."

I slam my eyes closed, determined not to cry or beg for another answer. As much as I want one, I'm terrified of what it would be. Of the gruesome details she'd be ready to supply, outlining exactly what she means by her last two sentences.

"Kara, darling," she continues, with the sugary reassurance of a mother consoling a child. "Follow your head here, not your heart. The demon blood running through your veins is your greatest gift. Your most valuable asset. And you get to pass it on to ensure that your children are even stronger. And once you do, you'll understand how important you are to all of this. Too important to give in to these other cravings. That means you must put any mortal into the back files for now. After you've served the cause, you're a free woman. You can have whatever affairs you want, where and whenever you want."

"I don't want to have affairs."

I don't scream it, but I yearn to. Even the thought of one affair, let alone many, turns my stomach. I want to *be* with someone. Fall in love with that person. Follow my dreams. I've never known it with such certainty until now.

Mother sighs quietly. "The best way to manage this is to eliminate the temptation, I suppose. I'll talk to the university and have Kane removed for this behavior. There has to be some policy he's violated. He had his hands all over you."

Panic makes me jerk my stare up. "No!"

She lifts an eyebrow in challenge. "What else would you have me do? This doesn't look good. And it's only going to get worse if you two are involved in any way, academically or otherwise. Mark my words. This ends today."

I'm drowning in dread now. I can't hide the pleading in my eyes. Except my mother's returning gaze is far from a life raft. It's more like she's tying a boulder to my ankle, determined to sink my dreams once and for all. And along with it, my spirit.

I swallow hard, already devastated by what I'm about to say. Of all the consequences I envisioned, I never expected this one. But she's leaving me no other choice. And no one will be happier than her to hear it. I'm not fooled for a second by her surface-level sorrow.

"I know this is difficult for you, Kara, but—"

"I'll quit."

Thick silence fills the room. As if the energy between

these walls wasn't unbearable enough, I pick up on the hint of her reaction before I witness it in the sudden relaxing of her shoulders. Relief. Overwhelming relief.

Exactly what I expected.

So why am I still so devastated?

I close my eyes briefly, refusing to let the burning tears behind them escape. "I'll drop out."

"Are you certain that's what you want?"

She's only asking because she already knows the answer. And because she wants me to be clear about mine, no matter how badly my throat already burns with heartbreak.

"Of course it's not what I want, but I won't destroy Maximus's career over this. It's my fault, not his."

But given the chance to do it all again, I wouldn't change a single action or word. Not even as my mother folds her hands neatly in front of her like she's just negotiated a deal with favorable terms.

Checkmate. She wins.

She always wins.

"If that's your choice—and it *is* a choice—then I will accept that."

I linger in the kitchen for a while, make myself some tea, and contemplate sneaking out to the guesthouse. But I don't know what I would say once I got there. Gramps doesn't need the weight of this on him. For his own reasons—not even including how he'd be part of my punishment—he'd probably agree with my mother's position on this matter anyway.

Damn it.

I'm in psychological quarantine here.

The recognition has me shaking my head in utter disbelief, the same way I have at least a hundred times before when contemplating my future. Why haven't my visions for it ever held a glimpse of this path that's been charted for me? Why haven't I latched on to some of it as inevitable and real?

Even when I've accepted it in my mind, it never reached my heart. I don't think it ever will. Not with children. Not with fame and more money. Certainly not with the slow death of my dreams. And not without Maximus . . .

"There you are."

I turn at the sound of Arden's voice, self-assured as ever. I can't muster a greeting or even the words to ask why he's like a stray dog around here lately. Cute but unasked for— and always hanging out where the air smells the tastiest.

Except I'm not in the mood to entertain his presence right now. My whole world has come crashing down in a matter of hours. My heart's been shattered, and I'm pretty sure I'll never be whole again. Maximus doesn't even know we're over. That truth cuts me deep enough to threaten a wave of tears I'm certain Arden would be entirely immune to.

He drapes his jacket on one of the stools and walks over to where I'm standing at the sink. He leans his hip against the counter and looks me over.

"You're upset," he says quietly.

"I don't really want to talk about it." *Not with you. Not with anyone.*

"You don't have to. Your mother brought me up to speed."

I roll my eyes. "So glad her art dealer is up to speed on our family drama."

He doesn't flinch. Just considers me thoughtfully for a long moment.

"I think we both know I'm more than that, Kara."

I blink up at him, my lashes beating in time with my thudding heart as I search his expression for meaning. What I find is too much certainty. Too much bold, presumptive possessiveness. He tilts his head slightly.

"You really have no idea, do you?" He brushes the backs of his fingers against my cheek. "Lucky for you, even your naïveté turns me on."

I jerk away, my eyes narrowing. "Don't touch me."

His nostrils flare, but he drops his hand.

"Your little rebellions are over. No more stalling. And no more dalliances in the professor's office either."

I take another step back, heat prickling my palms. "Excuse me?"

He answers with an unpleasant grimace. "I had a feeling someone might be distracting you. Then I saw you at the fundraiser, and it all made sense. The minute that oaf barreled into our conversation, I knew you two were involved. Neither of you can lie worth a damn."

I fold my arms across my torso as if it can protect me from what Arden already seems to know.

"I have to admit, after I followed you out and saw you pressed against his window four floors up, I was pretty pissed off." He bares his teeth slightly with that admission. "I was even tempted to go find you and straighten things out myself, but I figured I'd let the chips fall as they may. If you broke your vow, I could at least take pleasure in dragging you back home." Something devious flickers across his gaze as he flexes his fingers, fisting and unfisting them. "And by home, I don't mean that adorable little place you've got in the Hills."

Now my mind can't find a single word, spoken or unspoken, of reaction. I'm blank. A void. Buried in a snowdrift of disbelief.

I really can't believe what I'm hearing.

It can't be . . . He can't be . . .

"No," I finally gasp. "You're not—"

"I'm your incubus, Kara. And as much as I would have enjoyed tormenting you on your way to hell, I'll be honest, I'm much more interested in fucking you here on earth."

I open my mouth to speak but again have no words. The shock is still lodged in my throat.

He has the audacity to laugh as he straightens. "Are you so surprised?"

Surprised? I didn't think any more devastation could rain on me today, but I was so very wrong. Perhaps if Maximus hadn't been consuming my thoughts these past two weeks, I would have figured Arden out myself. Seen through to his true intentions. His true purpose.

The purpose he's withheld from me. But not all on his own.

I shake my head, fresh tears burning at the corners of

my eyes. My mother knew. She knew this whole time.

"Wh–Why didn't you just tell me?"

"Your mother thought it'd be better to ease you into it. Play with you a little before pouncing." He smirks, like this is all some fun game that I should be laughing at.

Except I'm sick over it. Sick and disgusted and devastated.

I need to get out of here.

I turn and rush through the house. I'd love to give my mother a piece of my mind, but creating space between Arden and me is more important.

Except he's on my heels, whipping me around to face him once I reach my car.

"Let me go!"

I try to twist away, but he makes it impossible.

"I don't think so, my love."

He presses me against the door of the car, using the length of his body to pin me there, forcing me to feel more of him than I'd ever want. He twines his fingers in my hair and cinches a handful in his grip so any attempt to move away is painful. A whimper escapes before I can help it, but that only feeds the force of his grip. He brings our faces close, so close I can see the fire in his eyes now. Or maybe it's a reflection of my own.

"You're mine now, Kara."

I could scream, but it would do no good. Nobody inside the mansion will lift a finger to help me. This is how it is now. My duty is relegated to becoming this demon's intended bride. His plaything. His property.

My mind is blasted by words now. They tear like a growl from my chest. "I'll *never* be yours."

His answer is an evil smile that makes my stomach roil. "You *are* mine. You're a gift. Made just for me." He brings his lips to my neck, then his mouth to my ear to whisper, "I'd take you now whether you want it or not, but the Valaris are becoming a favorite with the powers that be. So I'll play nice if you will. And if you know what's good for your family, I won't have to tell anyone downstairs about your little slip with the professor."

I'm breathing hard now. My heart's flying. It's taking everything in me not to fight back and claw him off me. He's stronger and inherently more dangerous. I just need to get out of his clutches, even if that means playing nice... for now.

He drags his mouth down my neck. "What do you say, love?"

"I don't want to fight." I barely breathe the words. "Please."

He draws back in degrees, so gradually I'm not convinced he's going to let me leave. But he takes a full step back. Then another. Just like that, he manages to mask the ruthless demon inside him. He slips his hands into his pockets and shoots me an easy smile, as if we have a rapport. How pathetically wrong that is, but I'm not about to point it out.

"Dinner next week, then?"

I respond with a jerky nod, willing to agree to about anything if it gets me out of here faster. I draw in some much-needed air and get into the car. I start the engine with shaking hands, determined to get as far away from him as fast as I can. And as I pull through the gates of the place that will only ever feel like a prison, I make a new vow that I'll never go back.

Never.

Once I'm back on Sunset Boulevard, I drive a few blocks and cut a sharp right onto Beverly. Luckily, there's a spot on the curb beneath one of the big palms lining the municipal park here. I sit for a few minutes in silence until the trembling through my body eases. Once it does, I ring Kell.

She answers with a yawn. Then, "Hey, K-demon. What's up?"

"Where the hell have you been?"

"I've been at the spa all afternoon. I just turned my phone back on. Why? What's going on?"

"Everything." A sob threatens my voice. I deep breathe it away. "Everything is a fucking mess."

"Can you elaborate?" She pauses a second. "Oh, wait. Oh, shit. I see it now. Oh, *Kara*."

"On *Star Passion*?"

"On . . . everywhere. My phone's blowing up."

Shit. When news like this drops, it either falls flat or spreads like wildfire. There is no in-between.

"I should have been more careful."

"Careful? You shouldn't be canoodling with the man in the first place!"

"You canoodle, Kell. Don't lie to me and tell me you haven't messed around."

"That is *none* of your business. I'll admit it when I get caught, which I'm not stupid enough to do, like someone else I know. What's Mom going to say?"

"I already talked to her."

A few empty seconds pass. "And?"

"And I'm dropping out of Alameda. She threatened to get Maximus fired. I had no other choice."

Her heavy sigh speaks to the disappointment—and fear—she's not sharing out loud.

"But it's actually worse than that, if you can believe it." I blink back the tears that have been wanting to release for hours.

"Worse? How can it be worse?"

I restart the car and hook a U-turn back toward Sunset. The move is likely five kinds of illegal, but no way do I want to be even a block closer to the heart of Beverly Hills right now. Kell's question taunts me, despite how I invited it. How could anything get worse? I'm on the brink of losing everything I truly care about.

"They sent someone for me."

Another long silence. Long enough that I know Kell understands the full gravity of it.

"Who is it?"

"He's the art dealer Mom's been pushing on me to get her art collections going. Arden Prieto. He and Mom thought it'd be fun for me to get to know him before they broke the news to me. I guess today's paparazzi fun cut their private party short."

"Fucking hell."

"That sounds about right," I mutter under my breath.

"What are you going to do?"

Her tone is more sympathetic now. I have a pretty good idea why. She'll be next. No matter what happens with me, her fate is sealed just like mine. If only it weren't. If only we could find a way out...

"I need to think. Thankfully I got away from Arden before he could do anything more than a clumsy caveman thing he's probably been rehearsing for years."

She sucks in a shocked breath. "Are you kidding me? He came on to you already?"

"Why wouldn't he? What do you think this is about, Kell? This isn't nineteenth-century courtship. He isn't going to show up with flowers and ask me out for a stroll, hoping for a stolen kiss. He's a fucking demon. He's ready to eat me alive."

"Right. *Shit*. Well, just come home and we'll talk this out."

"I'm not coming home tonight." I hit the gas and speed through a yellow light.

"*Kara*."

"You sound like Mom when you take that tone."

"That's because you need to hear the sound of reason. Do *not* go to see him right now."

It doesn't matter what she says. The second I peeled away from Arden, I knew exactly where I'd go. I have to see Maximus again. Even if it's for the last time.

"Don't worry about it, okay? Things can't possibly get any worse."

"That's one thousand percent untrue. I can think of a dozen scenarios right now that will be worse. For you and for both of us. Now just turn your ass around and come home so we can figure this out."

Home. Her repetition of it brings a deeper sting. My skin prickles with more of the sensation as I recall Arden's take on the subject. At this very moment, he and Mother are probably figuring out how best to enforce his mandate. The writing is on the wall. These are the last few hours of the treasure I once called my own life.

"There's nothing to figure out, Kell. It's follow the rules or break them at this point."

"What's that supposed to mean?" Her voice has taken on a panic-level octave.

I sigh. Exhaustion is tugging at me. Everything about today has been a toxic drain. "I promise you, there's nothing you need to worry about. I'll be home in the morning."

"Kara…"

It's her last plea, I can tell. I have to kill the last of her hope and buy a shred of her trust.

"Just do me one favor. Don't tell Mom."

She huffs. "Damn you, Kara. Fine. Just don't do anything stupid."

CHAPTER 22

Kara

"**D**ON'T DO ANYTHING STUPID," I mutter to myself.

The whole drive here, I never considered turning around. Not once. The magnetic force that exists between Maximus and me seems stronger than ever, stretching across the city, bringing me here to his doorstep.

The day has melted into night, making the energy floating on the air a little quieter. The night always brings a kind of peace with it, but deep in my bones, I know Maximus is the only chance I have at peace. I want to see him so much it hurts.

I can hear the low, gentle beat beneath a jazz-blues instrumental on the other side of his apartment door. Only hours have passed since I left him at the bookstore. So much has changed since then . . .

I finally force myself to knock and step back. A few seconds later, he's there, swinging the door open. His sudden presence is like a gust of wind that threatens to knock me over. But I hold my ground and steady myself from the impact of being this close.

His eyes are dark in this light, his expression impassive. He's not angry. He's not anything. Just still and quiet. He takes up the doorway, his upper body tense as he grips the edges. It's the only hint that my being here is affecting him at all.

Still, seeing him is a relief, even if he looks like he's ready to tear the door off the hinges.

"Aren't you going to say anything to me?" I hate the way my voice breaks.

His silence is killing me, eating away at the last of my hope.

He looks down at the floor. "I'm afraid if I say the wrong thing, you'll leave." He's quiet, like he's straining to get the words out.

I let go of the breath I've been holding but somehow resist the fierce urge to throw myself through this invisible wall between us, straight into his arms. Because I don't think the electricity between our bodies will be enough this time.

"I'm sorry... I'm sorry I pushed you."

"You pushed me *away*." He looks up. The dark blue rings around his eyes intensify. "You keep pushing me away. That's a lot worse."

"I'm sorry for that too." The last word gets caught in my throat. The emotion of today returns full force. I swallow hard, trying my best to hold it back. "And I'm sorry for dragging you into my life. You didn't ask for any of this.

I've just never felt this way about someone before. I should have kept it to myself. I shouldn't have pushed so hard for something more."

He closes his eyes. "Kara."

"I can't take it back now. I can't undo this. And I can't pretend like I don't want to be with you when you're the only person in my life I've ever thought about breaking the rules for." Hot tears roll down my cheeks. I drag in a painful breath and force myself to go on. "With you, I'm me. Even if I can't show you everything, I feel like you see *me*. And I don't want to lose that."

I choke through a sob. The dam is breaking. I can barely see through the tears.

"I don't know how much time I have left here, Maximus. All I know is that I want to spend it with you."

The stone column of his figure softens when he lets go of the door and crosses the threshold. "Come here," he murmurs before lifting me into his arms.

I curl into his chest as he carries me inside. He kicks the door closed. I don't bother looking around. All I can do is cinch my arms around his neck and burrow myself tighter against him. As close as I can get. Even as the unrelenting sobs are ripping me apart on the inside.

He hushes me softly and lowers us onto the couch. I'm curled up on his lap, my arms locked around him, afraid to move. I never want to let go. I wish I never had to ...

I shudder through another stab of emotion. Everything is bubbling over. Not just from today. From forever. My whole life. Every dream I ever held on to, hoping for a different outcome. A better future. No dream has ever been as perfect as this one.

"I don't want to lose you," I whisper.

"You're not going to lose me," he says, his voice deep and soothing.

I can almost pretend to believe him when he's skimming his hands across my back and down my arms. Brushing my tears away. Whispering reassurances against my ear.

But the inevitable truth is seared into me, so painful and real it overwhelms his sweet promises, no matter how badly I want to hear them.

"You don't understand. They'll come for me."

"They'll have to get through me first, Kara."

I shake my head, saturating more of his shirt with my tears. "It won't matter."

"If I make this my fight, it will. I'm pretty sure I'm a lot stronger than they are."

I collect myself enough to look up at him. The fresh determination in his stare shouldn't give me hope, but it does.

"And this *is* my fight," he adds.

Except he doesn't know what he's up against. He might be stronger. In fact, I know he is. But he doesn't have the advantage of knowing the enemy as well as I do. And I can't tell him. Not when my days are numbered anyway.

I glance down at the dark smudges on his shirt. "I made a mess of your shirt." I wipe frantically at my eyes. As miserable as I am, I wish he wasn't seeing me like this. I can't imagine how terrible I must look.

He leans forward, loosening my hold on him so he can tug the garment over his head and toss it aside.

"There. Problem solved."

His playful grin is already doing something to my insides. When he tucks me back against him, the full contact has my head spinning. Makes me wonder what it might be like with nothing between us. Just our bodies.

I bite my lip, unable to keep myself from tracing the contours of his muscled chest and abdomen with my gaze and my fingertips. Literature professors aren't supposed to look like this. It's unfair to the entire student body.

"You're really hot, you know that?"

"Thanks," he says with a laugh.

"You know how many girls at Alameda would kill to see what Professor Maximus looks like under his sweater-vest?"

"Hmm. How many?"

"Probably all of them. Funny thing, it's not even my favorite thing about you."

I meet his eyes. Something glimmers there. Warmth. Happiness. I don't have to strain to sense it. Pressed this close, everything he's feeling radiates right into me. A beam of sunshine through a cloudless sky.

He brushes his thumb over my cheek tenderly. "What's your favorite thing about me, then?"

I smile, already enjoying the list my mind is making. All of my favorite things . . .

"The way you read the cantos. Like you forget other people are in the room." I cover his hand with mine. "The way you touch me, like I'm ..."

"Like what?"

I close my eyes and rest my cheek against his chest. "Like I'm precious to you."

"You are. You should know that by now."

His heart and the way it speeds up when we're this close is a steady reminder of the sentiment.

I take in a deep breath, grateful how the pain in my chest is slowly receding. The simple gift of his presence is pushing the misery away little by little. Even if it all comes back tomorrow, I have this right now. This one perfect moment with him.

Our fingers hook and thread.

"Your turn," I finally say.

"My turn?"

"You have to tell me your favorite things about me."

He blows out a long breath. "Well ... That's a long list. You don't need me to tell you how brilliant you are, but I'll put it at the top. We could put everything else aside, and that alone would knock me to my knees."

I feel my cheeks warm at the compliment. I'm tempted to remind him about the time he tried to cut me from his class for my supposed shortcomings, but I resist. I knew better anyway.

"You surprise me ... all the time," he continues. "I never know what's going to come out of your mouth."

I laugh. "That's probably not always a good thing."

"At least it's real. You're real."

I sigh ... relax into him a little more ... wonder how it's

possible to be this content with someone else. I'm happier than I can ever remember being, even in the wake of all that's gone wrong today.

Everything . . .

But I refuse to think about that. Not now.

"What else?"

"Are you fishing for compliments?"

I smile. "You said it was a long list. I'm just curious."

"It's just a hundred other things that make you unfairly perfect. Your sexy little body. Your smile." He touches my chin, lifting my gaze to his. "And I'm kind of a fan of the way your eyes light up like a forest fire."

I bite my lip, unsure how to feel about that. I should be ashamed of the eerie abnormality, but what if I didn't need to be?

"How does that work anyway?" He murmurs it like it's a secret between us.

It could be.

I lift my shoulder and release my lip, feeling brave. "It's genetic."

He pauses. "Your mother too?"

"All of us. Well, not—"

"Not your grandfather."

I shake my head. "No." But I don't want to talk about that either. I want to talk about us. The way Maximus stimulates my mind and everything else. The way he flips every switch on my body. My thoughts race over our more intimate memories, making my skin heat. "It happens when I'm feeling things strongly. Usually when I'm really pissed off. And I guess when I'm...aroused." Suddenly shy, I look down. "The other night...I didn't realize that would happen. That's why I left so fast," I add quietly. "I don't have that much experience, if you couldn't tell."

He doesn't say anything at first. Every second that goes by, I worry I've said too much, until I can't take the silence anymore and break it.

"Does that bother you?" I ask, looking up.

His gaze intensifies. My attraction to him skyrockets when those cobalt rings in his irises are more defined. "Why would it bother me?"

"I guess it's one of those things people hype up to be more of a big deal than it is."

A corner of his mouth quirks up. "Call me a romantic, but it seems like a big deal to me. You trusting someone that much."

Light rain pelts the windows. I can hardly hear it over the rush of blood in my ears. My heart is beating wildly thanks to the intimate turn of this conversation. This slow dance of showing him pieces of me. Always afraid of revealing too much. More frightened than ever that I'll never have a chance to be with him. To make this real.

"I trust *you*." I flatten my palm over his heart. The tightness in my chest is back, except now it's made of longing. Anticipation. Hope.

How do I tell him all that? I brave a look into his eyes, only to be met with their heart-shattering intensity. Before I can formulate the right words, he sweeps his lips over mine. Tenderly. Maddeningly tentative. I pull myself higher, press myself closer, needing the contact to match the wild need building in me.

Except when I do, he brings his hands to my face, keeping me from going deeper. Tasting more. Taking more.

He pulls back and takes a couple of short breaths. "You should get some rest."

I frown. "Why?"

"Because it's been a heavy day, Kara, and it's late. You must be exhausted."

I am, of course. But I'm not. My heart is going a million miles an hour. Every nerve ending is hypercharged to respond to his touch. No way could I sleep right now.

Still, he's lifting me into his arms again like all this crying has somehow rendered my legs useless. But I don't mind the effort he goes to, walking me to the edge of his bed in the studio and lowering me gently to my feet.

"You can sleep here, all right? I'll take the couch."

He bends to kiss me again. A swift, chaste kiss that's a fraction of what I need it to be. I chase it, but he's moving away too fast.

Meanwhile the ache in my chest is spreading everywhere. Fire under my skin. A frantic pulse so fierce and so fast, I can hardly breathe. I need more than a kiss. I need his hands on me. I need to feel this connection between us in every possible way.

I'm done denying I can walk through this life without having it.

He's moving around the living room, tossing throw pillows off the couch. His face is so crunched in concentration, one might think he was in the midst of solving a complex equation. The equation is simpler than he realizes.

Me plus him. Not a shred of anything else. Not even the snug jeans that are giving his own arousal away.

I slip off my shoes and tug on the string that's holding my wrap dress in place. That's all it takes for it to loosen and slip off me. He can't possibly hear the flimsy fabric fall to the floor, but he looks up just then.

I don't think he's even breathing.

"Kara."

My name has never sounded like such torture. It might as well be a dying plea on his lips.

Except he's mine. My last wish.

My hero.

"Come here," I say.

His chest moves under labored breaths. Finally he takes a few steps closer, slowly, stopping several feet away. He swallows hard and takes me in, from my naked toes to my bare breasts, lingering on the lacy black panties I'd have stripped off too if I didn't want to save the task for him.

"I want to be with you, Maximus."

He tears his gaze away with a muttered curse.

"You said you wanted all of me."

"I do. God, I do." He slams his eyes closed and rakes a hand through his hair roughly.

"Just come here," I beg.

"If I touch you right now, this is over. I can't... I'm strong, but I'm not that strong."

"You don't need to be. We want the same thing."

He won't move. Won't open his eyes. So I go to him.

"Maximus," I whisper. "Look at me. Feel me."

Then we're chest to chest. He releases a jagged exhale and opens his eyes, looking every bit as overwhelmed as I feel.

"Just kiss me."

A long moment passes. He searches my eyes, feathers a soft touch over my lips. He looks me over with wild wonder, like maybe he can't believe I'm real.

And when he finally lowers, our mouths collide in a desperate rush. He kisses me like he might die if he doesn't. Or maybe that's the reflection from my own soul. My own agonized spirit. Every inch of my anxious body. I'm a mass of awakening and awareness, of need and urgency, of lust and longing. Never have I been drenched in a feeling like this. Already it's threatening to consume me.

He folds his arms around me and binds us tightly, lifting me off my toes. We're sharing breaths. And heat. And connection. So many chains of connection . . . but not nearly enough.

He moans my name. It's a desperate sound that reflects my own thinning patience. My own raw desire and commitment to fulfilling it. He captures my face and holds my gaze for another long moment.

"Are you sure?"

"I'm sure," I promise.

"We have time," he whispers.

"No, we don't."

CHAPTER 23

MAXIMUS

I BELIEVE HER. EVEN the last conviction she utters, with all three of the words threatened by the sob she's struggling to hold in. It's not the first time that's happened tonight, but this moment is different—in the best and worst ways.

This time, I feel her anguish too.

It's not telepathy or sorcery or any of the crazy reality twists we've experienced together before. Right now, in this moment of our shared breaths and fitted bodies, it comes down to simple human chemistry. Her tremors are mine. Her heartbeats too. That means all her fear and despair are mine too.

And every desperate drop of her lust...

Especially that. It's thick smoke in my blood, clinging tar along my limbs. As our gazes meet again, the heat in her eyes confirms her own losing battle with it. And her confirmation of how we're going to get rid of it. The only way.

By searing it off with a fire we can't fight anymore. A passion we can't control.

No. Not *can't*. I just *won't*.

Not now. Not even after today, when every valid objection I had to this was justified by a paparazzi invasion to rival a biblical locust swarm. Her family. Her unique place in that family. My job and all the ways this relationship continues to threaten it.

But all the dread that had churned in my head couldn't touch the fear of watching her flee from me. An intensity of feeling trumped only by the elation of now. The wonder of holding her like this, as rain beats at the windows and a flash of lightning flares through the room. Blue-silver light leaps across the air, illuminating the burnished nudity of the gorgeous creature in my arms. For an incredible moment, she's an angel of brilliance and boldness. Her gaze is like starfire, full of wonder that's born of innocence.

Innocence she's giving to me. Only me...

And I refuse to deny how I feel about that. To myself or to her. The truth is that I more than want it. I pledge to deserve it. To cherish the gift she can only give once.

I make that silent vow with a soft mesh of our lips first, using the moment to coax her body higher against mine. As soon as she spreads her thighs and locks them around my waist, I settle their apex along the burgeoning bulge of mine.

"You feel...so good," I murmur once we've pulled back to catch our breaths. As soon as she responds with an approving sigh, I go on. "And I'm going to make all of it good for you, beautiful."

"Maximus." Every syllable is a perfect whisper, curling through me more thoroughly than her gentle fingers in my hair. "I need you to promise me something."

"I'll promise you anything," I husk. "You know that."

She tightens her twists, prickling my scalp in all the best ways. "Promise me you won't hold anything back."

The plea cuts through my haze of desire just enough to make me tense and really think about that. Not holding anything back. In every fantasy I've ever had about taking her this way, I've done just that. But deep down, I knew if it came to this—having her in my arms, ready to give me everything—I couldn't unleash all of that onto her.

I force myself to relax and brush a gentle kiss across her lips. "How about you let me drive, little temptress."

A frown mars her brow. "All of me for all of you. That's how this works. You don't have to be gentle with me."

"The fuck I won't be gentle."

Her lips purse. "We'll see about that."

"The fuck we'll see ab—"

She cuts me off by ramming her mouth against mine. Fiercely. Flawlessly. Just like that, the woman has stolen my breath again. I deal with it by taking hers. In the moment I plunge my lips back across hers, a new flash of lightning spears the room. Every cell of my blood feels jolted by the same energy. It sizzles between our mouths, arcing and sparking and feeding us. Never have I wanted a kiss to continue and end in the same moment.

I linger for a while, reveling in how Kara's silken groan resonates through my system, before dragging my mouth free. I look away long enough to make sure I get us across the room and onto the bed. Those few seconds are all I can take without her filling my vision. As soon as I sweep her down onto my rumpled sheets and blankets, I drink her in again. No. I gorge my gaze on the glory of her.

She's graceful curves and sensual shadows.

Sultry darkness and passionate light.

Blatant need and open desire.

But most of all, she's mine.

I'm going to make that true, in every sense of the word. The promise floods my veins, coils my tendons, pushes at every fiber of my muscles. It's a physical force like nothing I've ever known.

She's still and sweet and impossibly stunning, her hair splayed on the pillows like dark wings, her face alive with rising lust. I watch, spellbound, as that expression intensifies...with every inch I tug at the soft lace of her panties. Slowly. *Slowly.* My fingers hardly understand the command from my brain, especially as she fists the sheets and hitches her hips a little higher.

"*Please*," she rasps.

I flare my nostrils, hoping to convey a wordless request for patience. Stupid move because my senses are widened to more of her scent, a blend of smoky honey and aroused spices that makes me dizzy with desire. Who's running out of patience now?

Somehow I manage to grate, "We'll get there, beautiful. Let me treasure you."

And what riches she does have for me. Unlike the

moments we stole in my office, I take the time to savor the decadent glory of her. All of her. I start at her feet as I slip the black lace totally free from her body. After kissing each of her delicate, red-polished toes, I slide my hands along the sleek curves of her legs. When I arrive at their crux, I roam my fingertips inward. She's already slick there, her channel welcoming my touch like a portal to secret wonders.

Wonders she's finally giving to me.

And the secrets? Perhaps now she'll trust me enough to impart those too. In return, I'll give her all of mine. All of *me*.

She bows into my touch with an achy whimper.

It's time.

I'm past ready.

And I know, as I raise my head to stare deep into her eyes again, that she is too.

It's agony to look away from those soft and smoky depths, but the torment speeds up my reach for the nightstand. I've barely begun the stretch when Kara closes her hand around my wrist. The strength in her hold doesn't surprise me anymore. The urgency of it does.

Before I can hike one brow, let alone both, she says, "We don't need one of those."

I draw breath for the start of a safe sex lecture when she cuts in.

"I want this the way it's meant to be. With nothing between us." She palms my jaw. "*Nothing*."

I clear my throat. "Kara—"

"You can't give me anything. Just…take my word, okay? It's impossible. Not anything. Not a disease, not an infection, and certainly not a baby."

The sorrow that threads her last claim—and the conviction with which I believe her—is enough to have me forgetting the nightstand. Her fingers dig into my beard. With her other hand, she reaches for the snap on my jeans and tugs the zipper down. It's practically torture. My cock is hot and heavy, forcing us both to wrestle it free from the denim.

But I'm just eager to strip the rest of what's between us, to get more of her skin against my skin, so I finish the task by pushing off the bed and hurriedly shucking my jeans. While rising back up, I hurl the pants against the wall. I don't even care that they hit hard enough to chip the corners of a few bricks.

But then...I freeze. And linger there a moment too long, just staring in awe. Kara's writhing harder against the sheet, her hands restless over the flesh I'm certain I could spend the rest of my life worshiping. Starting with tonight...

"Open up for me, Kara."

With a soft sigh, she does. And at once, I'm damn near reborn.

Everything about the sight, and the simplicity of her act, reaffirms how very ready she is for this. For me.

I'm lured down over her once more. I scoop her hands beneath mine, meshing our fingers and locking our palms, giving her the breadth of my being. I wish I could find the right words to show her every part of me that she's unlocked. Every secret she's made safe. Even the ones I've hidden in deep shadows. The frightening things. The dangerous things.

They don't frighten me anymore.

They pulse through me like the rain that's now become a storm. Flashing more lightning across the air. Bursts that are echoed in my blood, even pounding beneath my skin, as I mold more of my body against Kara's. Feeding from her fire.

"Now. I need to feel you now." Her plea weaves through me like dark, devastating magic.

I give in to it and reach between us.

And then I'm sinking.

Into her fire. Into the storm. Fused to her desire. Compelled by the perfect connection of her ... *us.*

So deep.

Need to be ... so deep ...

But I have to get there slowly, goddammit.

Between one thrust and the next, I remember the self-control I was so committed to before I got inside her. I'm the first man to take her like this. She's so small and brave, having to accommodate *me.*

And nothing about me has ever been average. Right now, it's not a bragging right. It's a circumstance I force into the forefront of my thoughts, no matter how thoroughly my body protests the point. Everything's working beyond my control. I'm so full and hot, compelled to push in farther.

Farther ...

I'm only halfway when she sucks in a sharp breath.

Full stop. I freeze and force my head up. "Kara ... I'm sorry." The words rush from me between brutal breaths. My chest is pumping, smashing into her erect, succulent nipples—which does nothing to help the craving to slam into her fully. "I know I'm—"

"You are." She punctuates the acknowledgment with a low moan and a catlike arch beneath me. "You're also . . . not deep enough."

The surety in those words is a rush of thunder in my lungs. Voltage in my veins. A potent antidote to all my paralyzing worry over hurting her.

"Stop holding back," she murmurs. "I said all of you. I *meant* it."

I can barely meet the demand when she shifts instead. Lifting her legs higher, wrapping her thighs tighter. Giving herself the purchase to pull herself up the very moment I can no longer hold anything back. I drive forward . . . until every inch of my erection is fully seated inside her.

That high cry that emerges from her becomes an electrode of awareness snapped into the right port of my brain at just the right time. So this is what she means by *deep enough.*

"Holy *hell.*" A blur of cruder language washes across my brain. None of it sums up the fire she's setting to my cock . . . The flames she's spreading everywhere through me . . .

She presses a featherlight kiss to my neck. "You stole my line."

I can feel her smile against my skin, but I'm past levity. Being this deep in her feels like life or death. Maybe both. I don't really care which, as long as we see it through. I draw in a shaky breath, taking more of her heavenly scent into me as I do. My angel. My sweet heaven.

"And you've stolen my soul."

Our gazes lock again. She gives me a look I don't know how to interpret, except for the liquid heat in her eyes that I'm sure is made of pure desire. I don't stop to figure the rest out. Because right now, it doesn't matter.

Right now, I can't stop.

I'm pressure and passion and tension.

Fever and flames and obsession.

I'm wrapped in her heat, plunging to the farthest cushions inside her until all I crave is more.

Still, I go deeper.

Even as wind howls at the walls and rain sheets the windows.

Harder.

As all the lights flicker, sputter, and then darken completely.

Farther.

As a plummeting tree branch slams against my window before crashing onto the ground below. Then another.

I barely notice. Neither does Kara. She clings like I'm *her* tree branch, scoring my shoulders with her hold and gouging my back with her heels. Her head is flung back, and her mouth is wide as she gathers air in harsh, hoarse breaths. And her eyes...

Her eyes might just turn me into a pyromaniac.

Their flames, whorling faster and faster around her irises, have me thrusting with deeper force. Driving into her like a man possessed. Maybe I am. My lust is futile without her fulfillment. My blood is just water without her fire.

"Maximus."

My world is consumed by the sexual smoke of her voice.

She's not pleading this time. She's calling me. Compelling me. The sound of my name on her lips is a raw, sexual sibilance, wrapping me tighter than the sweet tunnel of her perfect core.

"Kara." I speak it back as complete worship. Transcendent praise. "Are you good?"

I'm pretty sure of the answer already, but a weirdly vain part of me wants to hear her say the words.

"So . . . damn . . . good."

The words do me in even more. "Worth the wait," I whisper back.

"You're worth all of it. Everything—" Her own throaty cry is her interruption. "Oh . . . you . . . you're making me—"

"Yes." I husk it into her neck, already feeling the rhythmic shock waves taking over more and more of her shuddering frame. "Let it go, Kara. Give me everything."

Her breath stops.

Her stare combusts.

Just before her scream decimates the air. And her body demands *my* climax.

"Fuck!" The second I steal to expel the word is all I get before the heat hits, racing to my center like an ignited bomb fuse. I go off with similar force just as a crack of thunder seems to break open the whole sky over the city.

I empty all I am into her, chasing completion while praying for any way to draw out the pleasure. Wishing there was a way to extend this single incredible moment between us that's made up of all the others. All the longing that's been building up inside me since the day I met her.

I don't stop.

Because she hasn't.

Her climax is a fascinating marathon to behold, peppered with her dazed smiles, delighted laughs, and moans that will haunt me every night I have to spend without her. It goes on and on, and with every new phase, I learn I've got even more to give her. Not just because of the extra things my body is suddenly capable of. It's all the other things she's bringing out of me. All my willing smiles and laughter. My unending passion and desire...

And astonishment.

Because I've never experienced anything like this. Any*one* like this.

For all my lust-fueled prayers for this bliss to never end, I'm stunned by the completion I feel when it does. Everything—my restlessness, my anger, my confusion— simply melts with the quieting storm, like the gods spinning up the weather are finally sated too. They've found their way to some kind of peace...and so have I.

My heart is still pounding out uneven beats when Kara and I unpeel from each other and I collapse to my back next to her. Little tremors rack her between her heavy exhales. As I piece my brain back together, I remember exactly what we've just done. I should be taking care of her better than this.

I get up, walk to the bathroom, and return with a warm cloth.

She follows my journey with her heavy-lidded gaze. "What are you doing?"

"Cleaning you up." I settle against the mattress and lift her knee to open her to me. "Having nothing between us can get messy."

I run the cloth softly over her intimate flesh, though it takes tamping down a fresh flare of lust. *Christ.* That's even before she starts undulating beneath my touch, humming softly as I stroke all her sweetest places. I have little doubt I could devote hours to the study of her body, taking mental notes of what will give her the most pleasure. Knowing every inch of her better than anyone ever will.

I flicker my gaze to hers, finding her no less rapt. I hook-shot the cloth across the room, where it lands in the hamper. My thoughts are already swimming toward all the ways I can have her next. And when exactly that can be. How soon is too soon?

Pump the brakes, Kane.

If I wasn't fully obsessed with her before, I'm a lost cause now. That should worry me, but in this moment, I don't even care. All I care about is that she's in my bed, looking blissed out and well loved.

I do a double take when she captures her full bottom lip between her teeth, brighter glimmers igniting in her eyes.

"What is it?" I murmur, tracing my fingertips over her raised knee.

"I feel…" She lets go of a little sigh. "I feel so many things right now."

I answer with a small smile. "I can relate."

She blinks, more brilliant flecks flaring in her big irises. "You can?"

"Why does that surprise you?"

"Well... you knew what to expect." She blushes.

It's the most beautiful sight I've ever seen. A sound rumbles from the center of my chest. Not a laugh, but a weight lifting free. "Kara Valari, no experience in my life has equaled that of you." I feather tiny circles down her slender calves. "Tell me. What are you feeling right now?"

She rests her palm over her stomach and inches lower. "I feel... empty. Without you."

I swallow over my suddenly dry throat. If she had any idea how much I'd like to rectify that... All night long. Every night. I never want her to leave my bed.

"I also feel like I could stay here forever as long as you were touching me." She closes her eyes sleepily before opening them again to half-mast.

"I think you just read my mind."

She smiles. "When we were together, I felt you... so strongly." She reaches out and links our fingers lazily. "Like everything you were feeling flowed right into me, mixing with all these new sensations my brain could hardly keep up with. Usually when I feel you... you're *you*. And I'm still me. I can separate the two. This was different... like everything between us wove together and became something new. Something that was just... *us*."

I take in a half breath. If the act of making love to her tonight wasn't already imprinting itself on my brain as the best night of my life, I'm certain her words just now would solidify it.

I manage a response, my voice rough with new emotion. "Kara, you know I meant it, right? I've never experienced anything like this." I end the confession with a soft press of lips to her hand. I move higher, nuzzling up her arm until reaching her sweet mouth once more.

She weaves her delicate arms around me as I settle alongside her. All I can do is gaze into her eyes, letting myself get lost there. Because she's everything to me right now. *Everything.*

"Is it crazy that I want you again?" she whispers.

I shake my head. "We just had a hit of something really good. So intensely good, it's normal to never want it to end. Trust me, I'm there too."

She widens her eyes with the possibility.

I smile and kiss her gently. "Not yet. You need to rest. I'm serious this time. We have tomorrow and the next day—"

She presses her fingers to my lips, stopping my vow for forever with her. Fresh worry pinches her beautiful features. "Will you stay here with me? Just for now?"

The rough edges of her whisper make my heart squeeze tighter. "Of course I will." I press a kiss into her forehead. "I promise."

"You won't leave?"

"No." I cage her against me a little tighter, enjoying the perfect press of our bodies once more. "I'll always be here."

CHAPTER 24

Kara

I FELL ASLEEP IN Maximus's bed last night, cocooned by his strength and his heat, my limbs tangled with his, like extra anchors, keeping the inevitable storm from tearing us apart. For a few wonderful, peaceful hours, I could believe that.

I know now the storm was only stalled. And fire is in the forecast today.

I was awakened by my heart-stopping fear of it, launched into consciousness again in the early morning hours of this deceivingly peaceful Sunday.

Maximus is still asleep as I rise and creep quietly toward the picture window. The city is gray-blue before the dawn, city lights still blinking across the horizon. A few delivery trucks rumble up and down the shadowed streets, their headlights swinging around corners and into alleyways.

For once—maybe the first time in my life—I dread the sun. With it comes a day full of terrifying unknowns.

What happens now?

Does anyone even know what I've done?

Have I set off some cosmic alarm system that's got the powers that be meeting even now to decide my fate? If so, what will that fate be?

Or . . . is there an easier fix here? Do I just tell everyone I needed time to think, and return home like I've simply been driving around all night? When Arden comes to take me, can I fake my way out of all this? Pretend he's the first who's ever been inside me?

I shudder from head to toe. My stomach lurches, begging to eject its contents along with the concept repelled by my mind.

Pretending away Maximus would be like banishing the best parts of myself. But soon—too damn soon now—I'll have to do exactly that.

I wrap my arms around my middle and bring my cheek to my shoulder, covered now with the soft T-shirt Maximus shed in the living room last night. After everything that's happened between us, the fear of having to say goodbye to him once and for all has grown new thorns. Every second, the dread tightens its coil around my heart and pierces new wounds into my soul.

I'll have to leave soon. Arden will come. Whether guided by an underworld alert beacon or his own frightening cunning, he'll figure things out and find me. When he does, all the fires in hell won't come close to the pain of losing Maximus. Add in the agony of walking away from him on the arm of another. I suppress another shudder.

I can't even approach the idea of asking him to wait until I'm free again. What male, in this realm or any other, would willingly sign up for that humiliation?

Not that I'll have a chance to get that far with the explanation.

I have to figure out how much of the truth to leave him with. For all my hesitations and sidestepping, I feel flayed open after a night in his bed. It's difficult—damn near impossible—to think straight right now.

We've shared so much already... Pieces of my soul I'd never give anyone else. I'll never forget the magic of what our bodies can do. The vulnerability of those precious moments. The trust in them. Now, suddenly, keeping the rest from him seems more unfair than ever.

I'm so confused. So scared.

Maybe he'll see me differently once he knows everything. Maybe he'll feel betrayed by all my secrets. But maybe he'll keep looking at me the way he does now, like he'd walk through fire for me. Like I'm the piece he's always been missing, the way he's been mine.

I glance down at the street directly below. The sidewalks are littered with debris from the storm last night. People pass by every once in a while. Probably straggling home after a wild Saturday night. None of them loiter too long. That means, thankfully, that none of the paparazzi have figured out Maximus's whereabouts yet. Maybe the story is already old news and people are forgetting about his involvement with the one Valari who's tried so hard to be forgettable.

I close my eyes and rest my forehead against the glass.

If only those photos had never been snapped to begin with. Everything would be different. We'd have more time... Time is the one thing I'd pay nearly any price to have more of right now.

There's a sharp knock on the door.

I jolt and slam a hand to my chest, where my heart bangs frantically against my ribs. I glance toward the corner of the studio, where Maximus groans into his pillow. He's still half asleep. A rush of hope joins the terror in my pulse. Maybe, if I submit swiftly and quietly to Arden, Maximus will slumber right through this. Maybe he'll only think of me as the flaky student who screwed him and dropped out on him instead of the cruel creature who left him with the male she was really promised to.

A second knock. Louder. Harsher.

I jump again but swallow hard and move slowly to the door. On my way, I keep the tears down by telling myself to remember the small details of everything I pass. Books in bookcases, bracketed by natural stone bookends. Between them, framed pictures. One of Maximus and Jesse on the beach. Another of Maximus with Reg from the store and a pretty woman I've never met. The striations of blond wood between the darker slats beneath my feet.

All the little things... that will be the details of my only happy thoughts from now on.

With a shaky hand, I turn the handle and open the door a fraction.

It's... *Who is this guy?*

The man greets me with a curious smile, tilting his head

to the side as if he expects me to recognize him any second. But I don't. I'm certain I'd remember him. He's dressed well, if a little strangely for an early Sunday morning, in a dusty beige suit. His eyes are a deep ocean blue, mesmerizing me from under his straw fedora. His overgrown copper hair is tucked behind his ears, a glimmering contrast to the grays that dominate his trimmed goatee.

Hope blooms around my racing heart. Maybe he hasn't come for me. Still, he doesn't look like someone who'd be in Maximus's close circle, which, as far as I can tell, is rather small.

"Well, hello there," he drawls.

"Uhhh...hi."

"And who might you be?" His voice is textured and deep, but it has a lightness to it too, like he expects to burst into laughter at any moment. The boyish smirk accentuates the lines around his eyes and mouth.

His entire presence, so full of confidence but contradictions, is beyond disarming. I finally overcome my curiosity to manage an answer.

"I'm Kara."

"Kara." He lifts an eyebrow before giving me a quick once-over. "Hmm. That's lovely. You're very nice."

I cross my arms over my chest. He chuckles softly.

"Don't worry. It's just a compliment. My wife keeps me on a tight leash these days. Besides, I came to see Maximus. Is he home?"

I blink a few times. "Oh." I open the door wider and let him pass through.

He saunters in with a casual air about him that makes me wonder if he's been here before—or several times before.

I remember that Maximus is still sleeping just as he proves otherwise and sits up in the bed. His hair is mussed and his eyes are tired, but they're just as striking as ever. I allow myself to enjoy the visual of his chiseled chest above the sheet he knots around his waist before he marches toward us. Except he doesn't look too thrilled with our sudden company.

"Who are you, and what are you doing in my apartment?"

Oh shit.

My heart beats up my ribs again. If Maximus doesn't know this man, who is he? He said he wasn't here for me. I believed him. For some reason, I still do . . .

The man tucks his hands into his pockets, making no move to leave. "My, my, my, Maximus Kane. How you've grown."

I feel the shift on the air as Maximus's alarm twists into confusion. It takes over his face, freezing his bold features. "Excuse me?"

"You . . . don't remember me?"

"Should I?"

The man shakes his head again, some of his good humor fading. Already, I pick up on the disappointment he's fighting to hide.

"My dear brother must have tinkered with your memories." He blows out a tense breath through his nose. "Of course he did. It doesn't matter." He waves his hand gracefully. "Not right now, at least. We can resolve that, given a little time."

But Maximus isn't reassured. "You need to leave," he growls.

The man ignores him. Blatantly. He takes off his hat and walks toward the window I'd occupied moments ago. "Aren't you curious about who I am?"

"If you think we know each other, you must be a lunatic off the street, because I've never seen you before in my life. This is your last chance. Get the hell out, or I'll remove you myself."

The man laughs at that, shooting his deep-blue gaze back to Maximus. "I don't think so."

Maximus flares his nostrils at the challenge. I can sense he's ready to snap into action seconds before he does, crossing the distance to this strange visitor. The man doesn't recoil. His expression doesn't change. He barely moves except to raise his hand when Maximus is a mere inch away.

I scream when Maximus is launched backward so hard and fast that the couch he lands on is also sent several feet back. He's breathing hard now. When he looks over to me, we share a silent exchange. *What the hell just happened?*

"How did you ..."

Maximus's voice is barely a whisper, but the man hears it.

"Because I'm a god. That's how."

Maximus grips the couch cushion and leans forward. His gaze is flared. His chest is still heaving.

The stranger drops into a leather chair, crosses his legs,

and rests his chin on his fist. "We have a bit in common, you and I. Incomparable strength. The ability to miraculously heal." A soft smile returns. "And calling forth the weather with our passions, it would seem."

"The weather."

The man rubs his fingers together absently. Tiny bursts of electricity snap from them. He seems oblivious to the anomaly, his attention instead pulled to the storm-battered trees lining the front of the apartment complex.

"That was quite the storm you whipped up last night, my boy. Thank goodness. Otherwise I might have never found you." His gaze lands on me next. "Must have been quite a night."

I bite my lip, which does nothing to stop the flush creeping up my cheeks. He has no idea...

"Who. Are. You?" Maximus grits it out, straightening himself to standing once more.

The man twirls his hat on his knee. "Well, you could call me *Dad*. But seeing as you have no memory of me, maybe we can start with Zeus. Though the people around here look at me a little strangely when I introduce myself that way. How about Z? That has a modern ring to it." His smile broadens. "Yeah. I think I like the sound of that."

Maximus pales. Fists and unfists his hands anxiously. Shakes his head but says nothing. He simply stares at the man in stunned silence. I'm not even sure he realizes what's happening. The total truth that he's just been hit with. That this stranger *isn't* a stranger at all. Moreover, that he's not only Maximus's father. He's precisely who he proclaims to be.

And I believe him. With every molecule of my being, I believe him—not just because I have the most accurate bullshit detector in the room. Because, more importantly, it explains everything. Everything I was too lovestruck and scared to piece together before.

Maximus is the son of Zeus.

Zeus.

The king of gods. Walking among men. In Los Angeles.

And right now, sitting in Maximus Kane's living room.

"Holy shit," I mumble.

Maximus shoots me an exasperated look. "You believe this horseshit?"

One second into my own stunned silence, and I'm convinced he knows I do.

"Maximus—"

"Kara! Oh, come on!"

"It makes sense."

I take a step closer, sensing Z doesn't intend to do us any harm unless he's attacked. In which case, he can obviously hold his own.

"Your strength," I murmur, taking Maximus's hand. "Your mental stamina... Hell, your stature." And all the other little things that should have tipped me off, had they been slightly more believable in the moment. Most of all... "This explains *us*. The connection. The fact that we both felt it, not just me."

Maximus's shock melts into a grimace of frustration. He steps back from me, stabbing both hands through his hair. "Why would this nutcase have anything to do with us?"

The corners of Z's lips curve up. "Oh, this is precious." He lobs an amused half grin in my direction. "Don't tell me he doesn't know."

I'm the one breathing hard now. Does *he* know? Of course he knows. He's fucking *Zeus*. And if I didn't believe it before, I worry he's about to prove it. Shit. He really is about to prove it.

Maximus pins me with another taut look. "What don't I know?"

"Maximus." I manage to stammer that much, but tears clog my throat and blur my vision. "I—"

I what? Was going to tell him? I can't lie to him. Not now, when he's dealing with the fact that his own parents did the same for twenty-seven years.

"Kara? *What* don't I know?"

Z beats me to the truth, filling the moment with an exaggerated sigh. "My dear boy, I'm afraid you've just been to bed with a demon." His gaze lingers on me. "Never had the pleasure, actually."

Maximus takes a step toward him and points threateningly. "You'd be wise to keep your eyes and hands off her."

Z raises his hands in mock surrender. "Come now. I wouldn't dream of it. Demons aren't really my type. If you think humans are complicated…"

Maximus turns, facing me down now. "Kara." Something in his eyes softens, like maybe he's silently begging me to tell him his father is fantastically wrong. That this is all crazy talk. Oh, how I wish I could tell him that.

Instead, I swallow over the painful knot in my throat, cast my stare down to my bare feet, and rationalize that there'd never be a good time to tell him. This situation has been so fucked up. So royally wrong—but beautifully right—from the very start.

"He's telling you the truth. He's telling you what I should have a long time ago."

Several tense seconds pass. I almost wish Arden would show up now and save me from what Maximus's expression might hold. If I could just skip all the judgment and pain and hurt I've imagined passing between us when this moment finally came...

But when I do look up, he's a canvas of bewilderment. Just as beautiful and vulnerable as he'd been hours ago, making passionate love to me. His eyes are wide and stunned. His lips part to accommodate the harsh breaths he's taking in.

"A demon."

"Yeah." My voice is thick with tears. "Mostly."

"All right."

I gulp hard, wondering why the ball of shock doesn't rip my windpipe open. "All...right?"

"Well, what does that mean exactly?"

Z sinks his cheek onto his hand again, rapt and waiting like he's dropped in just in time for story time at the public library.

"What you read in my grandfather's screenplay... Well, it was true. Partly true, anyway. He didn't mate with my grandmother as a price for his freedom. He'd already escaped hell, and she was his punishment for getting away with it. She was sent to seduce him. She became pregnant with my mother before he suspected who she truly was."

"And who was she?"

I close my eyes briefly. "A succubus. A demon sent in the female form."

"His punishment was breeding with a demon. Is that what you're saying?"

"Part of it ..." My voice trails off as we get closer to the darkest part of this truth.

His jaw tightens. "What else?"

"When he found out about the pregnancy, he chose to stay. He wouldn't abandon his family, even if that meant eventually living in near exile from the rest of us. Even if that meant sticking around, knowing an incubus would eventually come for my mother." My lower lip trembles. "And for me."

His color is back to a warm, healthy flush. His muscles are coiled tight like he's ready to fight. I can hardly see the blue in his eyes for how blown out his pupils have become.

"No."

Everything's tied up around that one word. His disbelief. My rebellion. The inevitable consequences of both.

Z's countenance has turned into a cringe that nearly matches my own. "Well, damn. That's not good."

Max whips his glare to him. "Why are you still here?"

"Actually, you should be grateful I am." The older man rises with a sigh. "I might be the only one who can get you out of this mess. And believe me, this is a mess." He lifts his brows high and checks his watch. "Looks like I arrived just in time. Or perhaps a touch late." He casts his gaze to me. "Does your family know?"

I shake my head. "No. I mean, I don't think so."

"But they will soon." Z states it as the fact it is.

"Yes." I dip a shaky nod. "He's already here."

"Who's here?" Maximus asks.

"Arden. He's the incubus. He was sent for me."

His gaze is raging cobalt. "You *knew* about this?"

"I didn't know why he was here until last night." I can't help being defensive about it.

"Over my dead body will I let him have you." He growls the promise like it's truth etched in stone.

"It's too late for that anyway," Z chimes in. "If you've been together, then she's already defied the edict of Hades himself." With a soft but annoying cluck of his tongue, the king of the gods glances down at the sheet slung low over his son's hips. "Breeding out her humanity is a moot point. This kind of rebellion is cause for punishment of the worst kind. They'll be booking her a ticket to the underworld the moment they catch wind of this."

Maximus paces to the door and pivots. He drags his hand over his mouth. "This is insane."

"I get it," Z says. "Trust me. I do. You should hear about some of the crazy shit I've gotten myself into over the years." He follows Maximus to the door, placing his hat back on his head. "We should grab a beer. I could tell you some stories—"

"I don't care about your stories or your crackpot

theories about my parentage, all right?"

Z answers with a contemplative purse of his lips. Then, "Listen, I'm nothing if not an eternal romantic."

I resist the urge to roll my eyes. If half the stories are true, womanizer is the better word.

"This whole situation with your little devil…" He gestures toward me. "Let me make some calls. I might be able to get this sorted out."

Maximus laughs roughly. "Who the hell are you going to call? The god of the underworld?"

"Hades and I are *in fact* on speaking terms at the moment, which isn't always the case. I can't say the same for my other brother." His smile is tight then. "But we can talk that through another time."

Maximus reaches for the door and swings it open. "Out."

"*Maximus.*" I rush to him, ignited by a surge of desperate—and probably dangerous—anticipation. Still, I latch on to his arm, clutching as deeply as his clenched muscles will allow. "Wait," I plead. "Please, just wait."

"Wait for what? I think we've both entertained enough of this, don't you?"

"Let him help." Fresh tears burn at the back of my eyes. But this time, they're made of hope. My last hope. "Please. What can it hurt?"

A valid question. What *can* it hurt—because by now, I'm probably screwed in a thousand and one ways.

"I can protect you, Kara," he says more softly, like Z isn't watching the whole thing.

"I know you can, but…" I look to Z. "Do you really think you can change their minds?"

He shrugs. "Even if I can, everything has a price."

My heart falls. "What kind of price?"

"Theirs." For the first time, the lines etched across Z's face have hardened. "And mine, of course. You know how this works. I'm not going to stick my neck out to save a demon unless I get something in return."

Maximus's pissed-off glare returns full force. "How noble of you."

"Take the favor or turn it down, son. This is your grail to lose, not mine. If no one stands in the way, your beloved will be tossed into the flames of eternal torment faster than you can imagine. You can doubt me if you'd like. But before you do, take one look into her eyes and tell me if you think she does."

I tighten my grasp on his arm and press my forehead to his shoulder. A silent plea for his understanding.

"*If* I choose to believe you… and *if* I say yes… what do you want?" Maximus's voice holds enough resignation to give me another surge of renewed hope.

"I've been looking for you for nearly a decade, Maximus. I'd like a chance to get to know my son. Nancy robbed me of your childhood. In doing so, she robbed you of the opportunity to know yourself. To know your purpose. Your gifts. I just want a chance to make that right."

The tension rippling off Maximus would be palpable even if I wasn't so wired into him.

"If she wanted me away from you, she must have had good reasons."

Z's expression remains unaffected. "I'm sure she had reasons. I can't say they were good."

"Don't talk about my mother—"

"Do you want my help or not?" Again, Z looks more determined than amused. Another sign that there's a god under that suit used to getting his way. The confirmation should comfort me but doesn't. Somehow I already know he'll want more than a casual reunion with his long-lost son. He can't have traveled this far and searched for so long to settle for that. There's much more to the story here. Still, I can't bring myself to challenge him and risk the help he's offering.

Maximus wraps his arm around me and holds me against him protectively. The act is equal parts tender and possessive, and I hope it means he'll do anything to keep me there. Even if it means letting this stranger into his life long enough to save mine.

"What's it going to be?" Z taps his foot a few times.

Maximus squares his jaw. "If that's your condition, then make your calls."

Z simply nods. "Very well. Until I know more, she's under your protection. I'm not responsible for anything that happens on your watch."

Maximus strengthens his hold on me infinitesimally.

"She'll be safe with me."

I press closer to his side, conveying how much I believe his every word. How thoroughly I believe in him. In us. In return, I receive an influx of his energy, warm and strong and full of purpose. It's all I need right now. It's what I've defied my family for. For this man—this demigod—who has every part of my heart, inch of my soul, and minute of my life in his hands.

ACKNOWLEDGMENTS

Special thanks to my beta readers, Jonathan, Lauren, Jennifer, Martha, and Mindy, for your early insights and excitement for this story. It meant so much to get your stamp of approval when the story was so fresh.

Thank you, Scott Saunders, for your eagle eye and your thoughtful red pen. To know my words are always in such good hands means more than you know!

Angel, I'm so grateful for your enthusiasm and all the heart you brought to the page for this. I'm so proud of our book baby, and I can't wait to create more magic with you!

Thank you, Victoria, for the sprints and the check-ins, but most of all, for your friendship. I'm holding you in my heart through every word. We're going to get through this!

Lastly, this book is dedicated to my wonderful, beautiful friend, Mindy Moniz. Thank you for always being there for me and for the constant stream of memes that keep me sane. Love you.

— Meredith

There's no better place to start than the pinnacle of the blessings tower, where goddess Meredith Wild resides. What do I say here? How do I express this fullness of my heart and joy of my storyteller's soul? Impossible. I can only tell you that birthing a world like this has been so epic with a friend and guide like you. Thank you for teaching me with the words and inspiring me with your heart. You are such a beautiful blessing in my world.

Scott Saunders: The words sing with you to help refine, smooth, comment, and galvanize them. My gratitude to you continues to be boundless and bountiful. Thank you for caring so deeply and working so hard. We are so blessed with your editorial expertise!

Jonathan Mac, Robyn Lee, Amber Maxwell, Haley Boudreaux, Keli Jo Chen, and Dana Bridges: the best marketing and PR team a gal could ask for. You are my most steadfast pit crew. My heart's worth of thankfulness for everything you do on a daily basis. #WaterhouseKicksAss

Victoria Blue: You are my hero, in so many ways, each and every day. Thank you so much for all the things—and for knowing where the bodies are buried but loving me anyway.

Carey Sabala: How your deep heart, fathomless loyalty, and endless smiles have lent me strength on the days I need it most. If there's an Excelsior Award for girlfriends (and booth biatches!), I'm going to stamp that medallion into the middle of your gorgeous forehead. *Excelsior*, baby!

Martha Frantz: Thank you for keeping the wheels turning and the gears going. You are amazing!

Regina Wamba: WHAT A RIDE, woman! And the adventure has only begun. I believe in you so much. I *love* you so much. So many good, great things ahead on your journey—and I am so honored to be here to see it.

Writing is an impossible profession without goddesses to help one see the proverbial light at the end of the tunnel. The lights in my world are without compare. Jenna Jacob, Shayla Black, Rebekah Ganiere, Sierra Cartwright, Jodi Drake, Red Phoenix, Nelle L'Amour, and Helen Hardt: you women are pure magic, and such amazing vessels of support. Thank you.

The Payne Passion Army: you remarkable human beings are the fiber of my fortitude, and—many, many times!—the gas in my engine. Thank you for all of your encouragement, love, memes, madness, and support. I love you all so hard!

Brock O'Hurn and Jade McKenzee: Thank you for pouring yourselves into embodying Maximus and Kara. You both make me swoon, forever and ever and EVER!

The Waterhouse Crew of Tireless Ops Support: I love you epic people with a passion I cannot put into words. You are all so special to me! Thank you to Jennifer Becker, Kurt Vachon, and Jesse Kench for handling the details when we need them the most! You are ROCK STARS.

Stephanie Arrache: You are one of the most badass women I know—a real Olympian!—and I'm so honored for your presence in my world. Thank you for the super-uber beta read, and making sure we got everything right about Jesse. You are very much appreciated!

Last yet NEVER least: Mom, you are my rock, my friend, my inspiration—and the woman who showed me the meaning of the best motto on earth. *Work hard, be kind.* I admire and love you so much.

— Angel

ABOUT MEREDITH WILD

Meredith Wild is a #1 *New York Times, USA Today,* and international bestselling author. After publishing her debut novel, *Hardwired,* in September 2013, Wild used her ten years of experience as a tech entrepreneur to push the boundaries of her "self-published" status, becoming stocked in brick-and-mortar bookstore chains nationwide and forging relationships with major retailers.

In 2014, Wild founded her own imprint, Waterhouse Press, under which she hit #1 on the *New York Times* and *Wall Street Journal* bestseller lists. She has been featured on *CBS This Morning* and the *Today Show,* and in the *New York Times,* the *Hollywood Reporter, Publishers Weekly,* and the *Examiner.* Her foreign rights have been sold in twenty-three languages.

Visit her at MeredithWild.com

Photograph © Sharon Suh

ABOUT ANGEL PAYNE

USA Today bestselling romance author Angel Payne loves to focus on high-heat romance starring memorable alpha men and the women who love them. She has numerous book series to her credit, including the action-packed Bolt Saga and Honor Bound series, Secrets of Stone series (with Victoria Blue), the intertwined Cimarron and Temptation Court series, the Suited for Sin series, and the Lords of Sin historicals, as well as several standalone titles.

Angel is a native Southern Californian, leading to her love of being in the outdoors, where she often reads and writes. She still lives in Southern California with her soul-mate husband and beautiful daughter, to whom she is a proud cosplay/culture con mom. Her passions also include whisky tasting, shoe shopping, and travel.

Visit her at AngelPayne.com